Bound
BY
DECEPTION

JAYNE CASTEL

WINTER MIST PRESS

She's a 300-year-old Fae assassin with a bloodstained soul. He's the mortal High King's chief-enforcer, responsible for hunting and killing her people. Their marriage will be the breaking—and the making—of them both.

Outlander meets The Witcher and Throne of Glass. BOUND BY DECEPTION is a high stakes Fantasy Romance with enemies-to-lovers, slow-burn delicious spice, a mail-order-bride, and a dark and lush world inspired by Celtic myth.

Bree Fellshadow is a master assassin, but when she's sent to work as a spy in the enemy court, she finds herself out of her depth.

Killing the queen's enemies is easy compared to pretending to be a biddable wife or dealing with her obnoxious chief-enforcer husband—a powerful warrior-druid who both enrages and unsettles her.

Cailean mac Brochan is also worryingly suspicious, and she keeps drawing his attention. But Bree must gain his trust, to learn where and when the enemy will strike.

That is … if she survives long enough.

To Timbo. My sweetheart.

And to all of us who embrace the magic of new beginnings.

BOUND BY DECEPTION
CONTENT WARNINGS

BOUND BY DECEPTION is a fantasy romance set in a brutal Pict-inspired world. It's intended for mature (18+) readers. You can find a detailed list of triggers on the author's website.

https://www.jaynecastel.com/fantasy/the-enforcers-bride-duology

THE REALM
OF
ALBIA
THE SEA OF SORROWS
THE WESTERN ISLES
THE BALEFUL SEA
THE UPLANDS
THE WOLDS
Harra
The Spine
Darkmere
Morar Barrow
Morar
The isle of Laggan
Darkmere Barrow
Strath
Cannich
Bracebell Barrow
Rothie
The Ring of Ard
Crook Barrow
Loch Glass
Dunmorth Barrow
The Goatfell Mountains
Dulross
Doure
The Hallow Woods
The Ring of Caith
Baldeen
Loch Caith
The Ring of Starke
The Isle of Arryn
Dorne Forest
Golval Barrow
Duncrag
The Shiel Range
Deeping Barrow
The Golval Woods
Loch Lethe
The Firth of Fallow
Dunharra Barrow
Farnoch
Strathnich Forest
The Galan Peninsula
Dingford
Ordsheen
Loch Ord
Strathnich Barrow
Gavich Barrow
Muirport
Inverwich
Troon
Braewall

MAP

Visit my website to view a larger version of the Realm of Albia map.

"All warfare is based on deception."

Shee proverb

1: THE QUEEN'S ASSASSIN

Caisteal Gealaich
The Realm of Sheehallion

THE SEVERED HEAD stank—badly.

Screwing up her nose, Bree slid off the stag's back, her gaze shifting to the sack that hung from her mount's withers. The blood staining the thick linen had turned the cloth dark, and fat flies now buzzed around it.

Even the musky scent of rose, from the delicate white buds that climbed the walls surrounding the outer ward of Caisteal Gealaich, couldn't disguise the sweet, putrid odor of decay.

Take that foul thing off me.

Bree deftly untied the rope holding the sack fast. *Sorry about that, Tiv.*

In response, the mighty white stag tossed his head, glad to be free of the grisly prize they'd brought back from the north.

I know. she patted Tivesheh's sleek neck. *The stench turns my stomach too … but Mor wants proof.* The stag's dark eyes met hers, and their gazes held for a moment before she gently touched his mind with hers once more. *You did well … thank you.*

Tivesheh snorted and tossed his head. *I will be waiting for your call.*

Bree stepped back from the stag then, allowing him to turn and bound away. Tivesheh left the fortress through a vast gateway, where two sentries stood, their silver helms gleaming in the bright sunlight. Bree watched him go. After nearly two turns of the moon traveling, and hunting, with the stag, it felt strange to be parted from him. However, all she had to do was whistle, and Tivesheh would come once more.

She could always rely on him.

Shaking herself free of the odd mood that had suddenly descended upon her, Bree tightened her hold on the top of the sack and swiveled on her heel. Then, leather creaking and soft-soled hunting boots whispering on smooth white moonstone, she crossed to one of the sentries standing at the foot of the sweeping steps leading into the fortress. "Where's the queen?"

The male's mouth pinched slightly, his cool gaze traveling over Bree.

His assessment made irritation spike through her. She knew she likely looked, and smelled, terrible. She'd barely slept over the past few days—such was her haste to return to Caisteal Gealaich.

Her appearance didn't matter though, and she had no time for this underling's scorn. Suffering his stare a few moments longer, Bree's free hand strayed to the hilt of the long hunting dagger at her hip. This guard knew who she was. It was foolish indeed to insult the queen's assassin. "The queen?" she repeated.

"Her Highness is in the garden," he replied, sullen now.

Not bothering to thank him, Bree turned and stalked across the swathe of slippery white cobbles that led toward a rose-covered archway.

Entering the walled garden beyond, she made her way through an arbor where even more white roses trailed overhead. Like all the Shee, the Raven Queen loved these flowers and spent much time tending the roses herself in this garden. Raising her chin, Bree sucked in their rich, musky scent—anything to try and escape the reek of decomposing flesh.

However, she didn't slow her determined stride.

She was at the end of her mission now and just wished to rid herself of the evidence she'd brought, so she could sink up to the neck in a hot bath and enjoy a tall goblet of chilled apple wine. It would be a relief to put this job behind her—although soap and water wouldn't scrub away all the blood she'd spilled.

Bree's mouth thinned. *It's too late now to worry about that.*

And it was. How many souls had she dispatched over the years at Mor's command? She'd stopped counting after two dozen.

Bree found the Raven Queen standing before the fountain at the heart of the garden.

Fashioned of moonstone, like everything at Caisteal Gealaich—from its high walls to the pavers that lined the garden paths—the fountain was of a huge corvid.

Mor stood silently, her gaze upon the water that spilled from the Great Raven's open beak, tinkling over the stones below. A real raven, its glossy blue-black feathers gleaming in the golden late afternoon light, perched upon the queen's shoulder. Eagal—Mor's trusted messenger.

Bree halted a few yards back from her queen and cleared her throat. "Your Highness."

Mor jerked out of her reverie and turned, her obsidian gaze widening when it settled upon her assassin. "Bree," she greeted her, stepping away from the fountain. "*Finally.*"

Bree dipped her head, even as she fought a frown. "Grae led me on quite a chase, Your Highness," she replied, holding the sack aloft. "But I have his head."

Mor's attention snapped to the sack, which now crawled with large black flies.

The queen stilled then, a lovely statue among the roses. In contrast to the glittering white surrounding her, she was clad entirely in black. A shimmering gown plummeted into a deep cleavage at the front and clung to her tall, lithe form. A simple crown, decorated with tiny daggers and glass skulls, sat upon her head, while inky hair—a mane of tight, wiry curls—tumbled over the cloak of black crow feathers that hung from her shoulders.

Silence swelled between them before Mor's throat bobbed. "Show me," she whispered.

Wordlessly, Bree stooped and emptied the sack onto the ground.

Grae's partially decomposed head rolled onto the pavers.

Staring down at him, Bree pursed her lips. It was hard to believe that the elder of Mor's two estranged brothers had once been handsome, as now his long tightly-curled hair was matted with blood, and his skin—once a deep umber like his sister's—was the color of ash. His dark eyes stared sightlessly up at the sky, his mouth slack and gaping.

Sourness flooded Bree's mouth then. Since striking off her mark's head and stuffing it into the sack, she hadn't looked at him again. Grae hadn't been easy to find or kill. The Raven Queen had hunted her brother for years after his failed attempt to take her throne had resulted in his exile. She'd feared that he'd try to usurp her again—but she needn't worry any longer.

"Well done," Mor said finally. Both her voice and expression were veiled now. If Bree had expected to see a glint of vindication in the queen's eyes, she was disappointed.

Letting the filthy sack drop to the ground, for a servant to clear away later, she resisted the urge to step back and take her leave. It took much to exhaust Bree, yet her limbs felt heavy this afternoon. Nonetheless, she checked herself. One didn't walk away from the queen until dismissed. "I am your servant," she replied, dipping her head once more.

Moments passed, and when Bree raised her gaze, she found Mor watching her. Meanwhile, Eagal shifted upon her shoulder, his eyes gleaming like two shards of onyx.

An uneasiness stole over Bree. That bird had a stare that flayed the flesh.

"You will receive twice your usual payment for this," Mor said after a pause.

"Thank you, Your Highness," Bree murmured. Years ago, the queen's generosity would have excited her, although these days, she couldn't dredge up the same enthusiasm. It was only coin, after all. Of late, Mor had kept her so busy she barely had time to spend it. The truth was she was jaded. Exhausted. Maybe it was time for a well-earned break.

Mor's mouth curved then. "You are my best, Bree Fellshadow."

Bree smiled back. Such praise was rare, and she'd enjoy it. Nonetheless, there was something about Mor's expression that made the fine hair on the back of her neck prickle. The queen seemed to have forgotten her brother now, despite that his rotting head sat just a few feet from her.

"I have another job for you," Mor added then, and Bree's smile froze.

Iron burn her, she'd just got back from hunting Grae. Couldn't she have some time to recover, to let the fatigue that had settled deep into her bones fade? "So soon?" she replied, trying not to let resentment creep into her voice.

The Raven Queen's smile hardened. "Aye … although *this* task will be a little different."

2: A VEIN OF TRUTH

BREE TOOK THE stairs down to the archives two at a time, descending into the lower levels of the fortress with careless speed.

Cressets burned on the gleaming white walls, illuminating her way, and cool air feathered against her skin. Yet she took little notice of her surroundings; Bree's thoughts had turned inward, and her stomach had clenched.

Reaching the bottom of the curving stairwell, she stalked along a wide vaulted corridor, lined with much narrower passageways, before entering the archives.

Tall shelves made of oak stretched up to a high ceiling, crammed with leather-bound books, and scrolls. Grey-robed archivists worked silently within the space. Some carried armloads of rolled parchments, while others bent over documents at tables at the heart of the archives, quills in hand.

A tall, lean male with long golden hair tied back at the nape sat apart from his colleagues, alone at a table on the edge of the space. Gil squinted as he scratched his quill against a sheet of vellum, writing with painstaking care.

Bree strode up to him. "Brother."

Gil Fellshadow's chin jerked up, his tawny eyes narrowing as they fixed upon her. "Bree," he greeted her warily. "You're back."

Bree halted before him. "Evidently."

She was receiving censorious looks from the other archivists, for they preferred to work in silence down here. Ignoring them, Bree flung herself down onto a chair opposite her brother and leaned back, throwing her booted feet up and crossing them on the tabletop. She then heaved a sigh. "That's better." A moment later, she cast her gaze around. "Do you have any apple wine down here?"

Gil's mouth pursed, and he cut a glare at her dusty boots before shaking his head. "You look terrible."

Bree pulled a face. She could always rely on her brother to be blunt. "Aye, well … this job was harder than most."

Gil's lean face tightened. Glancing around him, he put his quill back in its pot and leaned toward her, whispering, "The prince?"

Bree stilled. She hadn't told her brother of her mark, although rumors must have circulated Caisteal Gealaich in her absence. "Dead," she murmured.

Gil frowned. A brittle silence fell between them, and Bree coolly observed her younger brother. He was disapproving and sanctimonious, but he was all she had—and she needed to tell *someone* about the mission Mor had just given her.

"I've got another assignment," she said finally.

"Already?"

Bree dragged a hand down her face then as a heaviness settled over her. "I *was* planning to take some time off," she admitted, aware just how flat she sounded, how weary.

Gil arched an eyebrow. "Getting tired of spilling blood, are we?"

Bree scowled. "Never."

"Come … you can't tell me that hunting Grae didn't prick your conscience. He wasn't some faceless mark … you *knew* him."

Bree's pulse quickened. As always, Gil knew exactly where to strike. Blades were her weapons, but his were words. Indeed, over two hundred and fifty years earlier, when they'd been younglings, Grae had been a friend. But that was a long time ago—before he turned on his elder sister—and she preferred not to dwell on their past friendship.

"It's just a job, Gil," she replied after a pause, before lifting a hand and gesturing dismissively to their surroundings. "You spend your days with your nose in boring, dusty tomes … and I eradicate problems."

Heat kindled in her brother's tawny eyes, and Bree swallowed a vindictive smile.

"You know who you sound like?" her brother asked, folding his arms in front of him. "*Father.*"

Bree stiffened. That was a low blow. "I'm nothing like him," she muttered.

Gil huffed a bitter laugh. "Aye, you are. You have the same arrogance … and intolerance."

Bree glared at her brother. "You forget, we were *both* a disappointment to him," she pointed out. Indeed, both their parents had been warriors to the core and their father hadn't wanted an archivist for a son, *or* a lowly assassin for a daughter.

"Maybe, but he too never missed the opportunity to belittle my choice."

Bree fell silent, uneasiness shifting under her ribs. Was she like him? Shades, she hoped not. As soon as she'd come of age, she'd done everything she could to break free of her father's oppressive rule—to forge her own path.

Awkward moments slid by, and Bree shoved thoughts of her father aside. It was time to bring the subject back to her new job.

Straightening up, she removed her feet from the table and pulled her chair close to her brother. His nose wrinkled, letting her know that she did, indeed, reek. She pretended not to notice his reaction and murmured, "This assignment isn't like the rest … this time I'm working as a *spy*."

Gil inclined his head.

"Mor's sending me to Duncrag … I'm to wed the High King's chief-enforcer." She swallowed then. Ancestors, her mouth and throat were parched. She really needed that apple wine.

Her brother's brows knitted together. "Mor wants you to live amongst the Marav?"

"Aye."

"But I thought she already had a spy at Duncrag?"

"She did … but he's gone silent. Now it seems the chief-enforcer has *ordered* himself a wife … and I'm to replace her."

Gil's mouth pursed. "A Maid of Albia?"

Bree nodded, even as her stomach hardened at the thought of impersonating such a fawning individual. Marriage was rare amongst their kind—the Shee preferred to take lovers or long-term consorts—yet the Marav did things differently. And some men, usually those with deep pockets, bought themselves a 'Maid of Albia'—a young woman schooled to be the perfect wife.

The cat-like pupils of Gil's golden eyes narrowed. "Does this mean you'll have to walk through a stone circle as well … to become one of *them*?" Distaste laced his voice now. Like her, Gil had little love for the mortal race who lived beyond the veil.

In the old tongue, 'Marav' meant 'the dead'. Indeed, their lifespans were pitifully short. Even the longest-lived amongst them rarely reached a hundred years, while the oldest of the Shee was said to have lived six thousand years. Time held a different meaning for their people.

"Aye," Bree replied with a shudder. Her skin crawled at the thought. "Unfortunately."

"Can't you just glamor yourself?"

Bree shook her head. "Not if I'm to wed an enforcer." Her pulse spiked then. She wasn't sure what was worse, being forced to rut with the most powerful of the warrior-druids or becoming a sniveling Marav woman. Once she passed through the stones, she'd be living in a frail mortal body. "He'll see right through it."

Gil sat back in his chair, observing her with a veiled gaze. "So, you're going to pretend to be a loving wife … to ingratiate yourself with the chief-enforcer and wheedle his secrets from him?"

"Aye," she muttered, screwing her face up even as her pulse quickened. "Something like that."

Her brother gave a dry laugh. "You won't last the distance."

Bree's stomach clenched. "Excuse me?"

"You're as cold as an Albian winter, sister. You're incapable of getting close to anyone … and even *feigning* it will be a challenge." Gil's gaze glinted. "Aye, our queen holds you in high esteem … but I fear she overestimates you now."

Bree sucked in a deep breath, heat washing over her. *Pompous, self-righteous ass.* Her hands clenched at her sides as she fought the instinct to lash out and knock that smug look off his face. *How dare he look down his nose at me?*

Nonetheless, her brother's harsh comment held a vein of truth. She was used to hunting and killing, not cozying up to warrior-druids and pretending to be someone she wasn't.

With just a few words, Gil had exposed the anxiety that had flowered inside her ever since Mor had given her this job.

They both knew the Raven Queen should have chosen someone else.

Dusk was settling as Bree made her way up to her quarters. When the queen's assassin was in residence at Caisteal Gealaich, she lived in a lofty tower. It was a journey—nearly a thousand steps—to the top, but despite that her mind and body felt unusually heavy this evening, Bree made the climb easily.

All the Shee were blessed with strength and endurance, and Bree was barely out of breath when she let herself into her quarters.

Golden light pooled on the pristine pavers through the open window, gilding the simple yet elegant furnishings within: a large canopied bed and furniture fashioned from oak and moonstone. As expected, servants had been up here already. Despite that it was never cold in Sheehallion, a fire flickered in the hearth. The servants had also lugged up water from below and used the fire to heat it for her bath—a large stone tub of steaming water awaited her before the window.

Bree heaved a deep sigh.

Unfastening the long dagger from around her waist, she placed it on the table by the doorway. She then unstrapped the knives at her thighs and removed the various blades sheathed in her boots and on her torso, before stripping off her stinking leathers and walking naked over to the bath.

As she'd hoped, a goblet and a ewer of apple wine sat upon the low table next to the tub. Moisture beaded on the ewer's bronze surface, indicating that the wine was properly chilled.

Despite her dark mood, Bree's mouth curved. *Small pleasures.*

Settling into the hot water with a sigh, she poured herself a generous goblet of wine, raised it to her lips, and drained it in a long draft. She welcomed the wine's coolness, its crisp sweetness. Usually, she savored it after a job was done, but not this evening. With another, heavy, sigh, she poured herself a second goblet and drained that too before sinking down into the silky water. The scent of musky rose, from the oil a servant had added to the bath, enveloped her, and she drew it deep into her lungs.

It was a beautiful spot to take a bath, by the large teardrop-shaped window that had a view across the meadows west of the fortress. The setting sun now gilded the sculpted edges of the great mountains beyond. However, the spectacular view, soothing hot water, and numbing wine couldn't make her forget her situation.

"Mor is making a mistake," she muttered then, her voice carrying across the silent chamber. "I'm an assassin … not a spy."

She hadn't admitted such to her brother—and she'd have had her tongue ripped out before doing so—but she *had* attempted to suggest the Raven Queen select someone with more experience in subterfuge. Nonetheless, Mor wouldn't hear of it. "This job requires spine, Bree," she'd cut her off. "You're the only one I trust not to disappoint me"

Despite being cocooned by hot water, Bree shivered. There had been a warning in those words, for no one disappointed the Raven Queen twice.

Mor hadn't given her much of a reprieve either. She'd be leaving soon, for the spring equinox was just three days away. There were no seasons here in Sheehallion—the climate remained forever warm and springlike—but Albia was different. On the other side of the veil, the Marav were readying themselves to celebrate The Day of the Hag, when the world shifted from winter to spring. The three stone circles that linked the realms only opened at certain times of the year.

Bree's breathing grew shallow then at the thought of going anywhere near a stone circle. Her people avoided them for a reason; these places were infused with druidic magic. However, she needed to put her aversion aside. If she missed the next opening, she'd have to wait until Bealtunn, which was one and a half turns of the moon away—by which time, it would be too late.

The chief-enforcer's bride-to-be had just set off toward the capital. Bree had been ready to intercept her, although Mor had instructed her Ravens—the queen's personal bodyguards—to kill the woman instead. They'd then meet Bree in Albia, at The Ring of Caith.

Everything was already in motion.

Bree slid down in the tub, so that water lapped her chin, and closed her eyes. Numbness settled over her then, and a heaviness pulled at her limbs.

Here we go again.

She'd hoped for a break, but she wouldn't be getting one. Most of the time, she lived under the illusion that she was in control of her destiny—that if a job didn't suit her, she could decline. But today had shown Bree that she couldn't say no to the Raven Queen. Despite the generous payment she received for each kill, she was Mor's servant, her *weapon*.

3: THROUGH THE STONES

Three days later …

BREE TRAVELED TO The Ring of Caith alone.

Leaving the white walls of Caisteal Gealaich at her back, she set off northwest toward the stone circle. Tivesheh ran swiftly, bounding over lush meadows and glittering streams, the moon rising above them and the stars winking in the inky heavens.

It took her all night to reach her destination, and by the time they drew up at the foot of a large hill, the sky was glowing to the east. Dawn was breaking with the promise of yet another lovely day. Swinging down from the stag's back, Bree placed a hand on his warm neck. *This is goodbye for now … I don't know when I'll be back.*

Tivesheh dipped his head. *Just whistle, and I will come.*

Bree sucked in a deep breath and turned away from her stag. She wasn't one to linger over farewells.

Squaring her shoulders, she strode toward The Ring of Caith. The ancient stone circle loomed above her, grasping toward the sky like a claw. Climbing the hill, she tried to ignore her quickening pulse.

Aye, she was nervous—only a fool wouldn't be.

There were many portals between the realms, most of them the barrows of long-dead kings. But traveling through the stone circles was dangerous to her kind, for Marav druids often lurked on the other side.

Although such places were important to the druids, they hadn't made them. Instead, the Ancients—a long-dead race who'd once inhabited Albia—had raised the giant stones and worshipped their gods.

Bree had never dared get this close to The Ring of Caith before and hadn't met anyone who'd crossed through this way. Mor's last spy at Duncrag—a healer named Bryce Elmsong, who'd lived amongst the enemy for two years before going ominously silent—had done it though.

The queen had assured Bree that traveling through the stones wouldn't inflict any lasting harm, although Bree had doubted her. As such, she'd gone down into the archives the day before and enlisted Gil's help to find texts about the stone circles. Her brother had been surly and reluctant, but she'd bullied him into helping. There wasn't much. Nonetheless, when Gil had dug deep, he'd discovered an old parchment, crumbling with age, that confirmed that it was safe for a Shee to pass both ways through the stones—an act that would kill any Marav who attempted it.

According to the text, when she returned to Sheehallion through the stones once more upon a solstice or equinox, she'd change back into her Shee form.

Halfway up the hill, Bree halted. She then drew her long thin steel-bladed dagger from its sheath, her fingers flexing on the bone hilt. She wasn't entering Albia unarmed. The Day of the Hag was a sacred time for the Marav. Although The Ring of Caith was far from the nearest village or fort, it was wise to be cautious. There might be a host of druids dancing on the other side. She needed to be ready for them.

The Shee were a powerful race, but there were two things they feared: the kiss of iron on their skin, and the earth magic of druids. Enforcers—warrior-druids—wielded both, which was what made them such formidable opponents in battle.

A grim smile compressed Bree's lips. Her people might not be able to summon earth magic, but they had many abilities that gave them the edge over their enemies. They were faster than the Marav, for one. They could also glamor themselves to take another form temporarily, meld with the shadows when they wished to pass unseen, and touch minds with animals.

Nonetheless, the race that lived beyond the veil in Albia wasn't to be underestimated.

Bree exhaled sharply. She had to walk between the two largest stones that beckoned like lichen-encrusted, gnarled, upthrust fingers against the lightening sky. The sun needed to crest the heavens, breaking free from the line of mountains to the east, and appear directly between those two stones, at the same time.

Trying to ignore the thud of her pulse in her ears, she glanced over her shoulder, looking for Tivesheh. However, like his name—Ghost—the stag had disappeared. She was on her own.

Facing forward once more, she kept walking. "It's just another job," she reminded herself. "You haven't failed Mor yet." Bree's fingers flexed once more upon the hilt of her dagger then. *There's always a first time.*

The sun glinted ahead of her, and she lengthened her stride. Dressed in her usual hunting leathers, her fine blue cloak rippling behind her, she glided across the dew-laden grass.

Bree crested the top of the hill and paced toward the two stones.

Up here, the air felt different, charged, as if a thunderstorm loomed overhead. On the hillside below, there had been the whisper of the breeze, and the chirp and trill of birdsong, but up here, an eerie silence settled.

Upon the stones, she caught sight of engravings, ancient markings that gave this place its power.

The fine hair on the backs of her arms prickled. Unlike the barrows, which her kind usually traveled through whenever they wanted to reach Albia, these stone circles were infused with earth magic. Being so close to druidic energy made sweat bead upon her skin.

Don't hesitate.

Setting her jaw, Bree headed for the gap between the stones. And the instant she stepped inside the stone circle, the rest of the world disappeared.

Suddenly, mist shrouded her, and the air grew heavier still, pushing against her on all sides. Pressure built in her chest, and she stumbled. It was like wading through a bog.

A high-pitched ringing began in her ears then, and her head started to ache as if a giant invisible hand were squeezing it.

Each step became more difficult than the last, and Bree leaned forward as if bracing herself against a strong wind, plowing ahead.

She had to make it to the other side. If she collapsed in the middle of the circle, she'd die.

Even so, keeping going was hard—harder than she'd expected. And as she moved forward, pain tore through her body.

Bree swallowed a scream, squeezed her eyes shut, and reached out before her, trying to part the air with her free hand and dagger. Sharp knives dug into her flesh, twisting and rending.

And through it all, she kept moving forward, step by painful step.

The ringing in her ears turned into a roar, dizziness assailing her. She staggered and nearly fell.

Only sheer, stubborn will and a toughness she'd honed over three centuries kept her going. She was a fighter. She wouldn't let The Ring of Caith defeat her.

Even so, fear flowered inside her as she gasped for air. Ancestors, it was as if she were being turned inside out.

Screaming a curse, she lunged forward, clawing at the air before her.

Then something gave way, and the pain—the pressure on her chest and skull, and the roar in her ears—disappeared.

Bree pitched forward and fell onto her face upon wet grass.

Heaving in deep, shuddering breaths, she lay there for a few moments before raising her head.

Mist wreathed the hillside, and the air was colder and damper than earlier. A raven's caw echoed through the murky dawn. When Bree twisted her head, she spied the dark outlines of the standing stones behind her.

She'd done it—she'd passed through The Ring of Caith.

She was now in the mortal realm. In Albia.

However, despite her relief at being alive, a chill washed over her.

Sitting back on her heels, Bree raised her hands before her, inspecting them. They were paler, her fingers a little shorter, than before. She then glanced down at the body encased in hunting leathers. The sleeves of her jerkin were too long, but the bodice and torso were too tight.

Pushing herself upright, she swore softly.

Her mortal body *did* feel different. Weaker. Glancing down, she saw that her leather leggings had bunched at the ankles yet strained against her thighs and hips.

She was both shorter and heavier than in her Shee form.

Drawing in a steadying breath, Bree raised a hand before her once more. To her consternation, it was shaking.

Her jaw clenched at the sight. *Shit.* She hadn't thought transforming into a mortal would make her this frail. She wasn't prepared for the sensations that rippled through her either. Before entering the stone circle, she'd been on edge about this mission.

But now, dread squirmed within her like a sack of eels.

Her legs were trembling and hardly felt strong enough to keep her standing.

Was this what it was to live in a fragile Marav body? No wonder they were such an inferior race.

Gripping the dagger tight while she tried to suppress her shivering, Bree raised her chin, peering into the wreathing mist. "Gavyn!" she called out. Her voice was her own, at least, although it was huskier than usual. "Are you there?"

A heartbeat passed before a cloaked figure emerged from the mist. Behind him, the outlines of four other Ravens also appeared.

Pale hair glinting in the dawn, the captain of Mor's bodyguard approached Bree in long fluid strides. His gaze raked over her, and then his nostrils flared.

Bree swallowed. "Just pretend I'm glamored."

His eyes, the color of thunder clouds, glinted. "I can't. You smell like … *them*."

Her pulse thudded hard. Of course, this wasn't a mere trick of the eye. Her people were both blessed, and cursed, with sharp senses—and to them, the Marav *reeked*. Trust Gavyn Frostshard to be so blunt though. A long time ago, they'd been lovers. The intimacy they'd once shared was but a memory, yet even now, there was tension between them.

She shouldn't have been surprised by his reaction. She'd likely respond the same way if he'd changed into one of the Marav. Nonetheless, anger coiled in her gut. Easy for Gavyn to sneer. Mor hadn't singled *him* out for this mission.

Squaring her shoulders, Bree folded her arms across her chest, noting as she did so that her larger breasts got in the way a bit. "Is it done?"

Gavyn nodded. "We intercepted Fia mac Callum and her escort on the road, south of Loch Caith."

"She's dead then?"

"Aye." Gavyn gestured to one of the Ravens standing behind him. "We have her clothing for you to change into … and her pony for you to ride." He paused then before holding out his hand. "Give me your dagger … you can't go to Duncrag with that."

Reluctantly, Bree handed it to him—although the moment she relinquished her weapon, she regretted it. She'd left her other knives back in her tower room, but that dagger was her favorite blade; she was loath to be parted from it.

The Raven approached and handed her a bundle of garments.

Bree didn't want to touch it, almost as if she expected the clothing to still be warm from the mortal woman's body. But, of course, it wasn't. Taking the bundle and a pair of stout ankle boots the warrior handed her, she set them down at her feet.

She then unwrapped the bundle, finding a plain blue, ankle-length tunic, and a matching woolen cloak within. The mantle wasn't half as fine as the one she'd just removed, but Bree couldn't travel to Duncrag wearing Shee clothing. Tugging at the straining ties of her leathers, she cast Gavyn a sidelong look. "What did you do with the woman's body?"

"Left it in a ditch with those of her escort," he replied curtly. "Out of sight of travelers, mind." He paused then, his face screwing up. "She was wearing an iron protection amulet around her neck, but I ripped it off before I strangled her."

Gavyn and the other warriors turned their backs then, to give Bree privacy as she stripped off her leathers and dressed in Fia mac Callum's clothing.

Ironically, the items would have fitted her Shee form perfectly—for the lass had clearly been tall and lean, as Bree had been a short while earlier—but in her new body, the clothing was slightly ill-fitting. The tunic was a little long, the boots pinched, and the bodice was far too low and tight. Bree hadn't expected her body shape to change so much. However, there was nothing to be done. Fia was expected in Duncrag in five days. She wouldn't have time to get other clothes made.

Clad in her new outfit, she cleared her throat.

Gavyn turned, his gaze narrowing once more as he assessed her. "Incredible," he murmured. "I'd never recognize you."

Bree's mouth pursed, heat smoldering in her belly once more. She was reminded then, of why she'd called things off with Gavyn years earlier. The smug bastard got on her nerves. "Of course, you don't," she muttered, "that's the point."

4: HUMBLING

MOUNTED UPON A shaggy bay garron—a pony that had once been ridden by the woman she was now impersonating—Bree followed her escort south. They weren't close to any settlements here; as such, Gavyn and his warriors didn't bother to put their glamors in place.

Nonetheless, the Ravens rode with their hoods up, their bright gazes glinting in the dull morning as they scanned their surroundings. And all the while, the mist wreathed, white and wispy like crone's hair, around them.

During her many visits to Albia over the years, Bree had always noted just how much darker and colder it was than Sheehallion. Even in high summer, it was as if a shadow lay over the land. Despite her warm clothing, she shivered.

Leaving The Ring of Caith behind, they rode through dense woodland—a tangle of sycamores, elms, and twisted oaks that formed a canopy overhead.

The forests of Albia were deep and dark, carpeted in moss and thick growths of nettles and bright-green ferns. The pungent scent of damp, peaty earth filled Bree's nostrils, although rustling in the undergrowth on either side of the road soon drew her attention.

Her instincts flared.

The woods were alive—and many of its inhabitants were dangerous to a Marav woman. Especially one who didn't carry iron. Thanks to Gavyn, Bree didn't have Fia's protection amulet, although she didn't want to wear anything made of that vile metal anyway, especially against her skin.

She didn't need to worry though, for the presence of her Shee escort would repel most of the creatures that lurked in the shadows. They too were of faery origin.

Myth spoke of a time when they'd all resided in Sheehallion together, but the Shee had cast the others out long ago. Some, like wulvers and broonies, were harmless enough unless angered, yet others, such as the Ben Neeya, were an omen of death. Others still, like the aughisky—a water spirit that dragged its victims to a watery death—were outright malevolent.

The day's journey took the travelers through dense copses of woodland, interspersed by meadows, where the first flowers of spring, snowdrops and crocuses, bloomed. They didn't speak to anyone they met on the road—merchants and farmers mostly, carrying their wares to the crannogs upon Loch Glass in the northwestern Uplands—and Gavyn and his warriors quickly put their glamors in place the moment they spied any other travelers.

The mist eventually cleared although the sky remained the color of smoke. And as the gloaming settled, they passed a ruined broch. Conical-shaped and made of stacked stone, it would likely have once housed a chieftain's household. Nearby, the scattered remains of squat mud-brick cottages, their walls covered by ivy and moss, spread out on either side of the road.

Bree slowed her garron and surveyed the broch. It had lost most of its roof, and half of its northern wall was missing. There were signs—charring on the remnants of the roof, walls blackened by soot, and rotting wattle doors hanging off their hinges—that this place hadn't been abandoned, but attacked. A feud between chieftains perhaps, which had resulted in a deadly raid.

It was a sheltered spot, one that would offer travelers protection against the elements. All the same, she knew what lived amongst ruins such as these. It wasn't a safe place to camp overnight.

The back of Bree's neck prickled. A warning.

Urging her pony forward alongside Gavyn, she glanced across at him. "The powries are watching us," she murmured.

His gaze glinted. "Aye, of course they are … vicious wee bastards."

They rode on, leaving the ruins, and the hungry gazes of the murderous imps that lurked there, behind them.

The light was swiftly fading when Bree and her escort made camp off the road, on the fringes of a beechwood. There, the Ravens unsaddled and rubbed down their horses. After seeing to her own mount, Bree picked up Fia's two saddle bags and carried them over to where one of Gavyn's warriors was lighting a fire. There, she settled down on the soft grass.

It was time to find out a little about the woman she was to impersonate.

Bree opened the first of the bags and pulled out the contents: neatly rolled tunics and shifts, and a lovely soft woolen wrap. Even in the murky light, she could see it was a beautiful color—that of the sea in summer.

This was clearly a cherished item, perhaps a gift for Midwinter Fire from one of the other maids of Albia, or from family. The clothing smelled of lavender, and amongst the contents of the pack, Bree found a small cloth pouch filled with the sharp-smelling flowers. At the bottom of the bag, there was a pair of slippers and a few pairs of woolen tights. Everything was scrupulously clean and folded neatly.

Bree's brow furrowed. *Neat.* She'd need to remember that.

Hauling the other saddle bag over to her, she repeated the process she had for the first. Only, this bag was far more interesting. Underneath a woolen robe, she found a small leather-bound diary with letters in a tidy bundle. This was a good find—for Bree needed to learn more about Fia mac Callum. Nevertheless, it was getting too dark to read now.

With a sigh of frustration, Bree put the diary aside and withdrew a bone-handled hairbrush and a hand-held looking glass from the pack.

For the first time, she glimpsed what she'd become.

The light was poor, and her reflection was a little distorted, the silver tarnished with age, yet Bree saw herself clearly enough.

A stranger stared back at her.

She'd once had flaxen hair and golden eyes like her brother, but now—although her features still belonged to her—everything had been dulled. Her eyes were hazel rather than dark gold, with strange round pupils, and her hair, although thick and wavy, was the color of oak. Her face was rounder, and her skin had a pinker tone with a scattering of freckles across the bridge of her nose.

She wasn't ugly. She just appeared … ordinary.

Mouth pursing, Bree put the looking glass away. Digging deep into the bag, she retrieved a clay bottle of lavender-scented oil and a large block of lavender soap. Fia had certainly loved this scent; the herby, woodsy perfume filled the air now.

Finally, Bree pulled out a leather-wrapped parcel. Unwrapping it, she cast a jaundiced eye over figurines of four of the five Gods that mortals worshipped—The Mother, The Maiden, The Warrior, and The Hag—all intricately carved out of rosewood and varnished. Unsurprisingly, there was no figurine of the fifth God. The Reaper represented death. It was bad luck to have his likeness drawn, carved, or sculpted.

Bree hastily rewrapped the figurines. These Gods meant nothing to her. The Shee knelt before their Ancestors and The Great Raven. Nonetheless, she was Fia now, and once she arrived at Duncrag, she'd need to put these idols on display.

With a sigh, Bree began to repack the saddle bags.

"Find anything useful?" Gavyn sank into a cross-legged position next to her, casting a jaundiced eye over the bags and their contents.

"Possibly," she replied, putting away the last of the items she'd examined. "There's a diary and letters … they should give me an idea of what Fia mac Callum was like."

"For what it's worth, she was plain of face and as timid as a fawn," Gavyn replied. "The lass froze when we killed her escort and didn't even try to run when I came for her."

Bree's heart sank at this news. "Iron bite me," she muttered. "How am I to pretend to be such a mouse."

Gavyn snorted, and Bree cut him a sharp look. She'd already weathered her brother's scorn; she wouldn't put up with her ex-lover's disdain as well.

Sighing, she then scrubbed a hand over her face. Just the thought of pretending to be sweet and meek wearied her. "Mor wants me to find out what happened to Bryce Elmsong as well," she admitted after a pause.

Gavyn raised a tawny eyebrow. "She thinks the healer is still alive?"

"Possibly," she replied. "Although if he's being held prisoner, I'm to find out what he's revealed and deal with him. The Marav likely have no idea that we can take their true form … it's a weapon best kept hidden."

"That's wise … but what if he's merely walked out?"

"I'm still to kill him. Desertion is punishable by death … you know that."

Gavyn's gaze narrowed. "Did he send back anything of use before he went silent?"

Bree nodded. "His last silver acorn revealed that the Marav are preparing to move against us. There are more ironsmiths than ever in the realm … and the overkings are building armies. Apparently, in Cannich, they're even drafting the Circines, Druthen, and Lothin."

"Really? I thought the hill tribes kept to themselves."

"Not any longer." Aye, Mor had good reason for ensuring a spy lived amongst the enemy—the Marav High King was a vindictive bastard who'd long nursed a grudge against the Shee.

Gavyn's gaze narrowed as he studied her. "So, it's up to you to earn the chief-enforcer's trust" —an edge crept into his voice— "and get him to whisper the High King's plans into your ear?"

"That's right." Bree glanced away, deliberately dismissive. Nonetheless, dread clenched deep in her chest. Her people hated *all* warrior-druids, but the chief-enforcer was the worst of them. "Although I'd prefer to kill him."

"Mor will want you to stay at Duncrag a while," Gavyn reminded her coolly. "Try to refrain from cutting his throat in the first few moons."

"I'll do my best," she replied, distracted now—for she'd caught sight of lights in the trees to her right. Beautiful golden flames that flickered in the gloaming and beckoned to her. A soft gasp of wonder escaped her, and she found herself wanting to rise to her feet and walk into the trees, to follow the lights.

"Careful." Gavyn's voice intruded then, jerking Bree out of her reverie. "Don't let the corpse candles beguile you."

Shaking her head to clear it, she muttered a curse. In her Shee form, the candles would never have drawn her in. She knew they led their victims into deadly bogs, swamps, or marshes, never to be seen again. "I hate feeling this *weak*," she growled, deliberately keeping her gaze averted from the corpse candles now.

Gavyn's grey eyes gleamed in the flames that curled up from the fire before them, and Bree wondered if he was secretly gloating at her situation. Their story had ended many years earlier, but he'd been bitter over it for a long while afterward. The edge she'd heard in his voice just before warned her that resentment still simmered. "This forced stay among the Marav might do you good, Bree," he said after a lengthy pause. "Who knows, it might be *humbling*."

Bree didn't get a chance to open Fia mac Callum's diary until the following noon. They'd stopped on the shore of Loch Caith, where a cold breeze rippled the dark water. Clouds scudded overhead, playing hide-and-seek with the sun.

Seated upon a mossy stone, Bree finished her meal of bread, cheese, and fruit, her gaze scanning the loch. The lochs in Albia were different from those in Sheehallion, for they had a brooding, watchful air about them that set her nerves on edge.

Nearby, her escort watered their horses, leaving her in peace for a short while. It was time to do some much-needed research. Untying the diary, she removed the letters. It made sense to start with these.

The first was a missive from Fia's mother. The lass had been from a well-do-to family, for the woman wrote well. It was a chatty, rambling letter, full of inane details.

Irritated, Bree opened the second letter, and a few moments later, a victory smile tugged at the corners of her lips. This was more like it, for this was a missive from the chief-enforcer himself, sent to his bride-to-be.

The man's name was Cailean mac Brochan. Compared to the wordy letter she'd just read, his style was refreshingly blunt. Nonetheless, there was nothing romantic about his words; it was as if the man was conducting business.

Bree snorted. Of course, he was. Mor's spy at Baldeen had assured her that the chief-enforcer hadn't even met the woman he'd 'bought'.

Nonetheless, some prospective mates would have included a few pleasantries in his letter, a little … softness. Not mac Brochan. Instead, he'd merely listed his 'conditions'.

"I require a wife who speaks softly and enjoys silence," she read aloud. "A woman who makes no demands of me. My role takes much of my time and focus, and my wife mustn't intrude." Bree halted then before pulling a face. *Arrogant prick.* "You are to keep our quarters in order, but you are forbidden from touching any weapons, papers, or books that I bring inside. My role demands that I'm away from Duncrag frequently, so I require you to be independent and industrious during these periods. As chief-enforcer, and a member of the druidic council, I am privy to sensitive information … as such, I will not discuss the High King's business with you."

Quietly simmering, she read the rest of the letter, where he outlined the wedding arrangements—a handfasting on the banks of the River Lethe, with the High King himself as witness, followed by a great feast.

Bree lowered the letter, scowling. She hadn't realized the handfasting would be such a big event.

"We need to move on," Gavyn called from a few yards away. The Ravens were already on their feet and readying their horses.

Nodding, Bree tucked the letters back into the diary. But as she did so, a frown creased her brow. The chief-enforcer's arrogance had rippled off the page. Fia mac Callum must have been desperate for a husband, to accept such terms.

Bree stood up and moved to her garron, stuffing the diary back into her saddle bag.

Iron blind me, I'd rather try and charm a powrie.

5: NO MATCH FOR YOU

CRESTING THE LAST hill before Albia's capital, Bree drew up her pony.

She'd never ventured this close to Duncrag before, for the fort lay around two and a half days' journey from the nearest barrow. Nonetheless, it was as grim as she'd envisaged.

Perched high upon a rocky escarpment, and catching the last rays of the setting sun, the vast broch—many times larger than the ruin they'd passed days earlier—commanded over the pinewoods and grassy knolls beneath it. Even the serrated, snowclad mountains that reared to the north couldn't intimidate it. The broch was windowless, and from this distance appeared like a giant grey beehive crowned by a turf roof. Below the broch, terraces packed with squat dwellings and lined by high stone walls wound their way down to where a bridge crossed the swiftly flowing River Lethe.

Mist wreathed up from the river, giving the fort an otherworldly appearance.

Bree's mouth thinned. This crude place could never compare to Sheehallion's ethereal beauty.

Tearing her gaze away from her destination, Bree glanced over her shoulder at her companions and frowned. "You'd better put your glamors in place now … before we near the gates," she muttered. "Faces as pretty as yours will give us all away."

Her comment drew smirks from the Ravens, yet they heeded her. Relations between Bree and her escort had been strained during the journey south. Gavyn was the only one who'd bothered to converse with her; although every time he had, she'd seen the distaste in his eyes. And each time, his reaction had vexed her.

She didn't need reminding of what she'd become.

A breeze whispered over the hilltop, bringing with it the sweet scent of rose—Shee magic. Moments later, the sculpted features of the four males, who were now mounting their horses, altered to resemble the more rugged, flawed, faces of Marav men. And instead of eyes with slitted pupils, like a cat's, their gazes were mortal. Just as Bree's was. Unlike her disguise, her escort's glamors wouldn't hold up under close inspection, especially if a druid approached. However, it would get them through the gates and into the fort.

"Come on then." Gavyn urged his horse forward. "They'll shut the gates soon."

Silently, they all followed him, closing the final furlongs to their destination at last.

But as they made their way back onto the road, Bree caught sight of something on the low hill that lay northwest of Duncrag. A cluster of figures wearing crimson robes stood atop the mound, their arms raised to the sky.

Bree's lip curled, while the Raven who rode behind her hissed a curse.

Sacrificers.

There were five paths a druid could take, and those who donned the red robe carried out ritualistic sacrifices to keep the Gods happy. They also conducted the blood-letting ceremonies, rituals that were said to refill a druid's well of power.

Bree and her escort were a distance from the sacrificers, although she caught the drone of their voices, carrying through the still, damp air.

Jaw clenching, she tore her gaze from the hilltop and kicked her garron into a brisk trot. Such sights would be commonplace here. She would have to get used to them. All the same, she now kept her gaze firmly focused on the high stacked-stone walls encircling the lowest level of the fort.

A short while later, the pony's hooves thudded across wood, crossing the wide bridge toward the gates leading into Duncrag.

The gloaming was upon them, and the guards, clad in leather and fur, were about to draw the heavy iron gates shut for the night.

Iron. A chill feathered over Bree's skin. She'd be surrounded by it here. In this form, iron couldn't hurt her—but the sight of it was unnerving, all the same.

"What's your business in Duncrag?" One of the guards at the gates greeted them. Like many mortal men, his features were lumpy, his cheeks high-colored.

"We're escorting this woman up to the broch," Gavyn replied, his voice rougher than usual. "Her name's Fia mac Callum. She's to marry the High King's chief-enforcer tomorrow."

Bree's pulse sped up at this announcement. Suddenly, it all seemed too real. This time tomorrow, she'd be married to a warrior-druid, living a lie while she hunted for the secrets Mor needed.

The guard's manner swiftly altered from aggressive to respectful. "Aye, we've been expecting you," he replied with a nod, curiosity gleaming in his eyes now as he studied Bree. "Just follow The Thoroughfare up to the broch."

Gavyn nodded, and their party moved on, clip-clopping over packed earth under the long shadow of the guard house and into a wide dirt space. Squat stone buildings lined the area, with awnings in front of them, where vendors were shutting up for the day. A group of youths was brawling in the center of the clearing, their coarse shouts echoing high into the damp air as they grappled with each other.

Ignoring them, Bree looked around. She wrinkled her nose then as the reek of piss, dung, and rotting food hit her. The stench was so foul that her stomach churned. Changing into a mortal had wrought many changes upon her body, including dulling her senses. But it hadn't dulled them enough.

How could these people live in such squalor?

Behind her, one of her escorts made a choking sound. Of course, Gavyn and the others would find the stink in here unbearable.

Urging her garron forward, Bree made for the road that led off the dirt square, and her escort swiftly followed. The same squalid low cottages with turf roofs lined The Thoroughfare—the wide main street that wound up from the gates to the broch. Along the way, Bree and her escort passed narrow wynds—dark lanes between the dwellings—where dogs skulked and washing lines hung like spiderwebs.

Another smell hit her then, one that caught in the back of her throat: iron.

It was late in the day, but they passed several forges where ironsmiths still labored. The glow of forges illuminated the gloaming from doorways while the clang of hammers echoed out into the street—as did the hiss of hot metal being plunged into water.

Bree's nostrils flared, and she resisted the urge to glance over her shoulder, to see Gavyn's reaction. She knew that he and the other Ravens would be struggling. The Shee wielded steel blades, which were stronger than iron. However, the Marav favored the latter, for they knew just being near iron drained their enemies of strength. Just the touch of iron to the skin of one of the Shee would leave a fiery burn.

Bryce was right, she thought as she suppressed a shudder. The ironsmiths of Duncrag were indeed working hard, forging iron weapons to use against the Shee.

They were halfway up the hill when a woman stepped out of a cottage and threw the contents of a bucket across the road. Liquid splattered to Bree's right, and her pony snorted, side-stepping.

Bree glanced down at her cloak, but she couldn't see if whatever that bucket had contained caught her. The daylight had almost faded now, braziers illuminating the fort. *Disgusting place.* Mouth thinning, she urged her pony into a brisk trot.

Fortunately though, the higher they climbed, the fresher the air became—and by the time they rode up the final incline before the huge iron-studded gates in front of the broch, Bree sucked sharp, cold night air into her lungs.

Once again, Gavyn introduced them, and again, they were ushered through, riding into a large open space, lined on three sides by low-slung buildings and stone walls, with steps on the fourth side leading up to the great doors of the broch itself.

Bree drew up her pony and vaulted off, landing lightly on the stones.

"Careful," Gavyn muttered from where he'd dismounted next to her. His voice was rough, betraying his tension. Being amongst the Marav and in such proximity to iron was taking its toll. "You're Fia mac Callum, remember. Move with a bit less grace."

Bree bristled at his command before she reminded herself that Gavyn had a point. Her new body didn't feel as nimble or strong as her Shee one, yet she still carried herself with the same confidence and elegance as the rest of her people—not a bumbling Marav.

Nodding, she handed her mount's reins to the captain. They both still had their hoods up, although she caught the glint of his silvery eyes as he watched her. "Good luck," he said finally.

Bree's brow furrowed. "I don't need it."

Their gazes locked then. The closeness Bree and Gavyn had once shared was in the past, but the ghost of it still lingered. For a moment, she thought the captain might say something else.

But he didn't. She could almost taste his impatience to be away.

Two heavyset figures approached from the gatehouse, big men clad in dark leather with fur cloaks around their shoulders.

"Give us your bags, lass," one of them greeted Bree. "We'll carry them up to your quarters."

Bree nodded, motioning to the large leather packs strapped behind her saddle. "This is all I have."

One of the guards collected her things, while the other, who'd greeted her, motioned to the enormous broch that loomed above them. Braziers had been lit by the doors leading into the round tower, ruddy firelight flickering on dull stone. "I'll take you to meet the chief-enforcer now."

Bree's belly clenched. She'd thought she might be given time to prepare herself for meeting her husband-to-be.

She glanced at Gavyn again, but he'd turned away, mounting his horse once more.

Standing in the midst of the yard, flanked by two mortals, her breath steaming in the chill, Bree watched him go. The other Ravens followed. None of them bid her farewell. They merely favored her with lingering glances, their expressions veiled beneath the shadows of their hoods.

That's it, Bree thought as her gaze tracked her escort through the gates leading back onto The Thoroughfare. The main gates would be closed now; they'd have to find lodgings for the night in the lower levels of the fort. *I'm on my own.*

"The Hag's nails," the guard who'd shouldered her bags muttered. "What have you got in here … rocks?"

Bree didn't answer. Instead, she lowered her gaze demurely. Best she started behaving like a meek maiden right away.

"Not a chatty one, are you?" His companion eyed her.

The guard holding her belongings snorted. "The chief-enforcer is a surly bastard. The last thing he'll want is a mouthy wife."

"She's comely though." Bree glanced up to see naked appreciation flare in the other guard's pale-blue eyes. A note of envy had crept into his voice. His boldness made her itch to punch him.

"A Maid of Albia isn't going to have a face like the Ben Neeya, is she?" His companion replied, impatient now as he nodded to Bree. "Come on, lass … it's cold enough to freeze The Warrior's balls off out here. Follow me."

Bree did, relieved to get out of the chill.

They crossed the wide yard and climbed the stairs toward the heavy doors above. Bree noted that she walked differently now—she no longer moved in supple, stalking steps as she once had. As she mounted the steps, her thigh muscles strained slightly. Her body definitely had lost some of its former strength.

Two more guards, these clad in chainmail with domed helmets upon their heads, flanked the oaken doors. Wordlessly, they drew them open for Bree and her escort.

Sighing as she stepped in out of the cold and damp onto a rush-covered floor, Bree pushed back her hood and glanced around. She'd expected to enter the vast hall within, but this space appeared to be the entranceway, with another set of doors ahead of her. A single brazier burned in the center of the chamber, the flames casting long shadows over the damp stone walls, while to the right, worn stone steps led upstairs. To the left was another, shadowy, set of steps. These led underground.

"This way," the guard, who wasn't carrying her things, grunted. He took the stairs up to the narrow landing on the floor above.

And, as before, Bree followed—even as her belly started to pitch.

Irritated by her reaction, she curled her fingers into fists. Curse this mortal body and its weakness. What had happened to her nerves of steel? Ever since passing through the stones, her emotions had run wild.

The guard she'd been following halted then and turned to the curtained entrance to his left. "Mac Brochan," he called out roughly. "Your bride is here."

Meanwhile, his companion, who lugged her bags, continued up the stairs.

A heartbeat followed before a low, powerful voice replied. "Show her in then."

Bree's breathing caught. That voice rumbled like thunder through the curtain, and it had a rough, *aggressive*, edge to it.

Ancestors forgive her. She hadn't even set eyes on her husband-to-be, and she was quailing.

Pull yourself together, she snarled inwardly. *The Queen's assassin doesn't shake in her boots before one of the Marav. He's no match for you.*

Repeating these words to herself, she waited while the guard stepped away. Then, Bree pushed the curtain aside and walked inside.

6: FIRST IMPRESSIONS

BREE STEPPED INTO the entrance to the alcove, feeling the draft against her spine as the curtain swished shut behind her, sealing her inside with the mortal she was to soon wed.

The chief-enforcer stood with his back to her, staring down at the crackling hearth.

The first thing Bree noted was his size. He was huge, standing at least six-and-a-half feet. Of course, the fur cloak he wore around his shoulders emphasized their breadth, but there was no denying the warrior-druid filled the alcove.

The second thing she noted was the giant dog lying to his left.

The beast was indeed *massive*—bigger even than the wolves that roamed the northern Uplands of Albia. And as she stared at the hound, it raised its head, golden glowing eyes fixing upon her. Bree's already fast pulse lurched into a gallop.

This dog, with its pricked ears and long moss-green coat, didn't belong to this world, but her own. Fae hounds guarded the territory around barrows, protecting the portals between the realms from the Marav.

Mortals usually feared these creatures, calling them 'harbingers of death'. Fae hounds were silent hunters, yet its bloodcurdling howl had been known to stop men's hearts.

Bree hadn't expected to find one *here*.

The dog watched her, its glowing eyes unnervingly bright. And then it cocked its head.

Sweat slid between Bree's shoulder blades. *Shit.* This was the last thing she needed. She wasn't glamored, but she now worried that the hound would see through her Marav shell, to who she really was inside.

Don't be a fool … of course, it can't.

Since passing through the stones, she'd noted that she'd lost the ability to touch minds with animals—a gift all Shee were blessed with. Fia's pony was a sweet-tempered beast, but his thoughts had been closed to her.

And just as well too; that way, this fae hound wouldn't unmask her.

Swallowing hard, she tore her attention from the dog, her gaze sliding over the stacked-stone walls surrounding her— where iron swords, axes, and pikes hung—to the low beams that crisscrossed overhead. The alcove itself was sparsely furnished with just a single wooden table lined by two benches. It was a meeting room of sorts—a decent-sized space—but the big man and his monstrous dog made it seem cramped.

Bree focused once more on the chief-enforcer. From the back, his neck appeared thick and bullish, his crow-colored hair cropped short to his head. He stood with his legs slightly apart, his hands by his sides, as if readying himself for a fight.

Drawing in a deep breath through her nose and then slowly releasing it through her mouth, Bree concentrated on steadying herself. Her arrival in Duncrag had knocked her off-course, but she needed to regain control of her emotions and senses.

She also had to remember that she was playing a role now.

She was Fia mac Callum—a 'Maid of Albia'—a young woman tutored to become the wife of a high-born man or a military leader. She'd recently learned that ordering a 'Maid of Albia' for a wife was costly, although these women were famed for their grace and good manners. From the age of twelve, they were taught how to please their men.

Burying her distaste, both for the woman she was impersonating and this world that she was forced to inhabit, Bree gently cleared her throat. "My lord?"

"I'm no lord," he replied, turning to her.

A pair of piercing woad-blue eyes settled upon her. They were startling in their hue—not a color she was used to seeing among her people.

But his eyes weren't the only startling thing about him.

From the back, the man's size had given the impression of brutishness. She'd expected a coarse, lumpy face with a heavy brow and bullish jaw—but her husband-to-be had chiseled, sharp features that gave him a hawkish look.

His jaw was strong yet lean and shadowed with stubble, and he had a well-molded mouth. There was a severity to his face though, as if it smiled rarely. Her gaze traveled down then, taking in his broad chest and narrow waist and hips. He wore a leather vest with a knife belt strapped across the front and tight leather breeches. His arms were bare and covered in druidic tattoos. A knotted swirl of dark-blue markings wrapped itself around his heavily muscled bicep and disappeared under his vest before traveling across his collarbone to his neck.

Bree glanced back up to his face. Aye, he was a Marav toad—and far less handsome than males of her race—but all the same, Bree had to admit that he wasn't foul to look upon.

Just as well, she reminded herself grimly. *For you will be spreading your legs for him soon enough.*

Pushing aside the disturbing thought—for the fact that she'd soon couple with a man responsible for hunting and killing countless Shee made her feel sick—Bree ducked her head.

"Like what you see?" The question was blunt.

Bree stiffened. She hadn't realized she'd been staring. She needed to watch that. A Maid of Albia didn't gawk. He'd wonder where her manners were.

Cailean mac Brochan moved close then, looming over her. "Lift your head," he commanded. Bree raised her chin and angled her head back to meet that unnerving gaze. Making such bold eye contact with him was unsettling, especially now that they were standing just a foot apart.

She inhaled the smell of him then: leather and male musk, with a hint of clove. It wasn't unpleasant, not like some of the foul odors she'd endured on the way up to the broch. However, he didn't smell like a male of her own people. Gavyn's scent was fresh as a mountain glade. This man's scent was darker, sharper.

In truth, he unsettled her. And this close, she could smell magic on him too—pine and campfire—an odor that made her stomach clench.

This was why she'd had to leave her old self behind. She couldn't come before this man glamored. But even though she was Marav now, worry crept in.

This man wasn't like others of his race. He was the chief-enforcer, a powerful warrior-druid who cloaked himself in earth magic and had a fae hound at his side. What if he smelled her lie?

His gaze roamed Bree's face now. Ever since turning to look at her, his expression had remained stony. She'd expected the Marav to be easier to read than her own people, but this man gave her nothing.

"You're not what I expected," he said after a lengthy pause, his tone disapproving.

"No?" she asked lightly.

"No."

Trying to ignore the sudden dampness to her palms, Bree forced a polite smile. "How so?"

"I thought you'd be fresher-faced, shy. But there's a boldness to you." Accusation crept into his voice.

Curse it. She wasn't doing a great job at pretending to be Fia. Bree ducked her head once more. "I'm just excited to finally meet you," she murmured.

"There's no point in acting meek," he snapped, scowling. "In your letters, you told me you were two and twenty … was that a lie?"

Bree swallowed, raising her chin to meet his eye once more. "No … I've always looked more mature than my age."

Even in her Marav form, she looked no older than a woman of twenty-five or so. However, this sharp-eyed individual had seen what she'd been sure he wouldn't—that her eyes weren't young.

He continued to stare down at her, and Bree resisted the urge to squirm.

Squirm? She hadn't felt this uncomfortable under a male gaze in years.

"Aye, well … you'll do, I suppose," he muttered after a pause.

Bree stiffened. *Rude bastard.*

In her Shee form, she was *beautiful.* Lovely enough to bring a mere mortal like him to his knees. "I hope that I'm pleasing to you," she said, careful to keep her voice sweet and low.

He gave a snort and stepped back from her then, before moving over to a shelf where a jug and a row of earthen cups sat. "Mead?"

"Aye, thank you." Bree's pride was stinging now, but she managed to swallow her annoyance.

The chief-enforcer poured them both drinks and passed Bree her cup. "We'll be wed at noon tomorrow."

Bree nodded; this announcement wasn't unexpected.

"You will sleep in one of the guest alcoves tonight," he went on before taking a sip from his cup. "And then, directly after our handfasting, you will move into my quarters."

"Will there be a wedding feast?" she asked, hoping there wouldn't be. The quicker this was over the better.

"Aye." His dark brows knitted together. "I told you that in my letter," he snapped. "Don't you remember?"

Bree kicked herself. She'd forgotten that detail. "Of course." She lifted her own cup to her lips and took a sip.

Quelling the urge to gag, she swallowed it. The drink was rough and pungent, not at all like the sweet beverages she was used to.

"What is it?" Her husband-to-be had marked her reaction. His gaze was hard and cold now as he studied her.

"Nothing," she lied, forcing a bright smile. "The mead is just a little stronger than I'm used to, that's all." And then, steeling herself, she took another sip and swallowed, ignoring her churning stomach as she did so.

Mac Brochan's mouth thinned. "You're an odd one … but that doesn't matter. I need a wife, and you understand my *conditions*."

Bree nodded, even as she fought a frown. Aye, she did remember those. The man had a nerve.

Silence fell then as they both nursed their drinks.

It wasn't a companionable pause though, but a tension-filled one. Mac Brochan's expression had grown even more severe than before. His harsh manner put Bree on edge.

This wasn't going well. The last thing she needed was for her the chief-enforcer to decide she wouldn't suit him as a wife, after all, and send her away.

A chill slithered down Bree's spine as she imagined Mor's wrath. No, she couldn't let him do that.

In truth, she was nervous to say anything else. After reading Fia's letters, she'd tucked them and the diary away without bothering to research further. At the time, she'd been confident that she knew what was expected of her, but so far, she was doing a poor job of being a Maid of Albia.

She'd have to make a start on Fia's diary later. She needed to get into the young woman's head.

Sipping her foul mead silently, Bree wished he'd terminate this uncomfortable meeting and send her to the guest quarters.

All the while, her husband-to-be stared her down. His scrutiny was unnerving. She could feel the weight of his judgment. He wasn't happy with her, that much was clear. Lowering her gaze, she waited for him to speak.

Eventually, the chief-enforcer downed the dregs of his mead before taking Bree's half-finished cup from her. "I shall let you retire now," he announced, his tone sour. "The queen's women will visit you in the morning and help you prepare for the ceremony."

Bree raised her chin to see that he wore a grim expression. Pulse quickening, she dipped her head once more. "Aye, I'm tired."

"Rest then … and ready yourself for tomorrow," he replied, dismissing her with a curt wave of his hand. "The next time we meet will be at our handfasting."

7: A DEAD WOMAN'S WORDS

ALONE IN THE tiny guest alcove on the floor above the chief-enforcer's meeting space, Bree whispered a string of gutter curses.

Iron smite her, that had gone terribly. Mac Brochan was insolent and unpleasant—and he hadn't hidden his scorn for her.

"You've got a challenge there," she muttered. "That cold bastard wouldn't trust his own mother."

She could hardly be surprised though. He was the chief-enforcer, after all.

Bree cast a scowl in the direction of the flimsy curtain that shielded her alcove from the narrow passageway beyond. Unlike Caisteal Gealaich, this broch didn't have internal doors. Anyone could burst in on her, and the lack of security put her already taut nerves on edge.

She hoped that when the queen's women came to ready her the following morning, they'd announce themselves first. Her breathing grew shallow then. She couldn't believe that tomorrow was her wedding day. Tomorrow, she'd meet the High King of Albia.

Bree's mouth twisted. If there was one individual the Shee hated more than the chief-enforcer, it was Talorc mac Brude. The High King held a deep loathing for her people—a reckoning twenty-five years in the making. His animosity had festered ever since his first wife disappeared. The Marav believed that she'd strayed too close to a barrow at sunset and been stolen away. However, the truth was that the woman had met a Shee warrior one day while out riding. They'd become lovers, and shortly after, she'd run away with him.

The incident had also scandalized the Shee—for the warrior who'd stolen the High King's wife was Flynn, Mor's youngest brother.

Rumor had it that, besotted by the Marav woman, Flynn had willingly passed through the stones, giving up everything for love. Over two decades on, no one had seen or heard from him again. Mor's wintry rage had settled over Caisteal Gealaich like a harsh frost in the aftermath.

Dragging herself from her thoughts, Bree turned to the pile of furs, where she'd sleep, her gaze traveling to her saddle bags. The alcove was dimly lit, the ceiling so low that a tall man would have to bow his head to avoid hitting it on the wooden beams overhead. A cresset burned above a table opposite the furs, while a lump of peat smoldered on the hearth against the outer wall.

Bree wrinkled her nose at the pungent peat smoke. There was a vent that let some of the smoke out. However, there were no windows in this foul place to let in any fresh air. Crossing to the furs, she opened her bags and unpacked Fia's things. She hung the clothing up on hooks protruding between the stacked stone on the walls and placed her shoes and boots by the curtained entrance. Fia's lavender-scented soaps, pouches, and oils went on the low stool beside her furs, while she placed the figurines of the Gods on a narrow ledge inset into the alcove wall.

Then, her unpacking done, Bree perched on the edge of the furs and picked up Fia's diary. She'd just untied the thong that held the diary and letters together when a young female voice called out from the other side of the curtain. "Supper."

Irritation spiked through Bree. Couldn't she have one evening to herself?

Swallowing her annoyance, she sucked in a deep breath before releasing it slowly. "Aye … come in."

Moments passed, and then a small soft woman of her own age with curly peat-brown hair and sky-blue eyes pushed her way into the alcove. Like most Marav women, she wore a long sleeveless tunic, girded at the waist with a leather thong, and sturdy leather boots. It was cold this eve, so a woolen shawl covered her bare shoulders. An iron pendant—a small staff—hung from a leather thong around her neck. A protection amulet.

The servant bore a tray of what looked and smelled like venison stew, and she favored Bree with a shy smile. "I thought you'd be hungry … after such a long journey."

Bree was going to deny it and send the woman away, for she just wanted to start on the diary, when her belly gave a loud growl.

"I'm Mirren." The woman gave another timid smile. "I'll be your handmaid when you move in with the chief-enforcer."

"I'm pleased to meet you," Bree answered, remembering her manners. "Thank you, for supper."

Mirren placed the tray on the small table in the corner, which had a stool beside it. "The queen's women will help you get ready tomorrow," she said, meeting Bree's gaze fleetingly before glancing away again. "But I will see you the following day … once you and your husband have had some time alone together."

Bree's stomach flipped over at these innocent, well-meaning words.

The thought of spending time, alone, with the chief-enforcer, of being plowed by the brute, made her feel queasy. When she was going after a mark with a blade in her hand, she was in her element. But this was uncharted territory.

Suddenly, her appetite deserted her.

Mercifully, Mirren didn't stay long.

Bree didn't engage her in conversation—eager for her handmaid to leave so she could research the woman she was impersonating—so after she'd delivered supper, the lass hovered awkwardly for a few moments. Then, her cheeks pink with embarrassment, she bid Bree a good eve and left her alone.

Leaving her ripe-smelling stew to cool, Bree got down to work. It was too dim to read seated on the furs, so she moved over to the table and sat down. Opening the diary upon the first page, she then began to read.

Mid-winter Fire—Year of The Warrior.

My time at the House lengthens, and I still have no offer of marriage. I begin to wonder if what Maisi said to me out of spite two winters ago is actually true. I am too meek, too plain. The suitors who come here and take their pick of us forever pass me over in favor of one of my Sisters.

Mother Gelda says I must be patient, that one day a man will visit who will see my virtues.

But until that day, I wait.

Life here is lonely ... sometimes. That is why I've begun this diary. The friends I made when I first came here have found their husbands. I haven't seen Ma, Da, or Bran for so long. They never visit, and Mother Gelda forbids any of us from leaving the House.

I think she worries that on a trip home, one of us might meet someone ... unsuitable ... that we will run away with him.

I wouldn't though. I'm too obedient ... too eager to please.

The first entry ended there, and Bree lowered the diary.

The lass's words—written in a neat, flowing hand—were unsettling.

Bree wanted to curl her lip at Fia's weakness. However, she didn't. She'd thought reading a dead woman's words wouldn't bother her—after all, she'd been just some foolish Marav wench. But there was a vulnerability in that entry, a deep loneliness.

Fia had been surrounded by others at the House of Maids, yet she had felt alone.

Alone.

Frowning, Bree closed the diary.

That was enough reading for tonight.

8: THE WILL OF THE KING

"YOUR MOVE."

CAILEAN gave a brusque nod and replaced the lid upon the small clay pot sitting in front of him. He then picked it up, methodically shaking the pair of dice within.

Across the table, Torran huffed an irritated sigh.

"Don't rush me," Cailean growled. He shook the pot for a while longer, deliberately taking his time now, before removing the lid and looking inside. "A three and a four."

Torran watched him carefully, his grey eyes narrowing. "Liar."

Cailean handed the enforcer seated opposite him the cup.

Torran peered inside, his mouth quirking. "I knew it!"

Cailean frowned. Indeed, he had lied—instead of a three and a four, there were too 'ones' inside the pot.

"That's your last life gone … I win," Torran pointed out. "Three games in a row. You're not normally this easy to read."

Cailean reached for his tankard and took a deep pull of ale. Indeed, he was usually better at playing 'Liar'. "I'm distracted."

"Poor loser." Torran flashed him a grin, his teeth gleaming in the lantern light. "Play again?"

Cailean shook his head.

"What?" Torran inclined his head. "Don't want a fourth thrashing?"

"No."

The two men sat in Cailean's meeting alcove, where he'd met Fia mac Callum earlier. They often relaxed in here after they'd finished work for the day. And Cailean usually enjoyed 'Liar'.

However, tonight, he wasn't in the mood.

"Cheer up." Torran set the pot down between them. "At least you aren't wedding a hag." He cut Cailean a sly look then. "Some of the lads got a look at your bride-to-be earlier … they say she's—"

"Enough," Cailean cut him off. "We aren't discussing her."

Torran minded him, although the glint in his eye made Cailean's hackles rise. Aye, he'd also noted Fia's attractiveness, and it unsettled him. Mother Gelda had promised to send her plainest Maid, yet a sensual woman with delicious curves and knowing eyes had stepped into this alcove. She wasn't at all what he'd expected. Not at all what he wanted.

Meanwhile, his friend topped up his tankard from the jug by his elbow. He then viewed Cailean, his expression veiling. "You *really* don't want this, do you?" he asked after a few moments.

Bitterness flooded Cailean's mouth. "I told you I didn't." He picked up his tankard and took another gulp. "I'm only going through with it to please the High King … he's obsessed about continuing the druidic bloodlines."

Torran nodded, although his brow furrowed. "For good reason … we're dying out."

Cailean screwed his mouth up in response. He knew all that, but let the other enforcers produce children—let *them* ensure there were warrior-druids for generations to come.

"There are worse things than taking a wife, you know?" Torran pointed out after a heavy pause.

Cailean grunted.

"I'm serious."

"So am I."

Torran folded his arms across his chest. Like Cailean's, they bore inked swirls of druidic tattoos. And like his captain, he wore a sturdy leather vest with a knife belt strapped across the front. His dark-blond hair was cut short, cropped against his scalp. "Maybe this marriage will surprise you," he said, his mouth curving once more. "Maybe you'll grow to enjoy her company."

"Shut it, would you," Cailean snarled.

Heedless of his warning, the warrior merely grinned. Out of all those in his guard, Torran was the only enforcer who didn't fear him. They'd entered the High King's guard together—new enforcers who'd worked their way up the ranks shoulder-to-shoulder.

These days, Cailean was chief-enforcer and Torran was his second.

But Torran still didn't mind him—even when he should.

"Miserable goat," Torran goaded, swirling the ale in his tankard. "I hope they teach the Maids of Albia patience … the lass will need it."

Cailean drained the last of his ale and slammed his tankard down on the table. The move was so violent that Skaal, who'd been dozing by the hearth, lurched up with a grunt, her golden eyes fixing upon him.

Meanwhile, Torran hadn't flinched. He was still watching Cailean, amusement twinkling in his eyes.

"That's it." Cailean pushed himself up from the table. "You and me in the training yard … now."

Torran arched a tawny eyebrow. "This late?"

"Aye … it's time I gave you a beating."

His second rose to his feet. "Go on then … but if you fight like you dice, it'll be *me* handing you *your* arse."

A while later, Cailean climbed the steps to his quarters. He was still sweating after sparring with Torran, and his ribs were bruised from the punches he'd received.

However, he'd bested his second in the end. Torran had limped off, spitting out a gob of blood, and Cailean had watched him go with grim satisfaction. The fight had helped, had taken the edge off the fury that simmered in his gut.

Only, it didn't change anything.

This time tomorrow, he'd be wedded.

Cailean's pulse thudded in his ears. Curse the High King, he didn't want to go through with this. But Talorc had made things clear. Take a wife or step down from his position.

Frustration surged up once more, making him clench his hands at his sides. By the Reaper's scythe, he didn't have time for this. The past year had been a blur of patrols and Shee-hunting expeditions. The High King's hatred for the faery race beyond the veil knew no bounds.

Cailean's mouth thinned. Before entering the High King's service and working his way up through the ranks to his current position, he'd never given the Shee much thought. Aye, they were as dangerous as they were beautiful. However, he'd always believed that if you left them well alone, they wouldn't do you any harm either.

There were plenty of tales though, of people who'd strayed too close to barrows at sunrise or sunset and been killed or stolen away; and other stories of babies ripped from their cradles and replaced by a sly changeling.

Cailean had hunted them, fought them, for years now—and carried scars on his body from every encounter—but unlike the High King, he couldn't bring himself to loathe the Shee. The campaign Talorc waged against them was wearying.

Skaal padded silently behind Cailean, claws clicking on stone. The hound's name meant 'Shadow' in the Albian tongue; indeed, the dog behaved like one. Silent, watchful, and always at Cailean's side.

Cailean cast the dog a glance. "What did you think of her?"

Skaal's golden eyes gleamed in the guttering light of the cressets burning on the walls. It was said that the Shee could communicate with fae hounds by thought, yet as a Marav, he'd never managed it. Even so, he sometimes swore Skaal understood him when he spoke to her.

He'd expected the blood to drain from Fia's face at the sight of the fae hound. Few people liked being close to Skaal—but his bride-to-be hadn't quailed.

"The woman is too bold," Cailean ground out. "She'll have to learn her place."

Reaching his quarters, which sat a few yards away from his meeting alcove, he shoved aside the heavy curtain and strode in. Skaal padded in after him and headed straight to the sheepskin rug in front of the large hearth. The hound was so big that she took up the entire space.

Cailean's gaze shifted to the platter of food that sat upon the scrubbed oak table in the center of the stone-walled alcove. A servant had brought up his supper, and it smelled like boar stew. He didn't have much appetite this eve; however, the mead he'd drunk earlier had left a cloying taste in his mouth, so he crossed to the table and took a seat.

After a couple of mouthfuls of stew, he threw down his spoon and leaned back in his chair, raking his hands through his short hair.

"The Mother's tits," he ground out. "I'm going to fucking regret this."

His gaze cut to the shelf above the hearth then, where the four rosewood figurines he'd whittled himself years earlier gleamed in the firelight. Mouth compressing, Cailean ducked his head in apology for his blasphemy, even as frustration still pulsed in his gut.

Torran thought he was making a fuss over nothing. Most warriors eventually took wives—and at thirty-three winters, he was the only unwed individual in the druidic council. But Cailean had sworn he'd never be shackled. The High King's command felt like a chokehold.

He'd sacrificed enough for Albia. Talorc could have spared him *this*.

Shifting his attention from the Gods, he surveyed the rest of his quarters: the swords, daggers, and axes hanging on the walls, and the single high-backed chair next to where Skaal dozed.

He'd given up the warmest spot in the chamber to his dog but didn't mind.

However, he'd need another chair in here—for his wife.

Cailean's mouth compressed. This place was his sanctuary. He liked solitude and looked forward to drawing the curtain on the world every evening.

But from tomorrow onward, a woman would be sharing this space.

It would soon look and smell different.

He glanced over at his sleeping nook at the far end of the rectangular alcove, his gut clenching when his attention rested on the pile of furs he retired to every night.

This would be his last night sleeping alone.

He wondered then if he'd have to remind Fia of the conditions she'd agreed to. She seemed to have forgotten them earlier. Aye, he would, especially since there was something he *hadn't* mentioned in his missive.

No, he'd have to spell it all out to the woman. It was best to make everything clear from the start.

Cailean spied items draped over the furs then—garments he hadn't left there earlier in the day. Pushing himself up from the table, he crossed to his sleeping nook. Halting, he surveyed the leather breeches and a beautifully embroidered vest. A golden torque sat next to the clothing—a snake swallowing its tail.

The Serpent of Infinity, a symbol of rebirth.

The irony of it wasn't lost on Cailean. Lips twisting, he bent down and picked up the torque. It was a fine piece of jewelry indeed. However, like the clothing, it didn't belong to him. The High King had provided him with garments and jewelry for the following day's handfasting. He would be expected to wear them.

Cailean's hand tightened around the torque, anger pounding inside him like a war drum. *Fuck new beginnings.* He was the chief-enforcer to the High King, a powerful warrior-druid who commanded a host of men and struck fear into the Shee. He'd worked hard to earn his place at Talorc's side.

But none of that mattered. He couldn't escape the will of the king.

9: WITH MY BODY AND MY LIFE

STANDING ON THE edge of the River Lethe, Bree tried not to fidget.

Her clothing was too restrictive. The women who'd dressed her earlier had tied her bodice so tightly that she could hardly breathe. She wore a silky emerald-colored vest laced with ribbon and a matching full skirt that brushed around her bare ankles. Spring was supposed to be upon them now, but she shivered in a cold wind.

Curse Albia's cold and damp climate.

It didn't help that her clothing was ridiculously thin and she stood barefoot on the mossy riverbank.

Gritting her teeth, Bree cast her gaze over the gathering crowd. The voices of the men surrounding her were loud and coarse. The odor of stale sweat drifted over the riverbank.

She noted too that there were robed druids amongst the throng.

Bree's eyes narrowed as she observed them. Counselors, sacrificers, seers, enforcers, and bards—each wore a different colored cloak to distinguish them. And she could smell their magic too, conifers and wood-ash, heavy and pungent.

Her pulse quickened in response, her fingers curling into fists. She preferred the reek of unwashed bodies to the stench of druids.

How did Bryce suffer living here for so long?

Thinking about her predecessor reminded Bree that she'd need to find out what had happened to him. As soon as this handfasting was over, she would begin her search.

Bristling now, as impatience thrummed through her, she concentrated on keeping her back straight while she awaited mac Brochan. Where was the brute? She'd had enough of being gawked at.

Bree's attention shifted then, over the crowd of retainers and druids, to where the High King stood next to his wife, son, and daughter upon a rise overlooking the river.

Talorc mac Brude was scowling as if he too was tired of waiting for his chief-enforcer. The High King was a big muscular man, although older than she'd expected, his face craggy and harsh. Next to him, the queen—a pretty woman with delicate features and auburn hair that she wore in elaborate braids—was considerably younger.

Bree's gaze lingered on the High King and queen consort a moment longer before shifting to their offspring. The prince was handsome and flamboyant. Like his father, he had swarthy looks, although his long dark hair, oiled and swept back from his face, wasn't yet threaded with grey. A bronze torque gleamed at his throat. His sister stood silently beside him. No older than twenty winters, she had a heart-shaped face and a mane of dark-auburn curls.

The princess glanced Bree's way then. Her full lips quirked into a half-smile.

Heart kicking, Bree lowered her gaze. *Don't stare so, you fool.*

Murmuring reached her then, and she lifted her chin. An instant later, she spied a large figure cutting a swathe through the crowd.

There he was—her husband-to-be.

Bree's chest tightened, her breathing suddenly fast and shallow. She wasn't ready for this. She'd never be ready.

Clad in tight-fitting leather breeches and an embroidered vest, with a golden torque about his neck, the chief-enforcer also walked barefoot. The Marav always handfasted unshod; it grounded them and brought them closer to The Mother and The Maiden.

One of the queen's women had reminded Bree of that earlier.

To Bree's relief, the fae hound didn't follow him. She'd have to be careful around the beast. In her Shee form, she'd be able to touch minds with it—but even as one of the Marav, she felt a connection, like a thread pulling taut whenever the hound glanced her way.

Having the fae hound near was dangerous.

A black cloak rippled from mac Brochan's broad shoulders. Black was the color worn by the enforcers. Bree's skin prickled in revulsion. Of all the druids, enforcers were the worst of them, the ones who hunted her people.

The chief-enforcer closed the gap between them and stepped before her. Like the day before, his expression was severe, his gaze cold. He favored Bree with a brusque nod, and she nodded back. No words passed between them.

A tall, spare figure clad in golden robes approached then. A woman of around fifty, her angular face heavily tattooed, her grey-threaded black hair twisted into tiny braids.

Bree's stomach dropped sharply. *Fuck.*

She hadn't realized the arch-druid—the most powerful of them all—would conduct the ceremony; in truth, she'd thought one of the counselor-druids might. This was bad news, indeed, for if any of the druids could sniff an imposter out, this woman could.

But there was nothing to be done, for the arch-druid had halted before them, her dark eyes sweeping from Mac Brochan to Bree.

Slow your breathing and clear your mind … or she'll sense your agitation.

Despite the cold wind, Bree started to sweat. An instant later, she emptied her head of any thought, any feeling—a skill she'd acquired as an apprentice warrior—and focused on steadying her breath. She'd learned a long time ago that an assassin had to be the master of their fear.

The arch-druid's gaze rested upon Bree's face, and the woman stilled a moment.

She had a stare that could cut through stone. Bree's skin prickled. The arch-druid was probing into her thoughts. The tattoos on her neck glowed slightly now, a sign she was wielding her power.

Sweat trickled down Bree's back, but she stared back—her mind as empty as the sky.

Thank the Ancestors that her training had stuck with her, even through her transformation from Shee to Marav.

However, this was worse than she'd thought, for this woman was a seer.

The arch-druid's stare only lasted a few heartbeats, yet it felt like an eternity.

Mac Brochan cleared his throat then, and the woman's gaze snapped to him. Her strong jaw tightened, and then she unlooped a green ribbon from her belt. "Shall we begin?"

"Aye," he answered, his voice clipped.

"Face each other, and clasp hands."

Relieved to look elsewhere so she didn't have to make eye contact with the arch-druid again, Bree turned to face the chief-enforcer properly. A moment later, he reached out and took her hand.

Bree stiffened.

She wasn't sure what she'd expected his touch to be like. But the warmth and strength in the hand that held hers wasn't it. She hadn't realized the Marav had so much heat burning inside them. The underside of his hand bore rough callouses, a testament to how hard he likely trained and fought.

These were hands that had wielded iron weapons and summoned druidic magic against the Shee—hands that would *own* her later.

Dizziness swept over Bree before she gave herself a hard mental slap. *Control yourself.*

The arch-druid began to wrap the ribbon around their joined hands. "Cailean mac Brochan, chief-enforcer to the High King, I join you with Fia mac Callum of Braewall." The woman's voice carried through the cold, damp air. "May The Mother light your path. May The Warrior protect you. May The Maiden grant you a bounteous family. May The Hag bless you with long, healthy lives … and may The Reaper stay far from your door."

The arch-druid then focused on mac Brochan. "Say your vows," she ordered softly.

The chief-enforcer nodded, his jaw tight, and when he spoke, his voice was slightly choked as if he'd just swallowed nails. "I, Cailean, son of Brochan, pledge to protect you, Fia, daughter of Callum, with my body and my life."

Foreboding prickled Bree's skin. Vows made under the eyes of the Gods were sacred, and although she didn't worship The Five, she was superstitious enough to worry that her deception would rouse their wrath.

Silence fell then, settling uncomfortably, before the arch-druid's brow furrowed. "It's your turn, Fia … make your promise."

Swallowing, Bree forced herself to meet mac Brochan's eye. He stared back at her, his woad-blue gaze giving nothing away. Only the strain to his voice as he'd spoken his vow had betrayed him. "I, Fia, daughter of Callum, pledge to honor you, Cailean, son of Brochan," she said softly. "With my body and my life."

Queasiness churned through her as she finished speaking.

Ancestors, forgive me.

"You are now wed," the arch-druid announced as she unwrapped the ribbon that bound their hands. "You may kiss your bride, Cailean."

Bree's stomach lurched.

Of course, she'd never attended a handfasting before and knew little of the ways of the Marav. She'd thought that the ceremony ended with their vows. But it didn't.

The chief-enforcer's expression appeared carven out of stone at these words, and yet he stepped forward, a hand closing over her forearm. Once again, the strength and heat of his grip jolted through Bree. This man was a furnace.

She wanted to drop her gaze, to avert her face, but pride kept her in place, frozen like a hind in a hunter's sights.

A heartbeat later, heat ignited under her ribs. No, she wouldn't shrink from this beast. A kiss wasn't the worst of what she'd have to suffer from him.

Mac Brochan dipped his head then, his mouth brushing over hers.

The kiss was light, and his lips were soft and warm. For an instant, the scent of leather and ash, and the spicy hint of clove, enveloped her—before he pulled back.

Relief swept over Bree, the sensation so strong that her knees weakened.

That was it. The kiss was over. The ceremony was done.

10: NOWHERE OF IMPORTANCE

BREE SPEARED A slice of boar with her knife and placed it upon her trencher.

She then cut off a piece and took a bite, wrinkling her nose.

"What is it now?" Mac Brochan's irritated voice intruded, and Bree jolted. She hadn't realized her husband was observing her—yet it seemed that the chief-enforcer missed little.

Straightening in her seat, Bree forced an apologetic smile. "Nothing. The feast is a fine one … it's just different from what I'm used to."

His lip curled. "What do they feed the Maids of Albia then?"

Bree hesitated, unsure how to respond. Mortals ate such strong flavored dishes: venison, boar, and hare, seasoned with pungent herbs and served with dark bitter greens and coarse oaten bread. As hungry as she'd been the evening before, her first mouthful of stew had nearly made her gag. In the Shee realm, the food was far subtler; meals consisted of delicate cheeses, nuts, seeds, and fruits, along with custards and light soups.

"Pottage and goat's cheese mainly," she said, careful to keep her voice sweet and low.

He scowled. "No meat?"

"Only on special occasions." Bree took another bite of boar, chewing doggedly before washing it down with a mouthful of wine. It was plum, sharp and tangy, and it made her eyes water.

Everything about this world was an assault on the senses.

The noise in here—the clamor of voices and rough laughter—set her nerves on edge, while the cloying food smells blended with the fug of smoke from the hearths. The heat, coupled with the odor of too many bodies pressed close, was making Bree feel lightheaded.

Taking another bite of food, she surveyed her surroundings. Over the centuries, she'd heard much about the fabled hall of Duncrag. However, upon setting foot inside, she'd been disappointed. This space looked like a gloomy cave in comparison to Mor's fine throne room. Even so, the huge beams that rose above her, blackened from decades of peat smoke, were impressive enough.

Two enormous rectangular hearths dominated the circular hall. There were vents on the back wall to let out the smoke, but like the rest of the broch, this space was windowless. Curtained alcoves lined the hall, although the women who'd helped Bree prepare for her handfasting had told her that the royal family didn't sleep down here. Instead, they occupied the two top floors of the broch.

The tables had been placed to form a square around each hearth. One table was for the High King, his family, council, and highest-ranking retainers, while the second table was for the lower-ranking retainers and warriors.

The High King and his queen sat talking, their heads bowed together, flanked by their son and daughter. Prince Kennan was drinking heavily from his jeweled goblet, while Princess Lara talked animatedly to the woman next to her.

Bree studied the royal family for a few moments before her gaze traveled down the table, sliding across the faces of the druids and nobles seated there. Many of their faces were florid with drink.

Distaste knotted in Bree's gut. The Marav were so coarse compared to her people.

The dull gleam of firelight on iron caught her eye then, her gaze straying to the slaves circling the tables, ewers of wine and jugs of ale and mead in hand. Their faces were carefully blank, their gazes dull.

Bree watched them with interest. There were no slaves in the Shee realm, but she knew that the High King and his overkings all kept them. They were a sign of status among the Marav. However, the sight of those iron collars made Bree tense. If one of the Shee were ever fitted with such a thing, their skin would burn and blister before they choked to death.

"Why do you gawk, woman?" Once again, mac Brochan's deep voice intruded. "Haven't you seen a slave before?"

Glancing his way, she spied the sharp intelligence in the woad-blue depths of his eyes. The man hadn't spoken a word to her before or after the handfasting, but suddenly he wanted to talk. His manner bordered on hostile though, as if her mere presence at his side vexed him.

"No," she admitted. "My household wasn't wealthy enough to buy one … and the House of Maids has servants rather than slaves." Turds—that was quite a story she was weaving; she hoped it was true. She paused then, her attention returning to the young female slave who was being groped by a druid wearing a red robe. He was a tall, rawboned man with high cheekbones and a shaven head. The lass tried to wriggle away, but he pulled her onto his lap, one big hand kneading her breast.

"That's Gregor mac Hume," mac Brochan said, following the direction of her gaze. "The High King's chief-sacrificer." Sarcasm edged his gruff voice now, along with a note of disapproval. "His wife's not here tonight, or he'd mind himself."

Bree couldn't help it, her mouth thinned. If she saw a male handling a female like that back in Sheehallion, she'd cut off his balls. But she had to remind herself that she was in Albia now. The rules were different here.

She shifted her attention back to her husband, to find him scowling at her.

Reaching for her cup of wine, Bree took a careful sip. *Focus,* she counseled herself. *If you don't charm this whoreson, you'll never leave Duncrag.*

The reminder was sobering.

"How long have you lived here … husband?" she asked after a lengthy pause.

"A while."

"And before that?"

"The Isle of Arryn."

The largest of The Western Isles, Arryn was where druids trained. The greatest of the three stone circles in Albia, The Ring of Starke, sat at the island's heart. It was said that the druids drew much power from the stones during their initiation.

Bree had never visited Arryn, for there were no barrows upon the isle. To her knowledge, no Shee had ever set foot in the foul place.

"I've heard it said that druidic training is rigorous indeed," she said sweetly.

He grunted.

"How long did you study?" He didn't bother to answer, and heat washed over Bree. Iron choke her, she didn't have the patience for this. Right now, she wanted to grab an eating knife and drive it into his throat. Nonetheless, she plowed on. "Did you always know you'd be an enforcer … or did you choose your path later?"

His mouth twisted at this question, and Bree lowered her gaze so he wouldn't see her temper flare once more. Moments passed, and then she flicked him another glance under her eyelashes.

Mac Brochan's sharp-featured face was even stonier than usual. "It doesn't work that way," he replied coldly. "When your gift manifests … *it* decides your path."

"Where did you live before Arryn?"

"Nowhere of importance." His eyes glinted. "Do you have any other vapid questions?"

A meeker female would have quailed under the harshness of his tone, but Bree didn't.

She should have looked away, should have lowered her gaze and murmured another apology. But something within wouldn't let her.

He didn't intimidate her.

"It's our wedding eve … don't I deserve to know something of the man who is now my husband," she answered evenly, "before we *retire* together?"

Silence swelled between them as their gazes remained locked. Mac Brochan's eyes narrowed, and she swore she heard his teeth grind. "I hail from the north," he muttered. "From a village called Harra." He paused, taking another gulp of wine. "My father was a fisherman."

"He's gone then?"

"Aye … all my family are." The chief-enforcer wore a sour expression now, as if he were sipping horse piss rather than wine.

Sensing that he was moments away from losing his patience with her, Bree looked away and helped herself to some braised kale. Getting the chief-enforcer to talk about himself was like wringing blood from a turnip. Killing for a living was so much easier than this new role Mor had thrust upon her.

Fire kindled in Bree's stomach then, stubbornness rising within her.

Mac Brochan was a rude, aggressive whoreson, but she wouldn't let her dislike for him stop her from achieving her goal. No, she'd unpeel his layers, one by one. Eventually, no matter what it took, he'd tell her *all* his secrets.

11: MUMMERY

CAILEAN PULLED ASIDE the curtain to his chamber, allowing his wife to enter before him.

Fia brushed by, leaving the scent of lavender in her wake.

Gritting his teeth, he followed, letting the curtain swing shut behind them. It was late. The feasting had concluded with the newlyweds sharing a cup of mead and feeding each other honey cakes. Cailean had nursed his drink for as long as he could—but, eventually, he hadn't been able to put this off any longer.

Skaal was gnawing a mutton bone by the hearth. The dog glanced up when Fia entered, her tawny eyes spearing Cailean's bride.

Fia's step faltered, and Cailean nearly ran into her back. "Skaal makes you nervous, does she?" he taunted, vindicated that the woman was intimidated by his fae hound, after all.

His wife cast him a sharp look before hurriedly softening her expression. "Aren't these beasts dangerous?" she asked huskily. "I've heard that hearing three of its howls will still your heart."

"It will."

"So, why do you own one?"

Cailean snorted. "I don't *own* Skaal … she chooses to remain at my side."

Fia's hazel eyes widened. "How is that possible?"

He shrugged, even as irritation simmered.

Heedless, his wife continued. "Doesn't it make you nervous … living with a beast that usually serves the Shee?"

"No."

"But most folk fear anything connected to them."

"That's because most folk are ignorant. The Shee are fickle and dangerous … but they have an understanding of things we don't."

Fia stiffened. "It sounds as if you *respect* them," she whispered. "Have you—"

"That's one too many questions, woman." Cailean moved past her to the table, where he poured them both cups of boiled water. Mead and wine had flowed during the feasting, and he wished to clear his head, not be interrogated. "Leash your tongue now."

He turned back to her to find his bride's eyes had narrowed, anger burning in their depths.

Cailean glared back at her. Gods, what had he married? The woman had lied to him in his missives, as had the governess of the Maids of Albia. Mother Gelda had assured him she'd sent him a dowdy lass who valued silence. Instead, they'd sent him a strong-willed woman who wouldn't stop talking. Her questions had been so incessant this eve that his temples now felt as if vicious imps had just taken hammers to them.

His temper simmered as he approached Fia and handed her a cup of water. "Let's get a few things straight." He paused then, fixing her with a gimlet stare. "I never wanted a wife, but the High King demanded it. And as such, I've done his bidding." He fought a lip-curl at this admission but pushed on. "However, our marriage is nothing more than an arrangement ... *mummery*."

Fia's sensual lips thinned. Earlier in the day, especially after the light kiss he'd given her to conclude their handfasting, Cailean had found his gaze returning to her mouth. He stopped himself now.

"We will sit beside each other at gatherings, and you will busy yourself in wifely tasks each day as a good woman should," he went on. "When we are alone together, you will learn to enjoy silence." He gestured then to the nook to his left. "We will share the furs ... however, I won't touch you."

Fia's fingers tightened around the cup she now cradled. "Why not?"

"My reasons are my own."

To his surprise, his wife stepped back from him and muttered something under her breath.

Cailean stiffened. "What's that, wife?"

Her gaze met his once more, and he could have sworn he saw relief flare in her eyes before her mouth pursed. "Nothing," she replied, her voice clipped. High spots of color had risen to her cheeks.

Cailean drained his cup of water, took his wife's empty cup, and turned away from her, returning the vessels to the table.

"Our union is an arrangement … nothing more," he informed her coldly. He deliberately didn't look her way as he spoke. "I get a bride, and you have the *honor* of being wed to the chief-enforcer. You will be protected within these walls, shielded from poverty and hardship. That will be enough."

Silence followed before she answered, "You never mentioned *this* 'condition' in your letter."

Cailean glanced over his shoulder to find her scowling at him. "No, I didn't," he replied. "For obvious reasons."

"You deceived me."

"Aye … and I won't be the first or the last to do so."

"I don't—"

"You lied too," he cut her off as he removed his vest and threw it onto a chair. He then started unlacing his leather breeches, his back still turned to her. "The letters you sent me gave the impression of a quiet, obliging young woman. Instead, I get a mouthy shrew who must always have the last word." He hardened his voice then. "From this moment on, it will cease."

With that, he kicked off his breeches and strode naked past her to the furs.

Bree watched mac Brochan climb into the sleeping nook.

Fury pulsed like a stoked ember in her gut, although the sight of his nudity flustered her. Of course, she'd seen a naked male before—but she'd been unprepared for the sight of *him*.

The light of the fire and the single cresset that burned upon the stacked-stone wall played across his tattooed skin. The chief-enforcer was all brawn, his muscles rippling as he moved. He bore several scars, many of them silvered with age, upon his chest and back, and one, still slightly pink, upon his right thigh.

The males of her race were tall and lean, even if hard-muscled. But this mortal's brute strength was unsettling.

And she couldn't help herself—her gaze dipped to his groin as he strode past her, to what hung between his thighs. Even unaroused, he was big.

Bree swallowed, weakness flooding over her. Of course, she was relieved he wasn't going to rut her. She certainly didn't want him forcing *that* inside her. And yet, a different kind of heat ignited in her lower belly at the thought—one that she hurriedly quashed.

Shades, she'd nearly gotten herself in serious trouble moments ago, for she'd muttered a damning insult regarding his lack of sexual prowess under her breath. She was lucky he hadn't caught her words.

Even so, as her anger slowly ebbed, she cursed herself for not handling her husband better. Gil's comments came back to taunt her then. *You won't last the distance … you're incapable of getting close to anyone … and even feigning it will be a challenge.*

Iron smite her smug brother, how right he was. She'd only been in Duncrag a day, and already she was losing control of the situation.

Nonetheless, even an obliging Maid of Albia would chafe at this bastard's lack of manners.

Bree curled her hands into fists and let her fingernails bite into her palms. The pain steadied her, reminded her that, as tempting as it was, she couldn't accept his refusal to lie with her. Mor hadn't ordered her outright to couple with her husband, but the requirement had been unspoken. Marital intimacy would help lower his defenses. Many secrets had been told between lovers after a vigorous tumble.

Bile surged up, stinging the back of Bree's throat. There was no getting away from it—as much as the thought turned her stomach, she was going to have to seduce him.

Jaw clenched, she unlaced her vest and slipped out of her pretty skirt. Meanwhile, the chief-enforcer had pulled a fur over him and turned toward the wall.

Glaring at his back, she pondered her next move. Although she usually slept naked, she was tempted to leave on her flimsy undertunic. Her mouth thinned as she smoothed her hands over the shift that reached mid-calf. *It's too late for modesty now,* she reminded herself. *Do what needs to be done.*

Despite her husband's terse announcement, she'd seen how his gaze dipped to her mouth a few times during the feasting earlier. She'd even caught him looking at her cleavage when she'd reached forward to help herself to some bread. He did his best to hide it—and hadn't likely even admitted it to himself—but he *was* attracted to her. And she knew instinctively that her boldness stoked it. The chief-enforcer had ordered a meek bride, but what he really wanted was a hellcat—a wild woman who'd rake her nails down his back.

But could she force herself to play this dangerous game?

Bree stripped off her undertunic so that she stood naked. Glancing down at herself, she observed her new body—with lush curves, large rose-tipped breasts, and fair skin scattered with freckles. It was a far cry from what she'd looked like before, but mac Brochan was drawn to this form, and she needed to find a way to fuel his desire.

Maybe ... but not tonight.

Relief fluttered through her once more. She had a reprieve, even if it was a short one—time to come up with a plan.

A fire burned in the hearth, yet cool air feathered across her bare skin, and she shivered. Steeling herself, and doing her best to ignore the chill, she crossed to the alcove and climbed into the warm and soft furs. The sleeping nook was wide, and there was a mountain of bedding between Bree and her husband. As such, there wouldn't be any accidental touching.

Lying on her back, staring up at the low stone ceiling, she willed sleep to come. However, it didn't.

She was too tense.

I could kill him tonight.

Aye, she could slip from the furs while he slumbered, help herself to one of the blades on the wall, and stab mac Brochan between the shoulder blades. She'd enjoy it too. But no, instead of killing him, she had to find a way to make him talk.

A far more difficult task.

Bree squeezed her eyes shut, silently praying to the Great Raven for fortitude. She was going to need it.

12: TIME AND EFFORT

BREE SLEPT POORLY. As such, she was awake far earlier than the chief-enforcer.

Glancing over at her sleeping husband—cast in deep shadow, for the fire had died to a faint glow overnight—she frowned. Without a window to let in the light, she had no idea if dawn had broken outside. All the same, she sensed he'd get up soon and likely leave without disturbing her.

However, she intended to *disturb* him, to give him a look at what he'd rejected the night before. Surely, it wouldn't take much to make the chief-enforcer forget himself. After all, males were ruled by their rods.

Bree rolled out of the sleeping nook and padded naked over to the earthen bowl. Her stomach clenched then. She didn't want to do this. She'd lain awake for most of the night, *dreading* it.

She wasn't a seductress.

She picked up a jug of water and poured it into the bowl, noting that her hands were shaky. Curse it, she couldn't let her nerve fail her. Silently praying to the Great Raven for the guts to see this through, she helped herself to a cake of rough soap and began to wash.

Across the alcove, the fae hound stirred from its sheepskin. Sitting up, Skaal stretched her long body and then sat up, those golden eyes settling upon Bree.

And despite knowing it wasn't wise, Bree stared back at the hound for an instant. *Traitor.* Fae hounds belonged to her world, not this one. The beast should be guarding a barrow, not sleeping in the chief-enforcer's chamber.

Skaal gave a low growl then, the sound rumbling through the shadows, and Bree cut her attention away. It wasn't a good idea to stare down a fae hound—and that wasn't why she'd left the warmth of the furs.

Goosebumps pebbled her skin, and Bree clenched her jaw to keep her teeth from chattering. The water was icy, and the air inside this alcove was as cold as a tomb. Maybe this wasn't her brightest idea. Right now, she felt as sensual as a plucked goose hung up on a butcher's rack.

All the same, she deliberately lingered, waiting for the chief-enforcer to wake from his slumber. And eventually, when she was chilled to the marrow and reaching for a drying sheet, he did.

The whisper of the furs and the thud of his feet hitting the wood floor warned her that he was, indeed, awake.

And then the alcove went silent once more.

Bree's breathing grew shallow. She could feel the heat of his gaze upon her back, slowly raking down the length of her naked body.

Moments passed, and she let him look his fill. Her skin prickled, and she slowly counted to ten. And then, clutching the drying sheet to her chest, she twisted, glancing over her shoulder.

Her husband stood just two yards behind her.

Bree forced herself to stiffen, her lips parting as if she hadn't expected to see him there. "Good … morning," she murmured, injecting a husky note into her voice.

The chief-enforcer didn't answer.

His face was set in harsh, disapproving lines, but his gaze betrayed him. Even in the weak glow of the hearth, she marked the heat in his eyes.

In this light, they looked dark, almost black.

Dragging in a slow breath, she let her gaze travel over his naked torso, over the tangle of tattoos and the scars that told their own story, down his muscled belly to the nest of dark hair between his thighs.

Victory surged in her chest—along with a jolt of panic—at the sight of his manhood at half-mast. Unaroused it was big, although now it was swelling to an intimidating size before her eyes. He'd just proved that last night's muttered insult was groundless. There was nothing wrong with his manhood.

Bree's breathing hitched, heat pooling in her lower belly.

Iron blind her, was she responding physically to this beast?

Jerking her chin up, she met his eye once more. She'd expected him to look embarrassed, for mortification now crawled over her naked skin. But he didn't. For her part, she itched to throw the drying sheet around herself, to hide the sweep of her back and exposed arse from his hot gaze.

But she resisted the urge.

The chief-enforcer might be easier to bend to her will than she'd thought. Maybe this seduction would be blessedly short.

But mac Brochan's mouth thinned into a severe line. Uncaring that his rod now bobbed before him, he strode across to the stool where he'd left his clothing the night before. And then, as Bree looked on, he pulled on his breeches and vest.

Shivering now, Bree turned from him and deftly finished drying. Once she was done, she wrapped the large drying sheet around her. She'd catch a chill if she stood here much longer.

"A servant will be up shortly to rouse the fire," her husband informed her tersely. She glanced over her shoulder to see him yanking on heavy boots. "Mirren will answer your questions about how things are done here." With that, he moved toward the curtain, took a fur cloak off its peg from beside it, and slung the mantle around his shoulders. And then, without another word, he left the alcove, Skaal padding after him.

The curtain swept closed, leaving his wife alone.

And the instant it did, Bree's knees wobbled.

Another reprieve, thank the Ancestors. She clenched her jaw hard then. No, she couldn't shy away from this.

Retrieving her clothing, she hastily dressed, her hands shaking from the cold. "It didn't go that badly," she muttered to herself. "What did you expect? For him to throw you on your back on the furs and give you a morning tumble?"

Her pulse quickened, even as her lower belly clenched at the mental image those words created. She needed to be realistic about this situation. Softening her husband up would require time and effort. Cailean mac Brochan was a warrior-druid, a man with rigid self-discipline. It would take more than one sight of her naked to breach his defenses.

Aye, if she wanted his secrets, she was going to have to work a bit harder.

Her breathing grew shallow, panic slithering through her. Shades, she didn't want to think about what that would entail.

Huffing another curse, Bree crossed to the wooden chest next to the sleeping nook and opened it. Firstly, she checked her small pouch of silver acorns—the only item she'd brought from Sheehallion—was still nestled amongst Fia's belongings. Then retrieving her four figurines of the Gods, Bree glanced around, looking for somewhere to put them.

Her husband already had idols on display upon a ledge set into the alcove wall, but she wanted to put Fia's stamp upon these quarters too. As such, she pushed mac Brochan's figurines along so hers could sit next to them.

Her mouth quirked into a wry smile then. *That'll vex him.*

A sigh swiftly followed. Of course, she was supposed to be charming her husband, not angering him. Turning, she returned to the open chest. There, her gaze rested upon the leather-bound diary. Reading that first entry upon her arrival here had made her uneasy. Nonetheless, the Maid of Albia's diary might yield secrets, or details, that could assist Bree. Unlike Fia, she hadn't been schooled in the art of pleasing males.

And frankly, she needed all the help she could get.

Bree picked up the diary and crossed to the hearth, pulling up a stool next to the glowing embers so she could read. Then, she opened the diary and read the second entry. This one didn't unsettle her as much as the opening page had. Fia prattled on about the wet winter they were having.

Bree skimmed the entry, and the next one, before starting the fourth.

A man came to the House today. He was tall and lean with hair the color of ripe wheat and eyes the color of the Baleful Sea. My heart stopped at the sight of him, and I knew that he was the one.

Bree halted here, her lip curling. "Eyes the color of the Baleful Sea," she muttered. "What drivel." Steeling herself for more of the same, she forced herself on.

We lined up in the courtyard, all dressed in our finest, and he chose three of us to take a turn around the gardens with him.

I was one of the lucky three!

How my heart sang as we walked together. He was charming and polite, with a voice that was both deep and musical. I could have listened to him all day. He asked me about my interests and skills. I told him that I'm an able weaver and that I play the lyre very well.

Of course, I remembered Mother Gelda's teachings and made sure that the conversation always returned to him. He's a prosperous wool merchant from the Galan Peninsula and recently widowed. His blue eyes are so kind.

Our meeting went so well. I was loath to be parted from him.

But now I must wait. Tomorrow, he will make his choice.

Bree paused once more and shook her head. "Foolish lass." Fia's desperation was raw. Turning the page, she then read the next entry. It was short.

He didn't choose me.

Fyona was his choice. She is lively and charming, with the curves and prettiness I lack. But she can't play the lyre as well as me, and she tends to babble.

I can't believe Fyona was his choice.

How can this be? He was the one.

Bree closed the diary. Earlier, she'd sneered at the woman's gushing words over her suitor, although she didn't now. Fia's tone was bewildered, hurt. Her joy had been too brief, much like her life.

She imagined Fia's last moments then—her terror as Gavyn loomed over her, his fingers tightening about her throat.

Bree winced, a sensation she couldn't identify fluttering deep in her chest. Of course, she had no aversion to killing—her hands would forever be stained with the blood of her victims—but she liked to tell herself that they'd all had it coming.

They were the queen's enemies.

Yet Fia mac Callum hadn't done Mor wrong. Her only mistake was agreeing to marry the High King's chief-enforcer and getting in the Raven Queen's way.

13: A GOOD SOURCE

"I'M SORRY THE fire went out, Mistress … I should have put a bigger lump of peat on last night." Mirren fell to her knees before the hearth and hurriedly started laying fresh kindling. "It won't happen again."

The tension in her handmaid's voice made Bree glance up from where she was spreading butter and honey onto an oatcake. Her breakfast was fresh off the griddle, and unlike the overpowering stews and bitter vegetables of the handfasting feast, this meal was to her liking. The oatcake was crumbly and still warm, the butter rich, and the honey scented with thyme.

The food reminded her of home.

"It doesn't matter," she replied.

Mirren swallowed hard, her face flushing. "Aye, it does."

"Spring is upon us." Bree shrugged. "You wouldn't expect it to still be so cold in the mornings."

"It's usually much warmer than this," Mirren agreed, her face relaxing slightly. "I had to sleep with an extra fur last night."

Turning, the lass busied herself with relighting the fire, and a short while later, a lump of peat glowed in the hearth once more, its heat suffusing the alcove.

Bree's gaze narrowed as she watched Mirren poke the peat with an iron poker. She'd avoided touching any iron thus far and had to keep reminding herself that it wouldn't hurt her now.

The maid dug into a pouch at her waist then and grabbed a handful of something before sprinkling it in a semi-circle around the hearth.

Bree leaned forward, gaze narrowing. "What are you doing?"

Mirren glanced her way. "Just sprinkling salt."

"Why?" The question left Bree's tongue before she had a chance to check it.

Mirren frowned. "Didn't your mother teach you to always sprinkle salt around a hearth after you light it?"

Bree shook her head, silently kicking herself.

The handmaid glanced at the vent under the lip of stone above the hearth. "It keeps the botach away," she replied, reaching up to touch the protection amulet around her neck. "He won't cross salt."

Bree nodded. Of course. She knew of the botach, a specter who took the form of an old man. He roamed Albia and was a troublemaker; to catch sight of him was an omen of bad things to come.

"My ma used to warn me that the botach finds his way into dwellings through smoke vents," Mirren went on. "As such, I'm always wary."

"Your ma's advice was wise, I'm sure," Bree replied. It was useful to know that both iron and salt offered the Marav protection from the faery creatures that inhabited their world. Now that Bree was mortal, details like these could prove valuable.

Indeed, her handmaid could be a good source of information. She'd be privy to gossip within the fort and might have heard whispers about what the High King was planning. And she might know what had happened to Duncrag's healer.

First though, Bree would test the water with an easy question.

"How often does the chief-enforcer join the High King for meals?" she asked as she finished up the last of her oatcakes and washed the crumbs down with milk.

Rising to her feet, Mirren brushed soot off her long skirt. "At least once every four days," she replied. "The High King likes to break bread with his druidic council often."

Frustration clenched within Bree. She needed an invitation to one of those suppers. Who knew what might slip out when food and drink flowed? However, in his letter, mac Brochan had made it clear such meetings were off-limits.

Nonetheless, Mirren's straightforward response was encouraging. She'd ask her something else. "Does the broch have a healer?"

Mirren nodded, her blue eyes clouding. "Aye … are you unwell?"

"No." Bree waved her concern away. "I just get headaches from time to time and would like something for the pain."

"I can call Eldra to you, if you wish?"

Eldra. The handmaid had just confirmed that Bryce Elmsong no longer served the High King.

Bree stood up. "No, I'll go to see her now."

Mirren nodded. "Of course, Mistress … follow me."

Leaving the chief-enforcer's quarters behind, the two women crossed the landing and descended the stone stairs to the entrance hall. It was a cold, damp morning. Bree had thrown a thick woolen shawl around her shoulders, although she couldn't imagine ever feeling warm in this depressing place and longed for the soft brush of sweet Sheehallion air against her skin.

"The healer resides underground," Mirren informed her, leading the way across the hall toward the steps that disappeared into the earth.

"Has she worked here long?" Bree asked casually.

"Aye … although she started out as the last healer's assistant."

"What happened to her predecessor?"

Mirren glanced Bree's way, her eyes shadowing. "I don't know," she replied softly before her gaze darted around them as if she was wary of being overheard. "The word is that Damhan left one night, never to return."

Bree inclined her head. "Really?"

Mirren nodded, taking a torch from a bracket and leading the way down the stairs. "There are whispers that he displeased the High King."

Bree took these words in, following close at her handmaid's heels. "You don't know what he did?"

"No, Mistress."

"And what normally happens to those who fall from the High King's favor?"

The maid cast her a hasty look over her shoulder. The lass reminded her of a frightened fawn at times, easily startled. "His Highness can be … harsh … with those who anger him," she admitted, her voice dropping. "Perhaps Damhan feared his wrath for some reason … and decided it was best to disappear." The handmaid's face shuttered then, her mouth clamping shut, as if she realized she'd been too candid. She then turned away once more and hurried down the steps.

Bree's brow furrowed.

She'd pushed things as far as she dared—Mirren was wary now—but she intended to continue this conversation.

At the foot of the steps, they turned right, their booted feet scuffing on damp, mossy stone as they made their way along a hallway that had been carved out of the rock. Around ten yards in, they passed another stairwell, narrow and steep, that plunged into the darkness.

"Where does that lead?" Bree asked, slowing her step and peering into the shadows.

"To the dungeon," Mirren replied. "Fortunately, Eldra doesn't reside there."

Bree frowned once more. If she had to guess, Bryce was either dead or a prisoner. He could be locked up down there— she needed to investigate as soon as she was able. She'd have to be careful though; she couldn't have her husband catch her sneaking around.

They continued along the hallway, eventually reaching a heavy curtain. Halting before it, Mirren cleared her throat. "Are you there, Eldra?"

"Aye," a woman called back. "Come in."

Mirren nodded to Bree. "You go on, Mistress," she murmured. "I shall wait out here."

Brushing past her handmaid, Bree pushed aside the curtain and stepped into a large chamber with a high, rounded ceiling. And in its center, two women were working at a bench.

One of them was statuesque and of middling age with silver-blonde hair. She wore mauve robes—the color of healers in the mortal realm—and was vigorously mashing herbs with a pestle and mortar. Her companion was a young woman with curly auburn hair; she was dressed in a fine ankle-length tunic with a fur cloak about her shoulders.

Princess Lara.

Bree abruptly halted. "Apologies … I'm intruding." She hadn't expected to see the princess rubbing shoulders with the healer.

"Don't mind me." Lara held up the plant with yellow flowers that she was shredding. "I'm just preparing woundwort." Seeing Bree's awkwardness, her mouth quirked. "I enjoy learning of the healing arts … luckily, Eldra indulges me."

"Knowledge of such things isn't lost on anyone," the healer replied, her full lips curving. Her gaze, the color of a winter sky, fixed upon Bree. "How can I assist you?"

The woman was clearly Marav, yet there was a regal bearing and directness to Eldra that reminded Bree of a Shee female. "I get headaches from time to time and can feel one looming this morning." She raised a hand and rubbed her temple, feigning a wince. "They can sometimes be bad enough to send me to bed … and I was wondering if you could provide me with something to take the edge off the pain."

Eldra's grey-blue eyes lingered upon Bree a moment, assessing, before she nodded. "I will make you a tincture now." Putting aside her pestle and mortar, the healer went to a shelf and started sorting through the vials, bottles, and wooden boxes stored there.

Meanwhile, Lara gave Bree a sympathetic look. "My mother is afflicted by headaches," she said. "They can be crippling to some folk."

Bree nodded, suddenly at a loss for words. It felt odd to be conversing with the High King's daughter. Lara's father had been responsible for hunting and slaughtering many Shee during his reign. He had his enforcers out regularly, scouring the land around barrows. Just eight turns of the moon earlier, they'd attacked a group of Shee in the far north of the Uplands, near Darkmere Barrow. Four Shee scouts had been captured and, according to Mor's spy in Duncrag, dragged back to Albia's capital for a public execution.

Bree's people had always traveled between the two realms. They never usually strayed far from their barrows, remaining on the fringes of Albia, but Talorc mac Brude wished to drive them from it altogether. If the High King had his way, every last barrow would be destroyed—but fortunately for Bree's kind, the mounds were heavily warded and could withstand even the strongest druidic magic.

Aye, the High King was a scourge to the Shee, and yet this young woman wasn't responsible for it. Even so, Bree was on edge around her.

The princess was observing her intently now—too intently. "How are you settling in?"

"Well, thank you, Your Highness," Bree murmured.

"It must be quite an upheaval … to move to Duncrag … and to marry a man you've never met."

You have no idea, princess.

Bree forced a brittle smile, wishing Lara would turn her focus elsewhere. "Aye, Your Highness … but I've waited a long while for this day. I'm honored to be part of your household."

"And you're welcome," Lara replied. However, her pine-green eyes were still intense, searching.

Clearing her throat, Bree looked away, shifting her attention to the healer once more. She watched Eldra mix a concoction of dried herbs and powders. "I hear you are new to this role," she said finally.

Eldra glanced up. "Aye."

"You assisted the former healer?"

"Aye." Eldra's pale-blue eyes narrowed slightly. She then cut the princess a glance. However, Lara was now focused on crushing the woundwort in the pestle and mortar that the healer had set aside. "Why do you ask?"

"I hear he ran off."

The healer nodded, her face shuttering.

Bree swallowed a growl of frustration. Getting information out of the inhabitants of Duncrag was going to be harder than she'd thought. Counseling patience, she glanced around casually before motioning to the neat rows of bottles and jars lining the walls. "Well, it looks as if he left your shelves well stocked."

"Aye," Eldra murmured, even as her gaze remained sharp. "Damhan didn't take anything with him."

14: A SILENT MARRIAGE

"BE WARY OF your bride."

Stiffening, Cailean met the arch-druid's eye. The two of them stood in the yard outside the broch. Cailean had come outdoors to see Raen off. She'd journeyed here specially to conduct his handfasting ceremony and would now return to the Isle of Arryn. Above them, the sky was the color of smoke, while the wind—The Sweeper this morning—pushed at them and scattered straw across the yard.

Raen fixed him with a steely gaze he knew well. "There's something odd about her."

Cailean fought the urge to snort. That was putting it kindly. The woman was mouthy, willful, and devious too. He'd known what she was up to that morning, lingering at the washbasin clad only in her skin, waiting for him to wake up. When he'd rolled out of the furs, his gaze alighting on Fia, he'd been greeted with a delicious sight: the sweeping curve of her back, with wavy oak-colored hair tumbling between her shoulder blades, and a delicious pale and rounded arse. And, of course, his prick had responded.

But Raen's concerns were likely different from his.

"She wasn't what I was expecting," he admitted gruffly. "But what is it exactly that bothers you, Wise One?"

"I touched her mind just before I began the ceremony."

Cailean nodded. He'd seen the tattoos on the arch-druid's neck glow briefly and knew what she was doing. Before being elected to her current position, Raen had once been a seer. She could read the bones and see patterns in smoke and the flight of birds. And she was powerful enough to be able to touch a person's mind and read—even sway—their emotions. "And what did you see?"

"Nothing … she warded herself from me."

Warded? Cailean stilled. "How does a Maid of Albia learn to do that?"

Raen's strong features tightened. "She doesn't." Her gaze narrowed then. "Of course, the lass might wield the gift."

Cailean frowned. The gift was the untapped druidic power that usually manifested at puberty. Cailean's own gift had shown itself just after his fourteenth winter. "You think she could be one of us, yet not realize it?"

"It happens … she's spent the last ten years locked away from the world. We have no access to the Maids of Albia."

Cailean considered these words. "Is it a problem … if she's gifted?"

"Possibly not." The arch-druid fixed him with a piercing look. "But something about her bothers me, all the same. Don't let your guard down around her."

Cailean pulled a face. "Don't worry … there's no risk of that."

The silence was getting to Bree. Digging her wooden spoon into the thick barley and pork stew, she cast a veiled glance in her husband's direction.

The man hadn't lied the night before: theirs was to be a silent marriage.

In other circumstances, she'd have been relieved—she didn't want to have anything to do with him—but the success of her mission depended on mac Brochan opening up to her.

Clearing her throat, Bree reached for her cup of wine and took a sip. "Was your day a fruitful one, husband?"

He grunted, helping himself to some bread.

"Mine certainly was," she said when it became clear he wasn't going to elaborate. "Mirren showed me around the broch … and I met Princess Lara." She paused then, toying with her spoon. "The fort is bigger than I expected. We—"

"I heard you visited the healer today," the chief-enforcer interrupted her. "Is something wrong with you?"

Bree stiffened. Had he been spying on her?

"She gave me something for headaches, that's all," she replied. "Sometimes it feels as if powries are stabbing my temples with their pikes … and I thought I was succumbing this morning.”

His gaze met hers. “And how fares your head now?”

“Much better … thank you.”

A heartbeat passed, and then he glanced over at the inset, where the collection of both their figurines sat. His brow furrowed, and Bree sensed his disapproval. She’d known putting her idols next to his would annoy him and braced herself to be told off.

However, she wasn’t. A moment later, her husband focused once more on his supper. Silence fell again.

Irritated, Bree started to tap her foot under the table. “Princess Lara has invited me to go shopping with her soon … on Market Day.”

Mac Brochan nodded, but he didn’t look her way. He chewed his meal doggedly, although with little enjoyment. It was as if it was a chore he had to get through.

“I would like to buy some clothing,” she went on. “Is that permitted?”

“Aye.” Finishing his meal, her husband leaned back in his chair and picked up his cup of wine, swirling it in front of him. “I shall leave you a coin purse on the table tomorrow … spend what you want.” He paused then before adding, “I will be away from Duncrag for a few days.”

Relief swept over Bree before she swiftly checked herself.

She couldn’t avoid this man. And if he was away often, it would take her far longer to gain his trust and gather information from him. Her pulse quickened then. Was he off on one of his Shee-hunting expeditions to the Uplands? If so, she’d warn her people. She didn’t want to waste any of her cache of acorns, but Mor needed to be kept informed.

"Where are you going?" she asked lightly.

His mouth pursed, and for a moment, she thought he might refuse to answer—or reprimand—her. Instead, he replied, "Braewall."

Bree affected a worried look. "I hope there isn't any trouble down south," she murmured. "I fear for my family."

"There's no trouble."

Bree waited for him to elaborate, but he didn't. Impatience bristled within her. If her husband was being tight-lipped about his trip south, there had to be a reason.

"In my father's last missive, he mentioned that King Dunchadh of Braewall appears to be raising an army," she said after a lengthy pause. "Is *this* the reason for the High King's visit?"

Her husband's gaze snapped to hers, and she caught the warning glint in his woad-blue eyes. A muscle in his jaw flexed, and a chill settled in the air.

Once again, she waited for an answer, but none was forthcoming.

"You seem tense, husband," Bree noted eventually, swallowing her frustration. "Would you like a massage ... all Maids of Albia are trained in the art of—"

"No." Draining the last of his wine, mac Brochan pushed himself up from the table. "I've got work to do." He gave a low whistle then. "Come, Skaal."

The fae hound rose fluidly to her feet and followed her master as he left the alcove without a backward glance.

As he'd warned, mac Brochan departed early the following morning, rising before the first glimmer of dawn lit the eastern sky.

Bree didn't bother trying to get up early to give him a morning show of the wares he'd yet to sample. Her seduction tactic hadn't worked the morning before, so she was going to have to be subtler, craftier.

As such, today she employed a different approach. As soon as he rose from the furs, she got up too and hastily pulled on a tunic.

"Go back to bed, wife," he ordered as she pulled a woolen shawl around her shoulders and padded over to the hearth, skirting Skaal's large bulk. "It's still early."

"I will," she assured him cheerfully. "But let me first give you some light to ready yourself by."

Rousing the embers, she lit an oil lamp and carried it over to where he was washing beside the sleeping nook. Keeping her gaze averted from his nakedness, for she found it disconcerting, Bree then went to the square table that dominated the center of the alcove and poured her husband a cup of ale.

Mac Brochan had finished bathing and dressed with deft military precision.

"Here," she said softly, handing him the cup.

He took it with a curt nod, draining the ale in a few gulps before handing the cup back to her.

"Do you need anything else, husband?"

"No," he replied tersely.

An awkward pause followed before Bree cleared her throat. "I shall see you … when you return from Braewall?"

"Aye."

"I shall wish you a safe journey then."

He nodded, even as his dark brows knitted together. Bree heaved a silent sigh. Shades, this man was suspicious of her now, looking for manipulation in every word, every gesture.

Their marriage hadn't started well.

She'd gotten little from mac Brochan at supper the night before, and then he'd stayed away for the rest of the evening. Bree had retired to the furs long before he returned.

And now he would be gone for a few days.

After he and Skaal had departed, the alcove seemed empty indeed without the force of the chief-enforcer's presence.

Bree moved over to the fire once more and warmed her hands over the flames. Her fingers and toes had been cold constantly ever since she'd arrived at Duncrag.

While her husband was away, she'd listen to as much gossip as she could. The High King's household was a big one, and no one saw as much as servants did. Some of them might have served Talorc when he spoke with his druidic council.

Some also might know what had happened to Bryce.

Mac Brochan's absence would give her more freedom to explore too.

Bree had just finished dressing when Mirren arrived, bearing a tray of oatcakes.

"Join me." Bree gestured to the table as she moved toward it. "There are too many of these for me to eat on my own."

Mirren's cheeks flushed pink. "I'll break my fast downstairs later, Mistress," she murmured. "With the other servants."

Bree waved her words away. "Nonsense. My husband is away at present, and I'd like company. Take a seat."

Mirren hovered there, her cheeks glowing like the sunset before she nodded, pulled up a chair, and settled herself opposite, watching as Bree helped herself to an oatcake and started to spread butter upon it.

Glancing up, Bree met her eye. "What's your opinion of the chief-enforcer?" she asked.

Mirren's sky-blue eyes snapped wide at her direct question. "I d … don't know," she stuttered.

"Go on, venture an opinion … I'd like to hear it."

Her handmaid drew in a deep breath. "He's … intimidating," she admitted finally. "Although his dedication to his work is admirable." She paused then, her mouth curving into a wry smile as she warmed to the subject. "Some folk here say he doesn't sleep."

Bree huffed a laugh. "Oh, he does … I've seen him." She then spooned some honey onto the oatcake and handed it to Mirren. "Here."

For a moment, she thought the lass might refuse to take it. However, despite that her embarrassment hadn't eased, she did. "Thank you, Mistress."

"Just call me Fia," Bree replied, picking up an oatcake for herself. "The formality gets tiring."

Mirren started at this before giving a hesitant nod.

Bree spread butter and honey upon her oatcake and took a bite. These *were* good. She finished her first oatcake swiftly and prepared a second, which she handed to Mirren, who was nibbling at her breakfast with one eye on Bree.

The lass was still wary around her, cowed by their difference in rank. Bree wouldn't get any valuable details from her unless trust was established.

"Are you from Duncrag, Mirren?"

Her handmaid nodded. "I'm the youngest of five daughters. My Da is an ironsmith."

Bree suppressed the urge to pull a face at this proud admission. It wasn't surprising though; Duncrag was full of them. "And do you have a man ... any bairns?"

Mirren shook her head, her pale skin flushing once more. "My father had debts to pay, so he sold me into the High King's service. I have more rights than a slave, but as an indentured servant, I cannot take a husband."

Bree frowned at this. Likely, most of the Marav knew of such an arrangement and wouldn't think it strange. Nonetheless, there were many things in this world that were new to Bree, and she had to navigate them carefully. "And that doesn't bother you?"

Mirren pulled a face. "Not yet." She paused then, a shadow flitting across her features. "It's an honor to serve the High King." Her voice was a little wooden as she ducked her head. "I need nothing else."

Bree snorted. "You're young and fair ... just because you can't wed, there's no need to deny yourself of pleasure." Mirren looked mortified at this comment, but Bree continued. "Why not take a lover in secret?"

Mirren froze in her seat, flushing a deep red this time.

"Is there someone you've noticed?" Bree asked, pretending not to see her embarrassment.

"No," Mirren gasped quickly—too quickly.

"Liar. Who is he?"

Mirren cut her gaze away and reached for the cup of milk that she'd just poured.

"Come on ... I won't tell anyone."

"His name is Torran," the handmaid whispered. "He's an enforcer ... your husband's second-in-command."

Bree's mouth pursed. Seeing her reaction, Mirren's brow furrowed. "They're not forbidden to take lovers," she assured Bree, clearly thinking propriety was the issue. She paused then, her features tightening. "I stay away from most of the enforcers though. They're rough and aggressive … with hungry gazes and filthy mouths." She halted then, alarm rippling across her face. "Not the chief-enforcer though … I'm sorry, I didn't mean to—"

Bree waved her apology away. "I know you weren't talking about him," she reassured the lass. "So, this Torran … he's not like the others?"

Mirren shook her head.

"Have you spoken to him?"

"Gods, no. He doesn't know I breathe."

Bree observed Mirren silently for a few moments. "Maybe it's time he noticed you."

"I can't approach him." Mirren's voice was strangled now. "I'd die if he talked to me."

Bree snorted. "Don't be a fool. He's an enforcer … not The Warrior himself."

Mirren giggled at this, the flush on her cheeks fading, and Bree, to her surprise, found herself smiling in response.

15: MARKET DAY

TAKING A TORCH, Bree descended the steps underground.

If anyone stopped her, she'd say she was visiting the healer. However, it wasn't Eldra she was searching for this morning, but Bryce. She had to hurry though, for she was accompanying Princess Lara to market later in the morning.

With her husband gone a few days, she'd seized a quiet moment—after breaking her fast, while Mirren worked in the bakehouse—to visit the dungeon.

There would be guards down there of course, but she had a story ready for them too. She'd tell them that the chief-enforcer had promised her one of them would give her a tour while he was away.

Bree strode along the passageway and turned left, down the dungeon stairs.

Although she'd tucked an eating knife in her boot—old habits died hard—Bree didn't plan to use it. Instead, she had to find out if Bryce actually was a prisoner here.

After that, she'd plan the next step: how to get close enough to question, and ultimately kill, him.

What she needed to focus on at present was charming the guards she encountered below.

Her lips pursed. *Easier said than done.*

The scuff of booted feet below jerked Bree from her thoughts then. Her pulse lurched. Someone was approaching.

Halting, she put out a hand to steady herself on the damp, moss-covered wall, debating whether to turn and flee up the steps. There was no time, for an instant later, a tall, lanky figure, clad in enforcer-black, appeared below her.

The warrior-druid had close-cropped dark-blond hair and grey eyes. She'd seen him at her handfasting feast, sitting at the table opposite. He was handsome, for a Marav, and smiled easily. However, there wasn't any humor on his face this morning. Instead, his mouth was compressed into a thin line.

Seeing her, the enforcer frowned. "Lady mac Brochan … what are you doing down here?"

Ignoring the thud of her pulse in her ears, and the instinct to draw the knife in her boot and lunge for his throat, Bree flashed him a bright smile. "Exploring … although I've no idea where I've ended up."

"These stairs lead to the dungeon."

"Do they?" Bree gave an embarrassed laugh. "How foolish of me." She met his eye then. "I don't suppose you could give me a tour?"

The enforcer's frown deepened. "I don't think so … this isn't a place for you."

Bree waved his comment away. "I've a strong stomach."

His handsome face hardened. "Cailean wouldn't approve."

Frustration beat like a caged raven in Bree's chest.

"No," she replied, forcing another smile. "I suppose he wouldn't." Bree then twisted and began the climb back up. After a few steps, she glanced over her shoulder. The warrior-druid was glaring at her back as he followed her. "We haven't yet been introduced, have we?" she asked.

"No … I'm Torran mac Rab."

Bree turned away once more and resumed her climb, her pulse skittering. So, this was the enforcer Mirren had gone giddy over? She wasn't surprised. He wasn't as cold or as intimidating as mac Brochan. Even so, the whoreson had thwarted her—and he'd likely tell the chief-enforcer that he'd encountered her on the dungeon stairs.

"My husband has spoken well of you," she said as they climbed higher, the light from their torches glowing against the wet stone. "He values your loyalty greatly."

Torran huffed a laugh, the sound echoing up the stairwell. "Your flattery is appreciated, Lady mac Brochan … but you're *still* not getting a tour of the dungeon."

"What do you think … the light green or the darker one?"

Princess Lara held up two swathes of linen, and Bree peered at them. "The darker one," she said after a moment. "It's the color of pine … and matches your eyes."

Lara's gaze glinted. "I knew there was a reason I asked you to come shopping with me," she teased.

Bree favored her with a tight smile. Her encounter with Torran had left her in a sour mood. "It's not an empty compliment, Your Highness … but fact."

Iron bite her, she hated fawning like this—and she *despised* shopping. Back in Sheehallion, she lived in her beloved hunting leathers. She had two sets of them and never wore gowns. The long tunics Marav women wore hampered her movement. However, when the princess asked Bree to accompany her, she couldn't refuse.

Lara laughed, the warm sound drifting through the mild, smoky, air. Up here, near the broch, the stench of the offal pits and drains dug into the lower levels of the fort wasn't quite so bad. "Aye, and your directness is another thing I like about you. It's refreshing."

Bree kept her smile in place, even as discomfort rolled over her. She'd seen a bit of the princess since mac Brochan's departure and had been initially wary of her, for Lara had a probing gaze and asked a lot of questions. Nevertheless, she'd quickly realized that the princess only sought her out because she craved company. Besides servants, there were few women her age living within the broch.

All the same, Lara's comment took her aback. She wasn't used to receiving compliments. It made her feel oddly flustered.

The princess turned back to the cloth vendor then and started to haggle. After a robust negotiation, she handed over a shiny silver coin for a bolt of fabric. He hurriedly wrapped it up, passing it to one of the guards that shadowed them.

These men weren't enforcers but members of the fort guard, clad in leather armor with domed iron helmets upon their heads. Unsurprisingly, the princess wasn't allowed to venture into the town without an escort.

"Come." Lara linked her arm through Bree's, steering her away from the cloth stall, through the press of the crowd. "Time to choose a necklace to go with the new pine-green tunic I shall have made."

Bree fell in step next to her, even as her gaze swept the milling crowd. Her training meant that she rarely relaxed in environment such as this.

All the same, it was a relief to be outdoors with the sun on her face—despite the ever-present tang of iron that stained the air here. The interior of the broch was dark and damp, and Bree was limited to certain areas.

The dungeon aside, she wasn't allowed to venture into the hall itself, or the levels above where she and the chief-enforcer resided, unless invited. Since mac Brochan departed for Braewall, Bree had become twitchy and restless.

Nonetheless, she was still kicking herself for letting Torran catch her earlier.

He'd say something to the chief-enforcer—she was sure of it—which would result in an interrogation by her husband.

Trying to ignore the way her belly tightened at the thought, Bree focused on her surroundings once more.

The market was an assault on the senses. It took up a large tract of The Thoroughfare, the winding road that led up from the gates to the broch at the crown of the promontory. Market Day took place once a moon and attracted folk from miles around. Indeed, it was busy. Noise assaulted her ears: the cries of hawkers, the raised voices of those who haggled, and the excited chatter of shoppers. The aromas of hot mutton pies and frying garlic sausage drifted through the crowd, a respite from less pleasant odors, and despite that Bree still found mortal food overpowering, her belly rumbled.

She wouldn't be eating for a while though. They were only halfway through shopping.

Already, Bree's feet ached, and boredom pressed down on her. Nonetheless, Lara was in her element here, chatting to vendors, bartering with ease, and greeting those she knew as she wandered through the crowd.

The young woman was sharp-witted and charming. And despite herself, Bree found it difficult not to like her.

Careful, she warned herself. *You won't find any friends here.*

There wasn't a great risk of her forming attachments, anyway. Bree had always been a loner. She took lovers when it suited her and ended things when they became tedious. She'd never bonded with any of them. Her profession wasn't a sociable one either, and when she was in residence at Sheehallion, other females were wary of her.

No one trusted an assassin.

"I'm pleased to see that Cailean finally found himself a wife," Lara said then, as they edged their way toward the throng gathered before a jewelry stall. She flicked Bree a veiled look. "It's a crime for such a man to remain unwed."

Bree arched an eyebrow. "Aye?" She hadn't realized that the princess was on first-name terms with her husband.

Lara's mouth quirked. "Aye … half the women in the broch lust after him … as well as some of the men."

Bree snorted. "It sounds as if *you* do too." Her response was bold, but she couldn't help it.

To her surprise, the princess grinned. "I'll not deny it." She met Bree's eye then, and her expression turned wry. "I've partnered him in the blood-letting ceremony three times now. It was an … intimate experience."

Bree arched both eyebrows at this, and to her surprise, a flush rose to Lara's cheeks. "It's not like that," she said hurriedly, clearly worried that the chief-enforcer's bride would be jealous. "The ritual requires a druid to mix blood with one of us common folk, and when you feel the earth magic rising, the sensation is … intense."

A chill swept over Bree, and she suppressed a shudder. "Will I have to take part in a blood-letting?" she asked, feigning a casualness she didn't feel.

Lara nodded. "Once a druid takes a spouse, they always partner in the ceremony."

Bree swallowed. Iron choke her, she had *that* to look forward to. Anxiety twisted her gut then. Although she was Marav now, her heart—her soul—was still Shee. Would the blood-letting unmask her? "How often does it take place?"

"A couple of times a year … more often if the druids draw deeply upon their magic."

Bree studied the princess, noting the wistful look in her green eyes. "I think you'd have made a better wife for the chief-enforcer than me," she admitted after a pause.

Surprise rippled across Lara's face at this candid remark, and she cast Bree a probing look. An awkward silence fell then before the princess heaved a sigh. "Even if I wished it, I was never destined to be the chief-enforcer's wife, Fia … father has other plans for me."

Bree inclined her head, encouraging the princess to elaborate.

"King Dunchadh of Braewall has done my father many … favors … of late." Lara lowered her voice. "And he's asked for my hand in return." Pulling a face, the princess glanced away.

"I take it, you aren't willing?" Bree noted.

Lara huffed another sigh. "He reminds me of a vulture." She flashed Bree a rueful look then. "But I shall do it … for the good of Albia."

They reached the front of the jostling crowd before the jewelry stall then and paused their conversation to inspect the wares. An array of pendants, necklaces, arm rings, and bangles gleamed before them. There were also elaborately-worked golden torques—an adornment that only the wealthy, men and women alike, could afford.

Lara wore one this morning; it glinted in the sun and complemented the sleeveless blue tunic she wore, a lovely garment that rippled over her body, swishing around her ankles as she walked.

The garments Marav women wore could be pretty, but Bree still missed her old clothing. Aye, her own dove-grey tunic, girded at the waist, and light sandals were attractive enough but not half as practical as hunting leathers.

Surveying the jewelry, her gaze alighted upon a bronze arm ring, decorated with intricate swirls. She didn't usually wear jewelry, but the arm ring was lovely. Indicating to the vendor, a keen-eyed young man, she tried it on.

"Oh, you have to get it."

Bree glanced Lara's way. "I'm not sure it suits me."

"Of course, it does!"

That settled it. Bree purchased the arm ring—although not before Lara had beaten the vendor down to a good price. The princess then bought herself a pair of amber earrings.

"A new wife should have some pretty tunics too," Lara said then, tugging her away from the stall. "There's a seamstress halfway down The Thoroughfare who makes beautiful garments … come on."

Bree swallowed a groan. The arm ring was a pretty thing, but she'd had enough of shopping for one day. Nonetheless, mac Brochan might appreciate her more if she made an effort with her appearance—and she *did* need more clothing, for Fia had brought very little with her from the House of Maids.

Lara towed her through the crowd, while her escort continued to shadow them. However, they'd only gone a few strides when a horn sounded, its mournful bellow cutting through the market's din.

Lara halted, her grip on Bree's arm tightening. "It's father," she announced. "He's home early."

16: ON EDGE

BREE TENSED, her pulse quickening. She wasn't ready to see mac Brochan again or to weather his unpleasant company. She'd enjoyed having their quarters to herself and spending the evenings chatting over a cup of wine with Mirren.

The bastard would shatter her peace.

Bree swiftly pulled herself up then, reminding herself that she *needed* him to return. How else would she get information from him? She'd hoped to discover things in his absence, but Princess Lara had admitted that she wasn't invited to any of the druidic councils either, and Bree's questioning of Mirren had yielded little of use.

The crowd below them parted, and standards bearing the High King's crest, a white wolf's head on black, loomed above the low turf roofs of the surrounding cottages.

The two women remained where they were, watching as heavy feather-footed horses bearing big, tattooed men clad in black leather, thick jet-colored cloaks rippling from their shoulders, appeared.

Bree's stomach clenched.

Enforcer scum. The bane of her people. Just the sight of them made her fingers itch. If she were armed with all her blades, she could take half a dozen of them down in moments.

But that wasn't why she was here.

Clenching her jaw so tightly that her ears started to ache, Bree forced the murderous thoughts down.

She'd expected to see her husband at the head of the escort, but mac Brochan rode alongside the High King and the prince, upon a charcoal stallion. Skaal trotted at his side, and the crowd parted further to give the fae hound a wide berth.

Bree's attention fixed upon her husband, taking in his proud bearing and the furrow of his brow. He was intimidating, and he wielded it like a weapon. She couldn't help but notice how many gazes in the crowd tracked *him* rather than the king.

Talorc mac Brude wore a severe expression. On the few times Bree had seen him, the man's hatchet face hadn't softened into a smile once. She wouldn't be surprised if it never did. His dark, deep-set eyes surveyed the crowd as he rode, mounted upon a grey horse, decked out in leather and iron armor. The High King sat easily in the saddle, one hand holding the reins, the other loosely clasping the hilt of the dagger he wore at his hip. It was the stance of a warrior; although getting on in years, Talorc wasn't a man to be underestimated.

Next to him, Prince Kennan also carried himself with assurance, but without his father's aggression. Sun glinted on the prince's long dark hair as he rode. Bree marked the way two pretty lasses he passed gazed up at him like mooncalves, their cheeks flushed with excitement at being this close to the prince. But Kennan didn't spare either a glance.

The High King spied his daughter then, and something flickered across his severe features. For an instant, his face actually softened. Yet the moment was fleeting, gone so quickly that Bree could almost believe she'd imagined it.

"Daughter," he greeted her, the barest warmth in his voice. "I should have known you'd be out here."

"Morning, father." Lara ducked her head, her mouth curving. "You've returned sooner than expected."

He snorted. "Aye, well … I concluded my business in Braewall swiftly." The High King's gaze flicked sidewise then, and to Bree's surprise, it settled upon *her*.

She stiffened. This was the first time since her arrival at Duncrag he'd even noticed her. Skin prickling, she stared back for a heartbeat before checking herself. "Your Highness," she murmured, lowering her gaze and dipping into an awkward curtsey.

The High King made a dismissive noise in the back of his throat. "Settling in well?"

"Aye, Your Highness."

"Eager for your husband's return I'd wager."

Bree's gaze flicked up, and she nodded. A few yards away, mac Brochan shifted uncomfortably in the saddle. He didn't like the High King singling her out for attention. Was he wary of what she might say?

A wicked impulse fluttered up then—to tell Talorc that her husband refused to bed her, to humiliate him in front of his liege. The High King didn't want them to be handfasted in name only. Mirren had explained that he insisted all members of his druidic council not only took partners, but that they had children.

Bree had been surprised to hear the druidic bloodlines grew increasingly rare—especially those of enforcers—and the High King wanted to ensure they prospered once more. She'd seen a few warrior-druids gathered at her handfasting but had discovered that there were barely more than forty of them at Duncrag. Not the small army she'd anticipated.

Aye, this was useful to know, and Bree wondered if she could use this information to her benefit.

Talorc urged his horse on, making it clear that their exchange had ended, and the company moved forward. The gathered crowd drew back to let them pass.

The chief-enforcer passed Bree then, and for an instant, his gaze seized upon her.

The censure in those hard blue eyes was unmistakable. The woman she was impersonating would have no doubt flushed and dropped her gaze under such a stare, but Bree didn't bother. That ship had sailed. He knew she wasn't a mouse.

And so, she stared back, fire quickening in her belly, answering his challenge.

Returning to the broch after their shopping had concluded, Bree accompanied Lara to her quarters, where they tried on the shawls and jewelry they'd bought.

But the princess seemed distracted. Her gaze had turned inward.

Seizing an opportunity to learn more about the politics of this realm, and the relationships within the royal family, Bree cast her a probing look. "Are you worried about the news your father brings from Braewall?"

Lara sighed, studying her reflection in the beaten silver looking glass before her. She'd just put on her new amber earrings, and they gleamed in the light of the cresset burning on the wall behind her. "I shouldn't brood on such things," she muttered. "But I know father will have discussed me with the overking there during his visit."

Her green eyes unfocused then. Suddenly, it was as if she were leagues away.

Bree cleared her throat. "What would happen if you refused to wed King Dunchadh?"

Lara jerked out of her reverie, her startled gaze meeting Bree's. She then shook her head, tension rippling over her features. "One doesn't *refuse* my father."

Cailean observed his wife under hooded lids.

Fia sat opposite him, winding wool onto a distaff. It was a womanly task, one that most lasses learned from their mothers. However, he noted that his wife wasn't skilled at it. She wound the wool slowly and kept tangling it.

Cailean fought a lip curl. Gods, what did they teach the Maids of Albia?

The quiet inside the alcove was ponderous this eve. Supper had come and gone, largely silent as usual. And now, to his irritation, Cailean found his attention drifting to the woman he'd wed.

He wished he didn't find her so attractive.

Firelight burnished her creamy skin, warming her long rich-brown hair and hazel eyes. She was wearing a sleeveless tunic, the color of moss, that hugged her curves indecently. And about her right bicep gleamed a delicate bronze arm ring. Her comeliness was earthy, and it called to a primal urge within him.

Cailean's jaw tightened, and he lifted the cup of ale he'd been nursing to his lips.

Fortunately, he'd long ago mastered the art of self-control.

His pretty yet vexing wife might tempt him, but he'd not succumb. Bedding her would be a mistake. She'd expect closeness then, would try to *bond* with him. Women couldn't help themselves.

But Cailean wouldn't attach himself to anyone. He'd made himself that promise many years ago, and he would keep it. Maintaining his distance from her physically would ensure they both remembered what their marriage was.

An arrangement.

Even so, tension rippled through him this eve, and his fingers flexed against the cup he gripped.

Fia glanced up from winding wool.

"You seem on edge, husband," she noted. "Is something amiss?"

Cailean fought the urge to scowl. "No."

"Did the trip to Braewell go well?"

"Well enough."

"Princess Lara told me today that her handfasting to King Dunchadh is likely."

Cailean gave a non-committal grunt. The Warrior's cods, this woman couldn't keep her nose out of matters that didn't concern her. "That's the High King's business, not ours," he replied.

He caught the flash of annoyance in Fia's eyes before she ducked her head. "Of course."

Silence fell then, before Skaal, who was soundly asleep by the fire, started to snore. Cailean winced and nudged the fae hound gently with his boot. The snoring cut off.

"I hear you met Torran today," he said finally.

Fia's shoulders tensed. Warily, she raised her gaze to his. "Aye."

"Why were you taking the stairs to the dungeon this morning?"

"I was exploring and got lost."

Cailean sighed, reaching up and massaging the tense muscles at the back of his neck. It was the same excuse she'd given Torran. His second hadn't believed her, and neither did Cailean.

Fia held his eye, her expression veiled now. "I'm sorry," she said after a beat. "I was just curious."

Cailean frowned, fixing his wife with a gimlet stare. He reminded himself then of the arch-druid's warning. He should keep a closer eye on his wife. "You are to curb your curiosity in the future," he said finally, his tone wintry. "Don't go down there again."

17: A SMALL WIN

"THERE YOU GO." Mirren slid the last pin into Bree's hair and stepped back. "It's done. … what do you think?"

Picking up a looking glass, Bree inspected her reflection. It had been a long while since she'd taken such care with her appearance. Nonetheless, tonight was Bealtunn—the eve that marked the passage from spring into summer—and she wanted to look her best. At dusk, the inhabitants of Duncrag would venture beyond the walls and gather on one of the hills to the north of the fort. There, they would dance around the bonfire and drink the first of the summer wine. Bealtunn was a festival that celebrated The Maiden, fertility, and new life.

It was the perfect opportunity for the chief-enforcer and his wife to spend time together.

Bree's jaw tightened then, her gaze narrowing as she stared at the hazel-eyed woman in the looking glass. A moon's turn had passed since her husband's return from Braewall. But she was no closer to gaining his confidence.

These days, she and mac Brochan had settled into a routine of sorts. Silent meals. Awkward evenings seated opposite each other while Skaal slumbered before the hearth. Sleeping just a couple of feet apart in the furs, yet never touching.

Bree had tried to soften him up. But every attempt at conversation was met with terse responses. She'd done thoughtful things for him too. She'd had baths brought up for him and asked Mirren to find out from the cooks what his favorite foods were—blood sausage and grouse pie—to ensure he was served them regularly. However, her efforts were always met with non-committal grunts.

He was a rude, ungrateful bastard, and being nice to him galled her.

She hadn't tried to seduce him outright yet—not after his response to her first, clumsy, attempt. Something told her he'd reject any advances she made, and she didn't feel like being humiliated. Instead, she'd embarked on a subtler path, one that had yet to bear fruit.

Bree's breathing grew shallow then. Time was passing. Mor would be impatient for a silver acorn. Unfortunately, she had little to tell.

"You're frowning?" Concern laced Mirren's voice. "Don't you like it?"

Bree shook herself out of her reverie and turned to meet her handmaid's gaze. She then flashed her a reassuring smile. "Aye, I love what you've done."

Nonetheless, Mirren still looked unconvinced, and Bree huffed a sigh. "Don't mind me … I'm a little out of sorts today, that's all."

A groove etched between Mirren's brows. "Why? It's Bealtunn … and the sun is shining."

Bree's mouth quirked. Her handmaid's cheerful disposition had been a balm since her arrival at Duncrag. Despite that Mirren was an indentured servant and could lack confidence at times, she had a remarkably positive approach to life.

And of course, like most of the women in the broch, the lass was excited about Bealtunn.

"You're right," Bree replied with a shrug. "I've no reason to frown." She then focused on her handmaid, running a critical eye over her curly mop of peat-brown hair. "You'll be attending this eve too?"

Mirren nodded, her sky-blue eyes gleaming with quiet excitement.

"Well then, since you've spent so long pinning my hair up, the least I can do is braid yours."

Her handmaid's cheeks flushed before a delighted smile stretched her lips. "You would?"

"Aye." Bree rose to her feet and gestured to the stool she'd been sitting on. "Come … let me get to work."

Mirren did as bid, eagerly settling herself onto the stool, while Bree took a bone comb and carefully brushed out her maid's thick hair. She then divided Mirren's unruly curls into sections, fastening them with pins, before she started to weave long thin braids.

Braiding was something she was good at, for, back in Sheehallion, she usually wore her hair plaited, especially when she was working.

Nonetheless, as she braided Mirren's wayward mane, Bree found herself pursing her lips. She was pleased to do something for Mirren, for she enjoyed the lass's company, but there was part of her that couldn't believe she—the Raven Queen's assassin—was plaiting another woman's hair.

Shades, what have I become?

"Will the chief-enforcer accompany you from the broch this eve?" Mirren asked, intruding upon her brooding. "Or will he meet us at the bonfire?"

Bree pulled a face, glad that Mirren couldn't see her expression. She'd tried asking mac Brochan the same question that morning, but he'd been evasive. "I'm not sure." She hesitated then before adding. "In truth, I'm not sure he'll join me at all."

Her handmaid sucked in a breath. "But he *must* … it wouldn't be right for the chief-enforcer's wife to attend Bealtunn on her own."

Bree frowned. Iron bite her, she was tired of trying to soften up her husband. She'd have more luck molding a lump of granite.

Mirren was right though. Bree would cause whispers if she attended Bealtunn without him—and mac Brochan was the only reason she'd asked Mirren to put up her hair and help her dress in her most becoming tunic: emerald with a plunging neckline. She'd made this effort for him, but if he wouldn't grace her with his presence this evening, she'd miss another, crucial, opportunity to get close to him.

It wouldn't do. If playing the part of the dutiful wife wasn't going to sway him, she'd have to employ a different, slightly riskier tactic.

"You're right," Bree replied after a pause. "I will seek him out after I've done your hair … and *ensure* he joins me."

Silence followed her comment, and when Mirren finally replied, her voice held an awed note to it. "The chief-enforcer doesn't scare you, Fia?"

Bree snorted. "No."

Aye, he was an intimidating bastard, but that wasn't why she minded herself around him these days. She wasn't afraid of standing up to him when necessary either—she just had to be careful not to compromise her position here.

"Well … he cows everyone else," Mirren replied, oblivious to her mistress's thoughts. "Although I must admit, he's scarier than ever of late."

Of course, he is, Bree thought bitterly. *He's got a wife he doesn't want.*

Later, Bree found her husband in the yard before the broch, talking to three of his enforcers.

Ignoring the fact that all the warrior-druids looked her way as she approached, Bree picked up her long skirt—she didn't want to dirty her lovely green tunic—and made her way toward them.

Mac Brochan's dark brows knitted together in a frown as she approached. He wouldn't appreciate her seeking him out. But her conversation with Mirren had made her realize that if she didn't act, their relationship would never change.

It was time for her to push things a little.

"Husband," she greeted him with a nod, halting a few feet back. "May I have a word?"

"Can't it wait?" he replied tersely.

"I'm afraid not."

One of the other enforcers smirked, while the remaining two exchanged looks. Marking their reaction, Bree focused her attention once more on mac Brochan, waiting for him to answer.

A muscle feathered in his jaw, his frown sliding into a scowl, and for a moment, she thought he might bark at her—and attempt to send her away.

Bree put her hands on her hips then and straightened her spine.

He would not.

Moments passed, and then mac Brochan made a sharp gesture to his men. "Leave us."

The other enforcers departed, although not without lingering, hungry looks at Bree.

"What do you want?" he asked the moment they were out of earshot.

"It grows late in the day," Bree replied, holding his gaze steadily. "The eve of Bealtunn approaches … yet you haven't told me of your plans." She brushed at the full skirt of her tunic. "As you can see, I'm ready."

Brochan's blue eyes darkened, and he folded his brawny arms across his chest. "Go on your own."

"I can't do that."

His gaze narrowed. "Keep Mirren nearby and no one will question my absence."

"The High King might."

The chief-enforcer stilled at that, and at the warning she'd deliberately injected into her tone. "Excuse me?" he said finally.

"I hear that Talorc is desperate for the druidic bloodlines … especially those of enforcers … to be continued," she said, inclining her head. "I imagine he'd be upset to discover that his chief-enforcer won't be fathering any children."

A beat of silence followed before mac Brochan dropped his arms to his sides and stepped close to her. "Are you threatening me, Fia?" he asked, his voice lowering.

Bree's pulse quickened, for his nearness flustered her a little. Nonetheless, she continued to hold his eye. "Do I need to?" she replied softly. "I'm not asking you to bed me. All I ask is for my husband to attend Bealtunn at my side."

He stared back at her, and Bree started to sweat under his scrutiny.

She'd told Mirren that he didn't scare her, but suddenly she wasn't so sure. The man could be menacing, and now he turned the full force of his cold glare upon her, she found herself wishing that she wasn't flouncing around in a pretty tunic with her hair pinned in elaborate coils upon her head. Instead, she wanted to be dressed in grimy hunting leathers and facing him with a dagger in her hand.

Moments passed, and Bree had no choice but to suffer his stare. However, as she waited, her pulse hammered in her ears. Perhaps she'd pushed things *too* far.

Eventually, mac Brochan answered her. "Very well, wife." His voice was rough, as if each word was an effort. "I'll fetch you from our alcove at dusk."

Victory surged through Bree.

It was a small win, but the fact she'd managed to finally sway him over something sang in her veins. Aye, she'd found a weakness in his armor. Cailean mac Brochan feared few individuals it seemed. But the wrath of the High King checked him.

But, to her consternation, the chief-enforcer stepped even closer then, bending to speak in her ear. "You get your way this time … for we shall give the High King a show." His breath tickled her skin, while the scent of leather, ash, and male enveloped her. "However, I'd counsel you against trying to blackmail me again."

18: PUTTING ON A SHOW

THE CHIEF-ENFORCER and his wife walked arm-and-arm up the hill behind the fort. Above them, a bonfire illuminated the night like a beacon, golden tongues of flame licking at the moths that fluttered about it.

Bree's skin prickled at the sight of the Bealtunn fire, and at the pounding of the drums—a steady, ominous beat that reminded her of a pulsing heart—that echoed through the night.

Her own people celebrated the passage from spring to summer, but their festivities were different. Instead of honoring The Maiden, they gave thanks to The Great Raven. Right now, in Sheehallion, younglings would be painting eggs for the festivities of the following day and the bakers would be preparing the festive breads studded with nuts.

A pang went through Bree then. How long would she be stuck here in Albia, living someone else's life? When could she finally go home?

When Mor calls you back.

Her breathing quickened, as she imagined year after year stretching ahead of her here. Pushing the chilling thought aside, Bree glanced over her shoulder at where Mirren followed behind them. The firelight burnished her maid's face. Catching her eye, Mirren grinned.

Envy clutched at Bree's stomach then—a response that caught her off-guard.

Had she ever been the sort to get excited about festivals? Not since she'd been a youngling, many years ago now. Ever since reaching adulthood, she'd adopted a cool disdain for such things. However, the time she'd spent with Mirren since her arrival at Duncrag had made her face just how cynical she'd become, and how her attitude colored the world around her.

Mirren was mortal. An indentured servant. And yet day-to-day experiences brought her more joy than even the highlights of Bree's long life so far had.

It was an unsettling realization.

Her husband's arm tensed then, and Bree cut her attention left to where he walked at her side. His profile was harsh, but like her, he'd made an effort with his appearance this evening, donning the golden torque he'd worn for their handfasting. A matching black leather vest and breeches that had been embossed with druidic designs clad his big body.

Not for the first time, Bree found herself silently admiring him.

Aye, he was the loathsome chief-enforcer. But he was also distractingly attractive.

Realizing she was staring, Bree looked away, her gaze traveling to the reason her husband had tensed.

The High King sat upon a raised wooden platform, a few yards back from the bonfire. His face flushed with wine and the fire's warmth, Talorc mac Brude was talking to his queen.

The chief-enforcer halted then, on the edge of where revelers danced around the fire. Bree recognized many of the faces—men and women who lived within the broch, as well as those who resided in the fort proper. A number of enforcers were present this eve too, and as she looked on, one of them grabbed a lass and hauled her into the dancing.

"Folk certainly seem to be enjoying themselves," Bree observed, glancing her husband's way once more.

Mac Brochan grunted.

"Perhaps we could join the dancing too?" Bree's belly clenched as she spoke. She wasn't a good dancer and indeed hadn't had much use for the skill over the years. Nevertheless, she was desperate this eve to force some closeness between her and mac Brochan. *So* desperate that she'd even dance.

However, her husband scowled at her suggestion. "Not yet," he snapped.

Bree clenched her jaw, irritation surging.

"Would you like me to fetch you both some wine?" Mirren asked then, appearing at Bree's shoulder.

"Aye," Bree replied with a grateful smile. Wine would certainly help. "Thank you."

She watched her handmaid weave her way through the press.

Torran walked past Mirren then. However, he didn't notice the lass, for his gaze was upon a woman with long red hair who waved to him a few yards distant.

Mirren's gaze tracked the chief-enforcer's second-in-command as he strode past, longing upon her face. Then, pulling herself together, she turned and hurried on, dodging another enforcer—a massive brute—who lurched toward her. Reaching a woman who was ladling out wine into cups, Mirren collected two before making the journey back to the chief-enforcer and his wife. On the way, she navigated lecherous looks and barely avoided spilling the wine when the same enforcer who'd approached her earlier attempted to block her way once more. Mirren nimbly skirted around him.

Nevertheless, the maid's face was red, her mouth pursed, when she returned to Bree and mac Brochan and handed them their wines.

"All is well?" Bree asked before lifting her cup to her lips and taking a gulp.

Mirren nodded and gave an embarrassed shrug. "Just the usual harassment."

"Harassment?" Her response drew the chief-enforcer's attention. "Who is bothering you, Mirren?"

Pinned under mac Brochan's stare, the handmaid's expression grew anxious. She then shook her head vehemently. "No one," she gasped. "I jest."

"That enforcer seemed intent on getting your attention," Bree noted, unwilling to let the subject lie.

"Which one?" her husband asked, his gaze narrowing.

Bree nodded to where the huge warrior-druid now loomed over another lass.

"That's Drago," mac Brochan admitted after a weighty pause, glancing back at Mirren. "What did he say to you?"

"Nothing." Mirren swallowed. "He wanted … a dance."

"Aye, well … tell me if he crosses the line," the chief-enforcer rumbled, scowling. "Is that clear?"

The handmaid nodded, her blue eyes wide, startled.

Bree smiled at her, attempting to reassure the lass, for Mirren was clearly flustered. "Go on … get yourself some wine and join the revelry," she urged her. "My husband will keep me company."

Nodding once more, Mirren backed away and then fled into the crowd like a frightened hind.

Bree watched her go, frowning. "That enforcer *did* harass her," she said after a pause, turning back to mac Brochan. "I saw him."

Her husband sighed. "Drago has already been warned about bullying women," he replied.

Aye, well … warn him again. The words burned in Bree's chest, but she swallowed them. She'd attended Bealtunn with her husband to build a rapport with him, not argue.

They fell silent then, each drinking their wine as the revelry played out around them. Besides black-clad enforcers, there were other druids amongst the crowd—Bree picked out flashes of blue, green, yellow, and red amongst the plain homespun of the locals. The drums increased in tempo now, as did the dancing.

Tension rippled through the air as if the night was building to something.

Across the crowd, the High King ceased talking to his wife. Instead, his gaze cut across the press and seized upon the chief-enforcer.

Talorc's dark gaze narrowed.

"See," Bree murmured, grabbing the opportunity the High King had just given her. "He wishes to see us together … we should ensure he thinks all is well between us."

Mac Brochan growled a curse, and Bree swallowed a smile. She had him.

Draining the last of his wine, the chief-enforcer tossed the cup aside. "Come then, wife," he muttered. "Let's dance."

Cailean led Fia to where men and women whirled around the fire and drew her into the melee.

And as he did so, anger pummeled his chest like the drums around him.

He should have realized she'd discover the High King's determination to further the druidic lines, and that the devious woman would try and use it to manipulate him.

Nonetheless, she'd caught him unawares today.

Cailean ground his teeth, his grip tightening upon Fia's as he swung her around him. Her long oak-colored hair flew like a banner behind her. There was no denying it; his wife was lovely to look upon.

He would have had to be blind not to notice her in her tunic when she'd interrupted him with his enforcers earlier. Her full breasts were at risk of spilling from its low neckline. He wished she would wear more demure clothing—perhaps he'd tell her so later. But at present, he found it hard to keep his gaze from straying to her lush cleavage.

This close, her scent kept distracting him.

Fuck it. He didn't want to dance with his wife. He didn't want to stay by her side tonight, drinking wine, and putting on a show for the High King.

But, ironically, Fia had been wise to suggest doing so. Talorc would be incensed if he suspected Cailean wasn't fulfilling his duties.

He pulled his wife close to him then before clasping her by the waist, lifting her up, and spinning her about him.

Fia's cheeks were flushed now, her full lips parted. And her hazel eyes—a gaze that had the power to both anger and unsettle him—gleamed.

Cailean's gut clenched. He was playing a dangerous game, defying the High King like this. He'd seen firsthand over the years what happened to those who vexed Talorc. He was quick to anger and slow to forgive. Aye, Cailean was his chief-enforcer, and the High King relied on him. But he wasn't indispensable. No one was.

Hopefully, seeing Cailean and Fia dance together before the Bealtunn fire, and taking part in the revelry, would be enough to convince him that his chief-enforcer was doing his duty.

19: TRAINED TO KILL

BREE HAD JUST left the chief-enforcer's alcove, when she met the healer on the stairs. Eldra was returning from the level above. A basket hung over one arm, and her purple robes whispered around her ankles.

"Good morning," Bree greeted the woman with a nod. She'd been hoping to see Eldra more frequently since her arrival. But when she wasn't working, the healer kept to herself.

Eldra's mouth curved. "Good day, Lady mac Brochan."

Bree's gaze lowered to her basket of healing herbs. "All is well?"

"Aye … the queen likes me to attend on her regularly, that's all." Eldra met her eye. "How are the headaches?"

"The tincture you gave me works wonders," Bree assured her, "although I've nearly run out."

"Visit me tomorrow morning, and I'll prepare you some more."

Bree flashed her a grateful smile. "I will … thank you." Hopefully, fate would be on her side this time and Eldra would be on her own. She couldn't ask probing questions with Lara present. All the same, Eldra wasn't an easy person to pry details from.

"I shall see you then." The healer moved on, disappearing down the stairs.

Watching her go, Bree wondered if Eldra would speak frankly with her. She was self-contained, with pale, knowing, eyes. They'd only crossed paths a handful of times since Bree's arrival at Duncrag, although she got the sense that the healer observed her as closely as she did her.

Shaking herself free of the discomforting sensation, she left the broch, pushing through the heavy doors and descending the steps into the wide yard beyond.

A cluster of white-robed figures had just passed through the gates and was coming toward her. Bree's mouth pursed. *Counselors.* It wasn't the first time she'd glimpsed the druids who advised the High King. However, she'd never seen a group of them walking purposefully together. A well-built woman, her brown hair plaited into thin braids, led the druids.

Annis mac Gord, the chief-counselor. Aye, Bree had learned the names of each member of the druidic council. Even so, she hadn't spoken to any of the others. The chief-enforcer was the only member of the council who resided within these walls; the rest dwelled with their spouses in cottages outside the walls of the broch.

The chief-counselor's gaze slid over Bree as she swept past, haughty and dismissive.

Bree couldn't help it, she bristled. Watching the white-robed counselors mount the steps, she wondered what their purpose was today. Was the High King wrestling with a difficult decision?

Had he called his chief-enforcer to him as well?

Thinking about her husband made Bree frown.

A few days had gone by since Bealtunn. The eve had passed well enough—her husband had even danced with her a few times—and they'd lingered a while at the bonfire. Long enough to appease the High King.

Bree had caught Talorc watching them several times throughout the evening. Aye, she'd discovered a chink in her husband's armor. In refusing to bed her, he was directly defying the High King. It was powerful knowledge to hold over mac Brochan, yet she was wary of wielding it.

Having the chief-enforcer punished, dismissed, or even executed, wouldn't likely help her.

All the same, she liked having something to hold over him, something she could use should things get desperate.

Bree muttered an oath under her breath then. She was brushing the edges of desperation now, for ever since Bealtunn, the chief-enforcer had barely spoken to her. Her plan to draw them closer hadn't worked.

Dragging herself from brooding thoughts, she surveyed the wide yard before the broch. Several low stone buildings with turf roofs lined this space—a stable complex sat at one end with an armory next to it. Across from the stables was a granary and the kitchen. The rich smells of cooking drifted out from the long, low-slung building, as did the rise and fall of voices. From outside, it sounded as if one of the cooks was shouting at his helpers, muffled curses spiking through the warm late-morning air.

Bree decided not to stick her nose inside the kitchen. She'd done so once, shortly after her arrival at Duncrag, venturing into the smoky space mid-morning. She'd hoped to find a chatty kitchenhand to question, although, in the end, she hadn't lingered. The cooks and servants within had all fallen silent, watching her nervously. Their reaction was vexing. Everyone knew servants loved to gossip; however, this lot seemed to have swallowed their tongues.

Bree huffed a frustrated sigh. She had so few within the broch that she could question. Lengthening her stride, she passed the kitchen, heading toward the bakehouse that was nestled into the back of the complex.

Mirren usually worked there at this time of day, baking the last of the bread that would be served with the noon meal.

Of course, Bree wasn't supposed to be wandering around as if she had no constraints on her time. She had a pile of her husband's clothes that needed mending and wool to be spun— but those tasks could wait. Sometimes, when the walls of the chief-enforcer's quarters closed in and the lack of sunlight drove her mad, Bree *had* to get out.

As often, she went looking for her handmaid.

Worry gnawed at her gut this morning, but Mirren would make her feel better.

Leaving the yard, she made her way down a narrow wynd between tightly-packed outbuildings. Ahead, the entrance to the bakehouse loomed, where the nutty aroma of oaten bread wafted out.

Bree's mouth watered. The bread and her morning oatcakes were some of the few foods she found palatable here.

Peering inside, she was disappointed to find the bakehouse empty. Where was Mirren? It was also odd that no one was in here to tend the loaves. Even from the entranceway, she could see that the bread was deeply browned and on the cusp of burning.

Maybe she should don some gloves and save the loaves?

Bree was about to step inside the bakehouse and do just that when a muffled cry drew her attention. Her senses sharpened at the noise, her warrior instinct stirring.

Emerging once more into the wynd between two buildings, she moved farther into the shadows, toward the narrow passage that ran beneath the high stacked-stone wall encircling the broch.

And as she stepped into it, she spied three figures struggling against the wall of one of the storehouses: a woman with curly dark hair, and two huge heavily tattooed men clad in black leather.

Bree stilled. *Mirren.*

One glimpse at the scene and two things were clear: the men were the High King's enforcers—and the lass wasn't willing.

Mirren twisted and fought in their merciless grip, tears streaking her cheeks.

One of them—the biggest of the two—had his hand over the lass's mouth, flattening her against the wall and pinning her arms over her head. Meanwhile, his companion, his bullish face slack with lust, had pushed up her tunic, exposing the lower half of her body. He gripped Mirren's naked hips as he rutted her from behind, yanking her up to meet him with each vicious thrust.

She struggled wildly, her eyes feral with pain and panic.

Recognizing the brute raping Mirren—it was Drago, the enforcer who'd tried to corner the lass at Bealtunn—Bree hissed a curse and glanced around for a weapon.

Neither man realized they had a witness to their rape, but they would soon.

"Hurry up and finish," the one holding her still rasped, his voice tight with excitement. "I want a turn."

"Aye, you'll have her," his companion grunted, sweat beading on his brow as he started to thrust harder and faster. "But not before I split this bitch open."

Bree spotted a broom leaning up against a storehouse then, no doubt left by a servant. It wasn't much, but it would have to do.

"Leave the lass be." Her voice echoed through the passageway. "Now."

The men cut their attention Bree's way, their gazes narrowing as they settled upon her.

"Fuck off," Drago growled, grinding himself into the lass so she made an agonized sound against the hand gagging her. "Unless you want me to take you next."

"She's the chief-enforcer's wife," his companion muttered, his expression darkening. "Maybe, we should—"

"Retrace your steps, bitch," Drago grunted, angered rather than worried by this declaration. "*Now.*"

Bree lunged.

The broom caught the rapist under the jaw. Her second blow broke his friend's nose.

Mirren crumpled to the ground as they released her. Her choked sobs ripped through the air as she yanked down her skirt and crawled away into the shadows.

Meanwhile, Drago hauled up his trews and drew one of the knives strapped across his chest. "I warned you," he snarled.

A heartbeat later, the two men launched themselves at Bree. Their tattoos remained dull; they clearly didn't think her a threat.

That was a mistake.

Mouth twisting, she stepped forward to meet them. *Careful,* she warned herself. *You're slower and weaker in this body.*

Aye, in her Shee form, she was deadly, but even as a Marav woman, armed only with a broom, her training didn't desert her. She could fight.

Ducking the swiping blades and meaty fists, Bree went for their eyes, throats, and groins, using the end of the broom handle to cause as much damage as she could. But the enforcers were druids, and just like her, they'd been trained to kill.

Their tattoos flared to life then on their naked arms, glowing as they drew on their magic.

Bree's heart jolted as the odor of pine and campfire enveloped her, before she checked herself. As a Shee, just the smell of druidic power would weaken her. But as a mortal, it didn't affect her. Nonetheless, summoning their magic made the enforcers even more formidable opponents. They worked together now, backing her up against the perimeter wall.

Sharp iron bit into her upper arm as one of their blades nicked her. Bree waited for an agonizing burn to follow, although there was nothing but a warm trickle of blood.

Jaw clenched, she ducked another meaty fist and spun, kicking Drago in the cods.

He grunted a curse and staggered. Such a blow would have brought down most opponents, but the warrior-druid recovered with alarming swiftness.

All the same, Bree couldn't believe these two idiots were taking her on. She was the chief-enforcer's *wife*. What did they hope to achieve—quell her before dragging her into the shadows to defile her as they had Mirren? Did they think she wouldn't breathe a word to her husband?

And then she saw the gleam in their eyes, the grim fatalism.

No, they both knew they'd gone too far. They intended to kill her. A dead woman couldn't betray them.

Above the pounding of her heart, Bree heard shouts nearby. The sound was steadily growing louder. Soon, they'd have company.

The enforcers had her cornered. However, she used the hard surface of the stone wall to spring back at them, kicking high this time. Her sandaled foot caught Drago, who'd recovered from the blow to the groin, under the chin, while she drove the end of her broom into the guts of his companion.

But she was panting now, her muscles burning from the strain of the fight. She wouldn't be able to keep this up for much longer.

Her assailants were down, but just for an instant. Blood pouring from his mouth, from where he'd bitten his tongue, Drago drew another knife. He came at Bree again, murder in his eyes.

He never reached her.

Something huge barreled into him. Bree reeled back, catching the blur of dark-green fur as she did so.

Skaal.

Hackles raised and teeth bared, the fae hound pinned Drago to the ground.

Snarling curses, the big man struggled wildly, yet a deep growl from Skaal, as she pressed her massive jaws close to him, made his face blanch. The glow of his tattoos faded.

A heartbeat later, the chief-enforcer himself pushed past Bree, an iron dagger clenched in his hand, and stabbed her second attacker through the shoulder, pinning him up against the wall.

The enforcer let out an agonized wheeze and tried to fight him off, but mac Brochan twisted the blade.

Grunting, the man sagged against the wall, sweat gleaming on his brow.

Bree leaned against the perimeter wall. She still grasped the broom handle in one hand, while she raised the other hand to her chest, against her pounding heart.

It was a humbling moment. *The whoresons almost had me.*

She glanced right then to where Torran looked on. He stood a few yards away, a knot of wide-eyed servants crowding behind him. The chief-enforcer's second's face was all sharp angles, outrage simmering in his grey eyes.

Swallowing, Bree tore her gaze from Torran to see that her husband had shifted his focus from the enforcer he'd just subdued. Instead, mac Brochan was watching her.

His gaze cut into her like an ax-blade, and Bree's stomach swooped.

Fuck.

Had she just unmasked herself?

20: FIGHT ME

"TELL ME WHAT happened."

The chief-enforcer's voice cut through the meeting room, piercing the silence.

"Those two brutes—" Bree began, but her husband cut her off.

"I wasn't addressing you." Indeed, mac Brochan's gaze was upon Mirren, who stood at his wife's side.

Head lowered, arms wrapped around herself, the lass was shaking.

Heat ignited in Bree's stomach. Couldn't he see Mirren was deeply distressed? She needed to visit the healer, not be interrogated. With effort, she bit her tongue; she'd already drawn far too much attention to herself this morning.

That was an understatement—she'd just landed herself in a steaming pile of shit.

The aftermath of the fight had been surreal, as if she were watching the scene from afar. The first thing she'd done was go to Mirren. Her handmaid had crawled deep into the shadows and curled up like a hedgehog, weeping. "You're safe now, lass," Bree had whispered, lowering herself to her knees before her. Mirren's throat had convulsed, her eyes still wild. And something had twisted deep within Bree's chest to see her terror.

Just yards from the two women, more enforcers had appeared. They'd then dragged the two men off in chains.

Bree had watched them go, fury kindling in her gut. Those two shit-eating bastards still breathed. How she longed to cut out their hearts.

"I w … was in the b … bakehouse," Mirren stuttered out the words finally. "T … they cornered me."

"The enforcers?"

"Aye … t … they followed me yesterday … when I was taking clothing down to the laundry … but I … I escaped them."

The ember in Bree's gut flared hot once more. *What?*

How she wished Mirren had confided in her—she'd have gone straight to her husband. She could have prevented this. Aye, Mirren had admitted that Drago intimidated her, but Bree had no idea that he and his friend had been stalking her like prey.

Bree cleared her throat. "When I found them, one of them was raping her while the other held her still."

Mac Brochan's gaze snapped to Bree then, pinning her to the spot. Ire burned in his eyes. Next to him, Torran also quietly simmered.

"Fia … told them to stop," Mirren gasped out the words, her blue eyes guttering, "and when they refused, she attacked them."

"With a *broom?*" The chief-enforcer's attention remained upon Bree then, a muscle feathering in his tight jaw.

"Aye," Bree replied, holding her chin high. "There was nothing else to hand."

A brittle silence filled the meeting alcove.

Mirren gave a choked sob then, her shoulders shaking. "W … will I be blamed?"

Bree jolted, shocked that Mirren would think such a thing. Acting on instinct, she stepped close to her handmaid and put an arm around her shoulders. The gesture felt odd; she couldn't remember the last time she'd comforted *anyone*. Nevertheless, Mirren's upset cut her to the bone.

"No, lass," the chief-enforcer replied, his tone softening slightly. "Those men committed a terrible violence against you … and they will pay."

Bree's mouth thinned. *They'd better.* If it were up to her, she'd string them both up by their balls first and let them cry for their mothers before she bled them. Her fingertips tingled at the thought.

Mirren nodded, even as she made another choking sound.

Bree tightened her grip on her maid's shaking shoulders. She then cut mac Brochan a sharp look. Couldn't he save his questions until later?

Their gazes fused, and a battle of wills followed, until the chief-enforcer scowled. He then nodded to his second. "Take Mirren down to the healer."

Bree stilled, an ache rising under her breastbone.

Mirren had admired Torran from afar for many moons, but this wasn't the first contact she'd longed for. And after what she'd just endured, the handmaid wouldn't want to go near any enforcer again.

Torran stepped forward. "This way," he said, his tone gentle, as if he were speaking to a wounded animal. Mirren's gaze flickered up. Her face was swollen and tear-stained, her eyes red from weeping, and she barely focused on the man before her. Instead, she gave a mute nod.

Bree steered the lass gently to the right, toward the doorway. She intended to go with them. Mirren was fragile at present; she needed her.

"Not you, wife," mac Brochan barked. "Stay where you are."

Bree cut him a sharp look. However, the thunderous expression on his face made her think twice about arguing with him. Swallowing her quickening anger, she dropped her arm from around her maid's shoulders and let her go.

Still hugging herself, as if fearing she'd crumble into pieces if she didn't, Mirren shuffled forward.

Torran followed her out of the meeting chamber.

An icy silence descended once husband and wife were alone. Meanwhile, Skaal sat at her master's side, her golden gaze fixed upon Bree.

The fae hound's baleful stare was even more unnerving than usual.

Eventually, the chief-enforcer spoke. "Please tell me, Fia," he said then, with exaggerated slowness. "How a Maid of Albia learns to fight like an assassin?"

Bree started to sweat. Ancestors help her, she had to talk fast, or the game would be up. "I had a tutor … at the House of Maids," she began, her mind churning to come up with a convincing lie. "An ex-mercenary, who taught us how to use our fists … and blades … to defend ourselves."

Mac Brochan folded heavily muscled arms over his broad chest. "I was told nothing of this."

"It's new … Mother Gelda decided that those Maids who wished to could learn to fight."

The chief-enforcer's gaze narrowed. "A wife does not need such skills."

"Perhaps not," Bree replied, forcing herself to hold his eye, "but the world is changing. Relations with the Shee worsen by the year, and there is unrest among our people too. Danger is everywhere, and Mother Gelda wishes us to be strong as well as trained in womanly arts." She raised her chin then, warming to her subject. "Wives must often travel throughout the realm … must look after themselves when their husbands are away." Mac Brochan scowled at this, but she pressed on. "If I hadn't intervened, *both* those animals would have raped Mirren."

"Enforcers aren't to be messed with." Mac Brochan stepped forward, looming over her. "They could have killed you."

His voice was flat and harsh, and yet something in the chief-enforcer's gaze made Bree still. Maybe she had pierced his armor after all.

"You were worried for my safety?" she asked softly, seizing the moment.

His stare drilled into her. "You are my wife," he replied, each word falling like a hammer blow. "I paid a lot of coin for you, and I won't see it wasted."

Bree flinched, even as her anger quickened once more. *Mercenary prick.*

"What are you going to do to them?" she demanded, lifting her chin in challenge.

"Their crime cannot be pardoned. They will be executed at dusk … I shall wield the blade myself."

Bree's mouth compressed. *Good.*

Underneath her satisfaction though, surprise flickered. Before coming here, she'd thought of the Marav as savages who couldn't care less if a woman was raped. But the chief-enforcer's response revealed that some did.

Mac Brochan stepped back. His gaze then swept down, from the crown of her head to her sandaled feet. There was no lust in his eyes though, just a cool assessment. "I'll admit, you are full of surprises, wife," he murmured. "Who would have thought a soft-looking woman could hold her own against two of my enforcers?" His mouth tugged into a humorless smile then. "I think it's time I tested your skills myself."

Bree frowned, not catching his meaning.

Her husband motioned to the doorway. "Come on, we're going to the training yard."

Bree followed mac Brochan into the yard behind the broch. Ringed by a high lichen-encrusted wall and lined by barracks, it wasn't an area she'd visited yet.

And the moment she stepped beyond the passageway that led from the main yard, she realized why.

It was a male domain.

Some enforcers sparred, stripped to the waist, their brawny torsos gleaming, while others sharpened their weapons on whetstones as they looked on. Like her husband, they were all heavily tattooed, their hair cropped short against their scalps.

And the moment Bree appeared, their gazes speared her.

Predatory. Assessing.

Bree's step slowed, her pulse thudding in her ears.

"Clear the yard," the chief-enforcer barked.

And to her surprise, they went quietly, although not without smirks and sharp looks at Bree.

"Is this wise?" Bree asked, frowning. "Surely, you don't want your men gossiping about your wife?"

"Too late for that," mac Brochan replied, turning to her. He then removed the heavy knife belt he wore across his chest, and the blades strapped to his hips and thighs, before tossing them to one side. "The servants who witnessed the fight will have already told half the residents of the broch. By this evening, even the fort's shit-shoveler will have heard."

Bree flinched. He wasn't likely wrong about that. She then lowered her gaze, feigning reticence even as her gut clenched. "I don't want to do this," she murmured. That was a lie. She longed to give this prick a beating he'd never forget. Frustration hammered within her. How she wished she could shift back into her Shee form. Even then, mac Brochan wouldn't be an easy opponent. Nonetheless, it would be a fairer fight.

The chief-enforcer snorted, and she raised her gaze to see that he'd lowered himself into a fighting stance. "Come on, wife." The goading edge to his voice made violence surge within her. "Imagine you hate me."

Bree set her jaw. *That shouldn't be too hard.*

Shifting back from him, she mimicked the same pose. Back in Sheehallion, she'd trained every day, even while she was hunting her next mark. She'd missed pushing her body.

They were alone in the yard now, the warm sun on their heads.

The back of her neck prickled then. Of course, many of the enforcers would be watching from the shadows. They wanted to see her thrashed.

"So, you want to humiliate me?" she asked, as they slowly began to circle each other.

He shrugged. "I want to learn more about the woman I married … a woman with secrets."

Bree snorted. "You've had plenty of opportunity to get to know me," she shot back. "But I'm usually beneath your notice."

His dark brows knitted together, and Bree almost smiled. She had him there, and they both knew it.

He lunged then, catching her off guard. His fist drove straight for her face, yet Bree ducked, her left hand snapping up and catching his wrist, while her right hand curled into a fist and punched toward his throat.

Mac Brochan jerked his head back, just missing having his windpipe crushed.

They sprang apart and circled each other once more.

But this time, the mood had changed.

Tension shivered through the warm air. Bree's blood started to roar in her ears.

What are you doing? Her pride made her want to fight him properly, to unleash herself on him, but to do so would be idiotic. Aye, she'd woven a lie about learning fighting skills at the House of Maids, but she still wouldn't have the same level of skill as a warrior-druid who'd spent many years training.

As much as it galled her, she had to let him have an easy victory, while at the same making it look credible.

And so, Bree forced herself to go on the defensive. Instead of aiming for his throat again, she focused on deflecting his blows.

The bastard was fast though. His knuckles grazed her jaw and glanced off her ribs. Both places stung, and the pain shocked her a little. Pain in this body was different, sharper and rawer. She could almost feel the bruises forming.

Again and again, she dodged, ducked, and side-stepped. Sweat slid down her back, while mac Brochan's eyes now burned into her.

"Fight me," he growled as he struck once more.

Iron bite her, how she wanted to. How she wanted to crush his nose with her fist and blacken both his eyes while she was at it. How she longed to smash his pretty face to a pulp.

Ducking under his guard, she caught mac Brochan square in the jaw with her fist and then drove her knee up into his groin.

Frustratingly, he moved to avoid the blow, and her knee collided with the hard muscle of his thigh.

And then, he kicked her feet out from under her.

Bree hit the ground hard, the impact driving the air from her lungs.

For a heartbeat or two, she merely lay there, mouth opening and closing, as she tried to recover her breath. Curse it, she'd fallen much harder than she would have in her Shee form. She'd never been winded like this before.

A shadow fell over her then, and she looked up to see her husband blocking out the sky.

"Bastard!" she gasped.

To her surprise, he flashed her a wicked smile—the first show of mirth she'd seen from him. "Not bad," he drawled. "Although don't think I didn't notice that you pulled your punches."

21: A COLD AND EMPTY LIFE

"I'VE GOT AN errand for you." Cailean greeted Torran without preamble.

His second was standing inside their meeting alcove, pouring himself a cup of mead, when Cailean strode in.

Torran nodded, handing Cailean the cup and pouring himself another. "Where to?"

"The House of Maids in Baldeen." Cailean walked to his desk in the far corner and sat down before pulling out a sheet of parchment. Unstoppering a jar of ink, he then dipped in a quill and deftly began to write.

All the while, he was aware of Torran's gaze upon him, but the enforcer had the wisdom to hold his tongue.

The missive Cailean wrote was short, blunt even. Nonetheless, he wouldn't waste words. Once he'd signed the letter, he sprinkled a couple of pinches of pounce over it, to dry the ink, before shaking the powder off and rolling up the parchment. He then sealed it with warm wax. While the wax was still soft, he took off his signet ring—which bore a wolf's head sigil, the mark of the High King's chief-enforcer—and pressed it into the seal.

Only then did he pick up his cup and take a gulp of sweet, frothy mead. "How is Mirren?"

Torran's features tightened. "The healer has tended her. She'll heal in a few days … physically, at least."

Cailean's fingers tightened around his cup. "I warned Drago what would happen if he harassed any more servants."

Torran pulled a face. "Leering at the lasses is one thing … dragging one into the shadows and brutalizing her is another."

"That's why Drago and Frang's heads are now on pikes outside the walls … I don't give warnings twice."

A tense silence fell then. Torran leaned up against the stone wall, long legs crossed at the ankles as he nursed his drink. "That should dissuade others in the future."

Cailean scowled, reaching up to massage a stiff muscle in his shoulder. "I lead a pack of rabid wolves."

Torran pulled a face. "Aye … the earth magic turns us all a bit feral … but the men all know rape won't be tolerated."

"Let's hope so." Cailean lifted his cup to his lips and took another deep draft.

"I hear I missed a show earlier," Torran said after a pause.

Cailean glanced his way, to see his second was smirking now. "You did."

"You went easy on her, I hope."

"Of course," Cailean replied with a snort. "Although I could see she was doing the same."

Torran barked a laugh. "You jest?"

"Do I look like I am?"

Torran's expression sobered. "She certainly held her own against Drago and Frang." He gave a rueful shake of his head then. "The Mother's tits … how is that possible?"

"Fia insists she had a fighting instructor at the House of Maids." Cailean rose from his desk and crossed to his second. He then thrust out the folded parchment to him. "Which is why I need you to ride there … and get me an answer from Mother Gelda herself."

"Have I gotten you into trouble?"

Sucking her finger, for she'd just pricked herself, Bree glanced up from where she'd been mending her husband's leather breeches. In truth, she'd been finding it hard to concentrate. Ever since her fight with the chief-enforcer, she'd been plagued with a feeling of impending doom. "No … why would you think that?"

Mirren straightened up from sprinkling fresh salt around the hearth, lowering her gaze. Her face was pale and puffy today, her eyes red-rimmed. "The chief-enforcer seemed vexed that you'd come to my aid yesterday," she said huskily.

"He wasn't angry about me helping you." Bree pulled a face then and shifted uncomfortably in her seat. After her fight with the enforcers—and then sparring with her husband—her body ached all over. "He thought he'd ordered himself a refined Maid of Albia … not a wife capable of breaking someone's jaw with a broom."

Mirren's gaze flicked up. "I've never seen a woman fight like that," she whispered.

"Aye, well … I was taught to defend myself at the House of Maids."

"You were?"

Bree nodded, studying her handmaid for a long moment. She'd told Mirren to take a day or two off, but the lass had refused. All the same, she looked too upset to be working. "How are you today, Mirren?" she asked gently.

The lass's throat bobbed, her sky-blue eyes glittering as she held back tears.

Watching her, Bree fought a tight sensation in her chest. "I'm glad my husband executed those pigs," she ground out. "Although he should have made them suffer first."

Mirren nodded, hurriedly knuckling away the tears that now trickled down her face. "I wish I were like you, Fia," she croaked.

Bree forced a smile, even as her ribs constricted further. Ancestors, she wished they could change the subject. "No, you don't."

A muscle feathered in Mirren's jaw. "But you're fierce. You aren't afraid of anything … and you know how to defend yourself." She paused then, her throat bobbing. "Will you teach me?"

Bree stared back at her. Of all the things Mirren might have asked her, this wasn't what she'd have expected. "Surely, you don't want—"

"I'm tired of being cowed," Mirren choked out, wringing her hands before her as tears flowed unimpeded down her cheeks. "Of shrinking to make myself smaller every time one of those brutes looks my way." She drew herself up, even as her small body trembled. "You don't live in fear … you *fight* … I want to do the same."

Bree drew in a deep breath. Curse it. She didn't have time to train her handmaid, and it wasn't wise either, not when her position here was so precarious. Not when her husband now watched her like a hawk.

The way things were going, Bree would soon have to flee Duncrag. Mor had wanted her to stay here a while, but at this rate, she wouldn't last the summer.

Aye, she had her own problems, but the pain and desperation in Mirren's eyes held her fast. She'd asked for her help, and Bree couldn't bring herself to refuse her. And so, she nodded. "Very well," she murmured. "We shall start tomorrow."

"What are you doing?"

Bree glanced up. She was sitting in the sleeping nook, propped up by a mound of furs, Fia's diary on her lap. Across the alcove, her husband sat by the fire, cup of ale in hand, Skaal at his feet.

"Reading my diary," she replied, surprised that he'd even addressed her. Usually, mac Brochan made a point of ignoring her all evening.

They'd had supper together, a tense and silent meal, before Bree retreated to the sleeping nook. It had been a frustrating day. She'd finally managed to go down to see Eldra. The healer had been alone, although she'd been more interested in questioning Bree about the incidents of the previous day. She'd also been frustratingly glib and enigmatic when Bree asked her about the man she'd once worked with. Eldra seemed convinced he'd departed Duncrag one night and never returned.

Bree didn't want to believe her—for Eldra didn't offer any explanation—but doubt had crept in. Maybe her predecessor *had* fled. Living here wasn't easy; perhaps he'd feared for his safety and was now hiding somewhere in Albia, doomed to continue living as one of the Marav. Bryce wouldn't dare return to Sheehallion now, not after failing his queen. A chill had prickled Bree's skin as she'd considered this possibility—for she was also close to messing up.

Mac Brochan cocked a dark eyebrow. "Why? Didn't you write it?"

Bree gave him a tight smile. "I did … husband … but reading my entries brings back memories." She shrugged. "These days, I feel like I'm a different person to the lass who wrote these words."

Her breathing quickened then. The chief-enforcer would never know how true those words were.

His head inclined. "How so?"

Uneasiness fluttered up, like a sack of released moths, in her belly. She didn't trust her husband's sudden talkativeness. Under normal circumstances, she'd have been pleased that he wasn't ignoring her. But after what happened the day before, she suspected there was a purpose behind his questions.

And yet, he was also handing her an opportunity. Maybe, if she engaged his sympathy, she'd draw him in.

"I was lonely at the House of Maids," she finally replied. Indeed, the entries after Fia's disappointment at not being chosen by the wool merchant had been tinged with melancholy and a growing sense of hopelessness. "I felt cut off from my family … and one by one, my friends all left."

The chief-enforcer grunted at this, his gaze flicking to where a lump of peat glowed in the hearth. It had been a cool day with heavy grey skies, and despite that they were now in early summer, the air was cold and damp inside the broch.

"It's best to make friends with loneliness," he said after a pause, still not looking her way. "The only person you can truly count on is yourself, anyway."

Bree stilled. Iron choke her, she didn't like to admit she had anything in common with this man. And yet, how many times over the years had she told herself those words?

Like her, Cailcan mac Brochan was a lone wolf.

Pushing aside the discomforting realization, Bree focused on the warrior-druid seated by the fire. "That's cynical," she replied finally. "Surely, there are those you trust within these walls?"

Mac Brochan's gaze cut her way, his lips compressing.

"What about Torran?"

Her husband snorted.

"But you two seem to be … friends."

"Aye, but that doesn't mean I *trust* him."

"That makes for a cold and empty life."

He shrugged. "Aye, just the way I like it."

Silence fell then. And once again, Bree felt an unwelcome feeling of kinship with this man. It took a rare individual to be comfortable with being alone. She'd met few, besides herself, who'd mastered it.

Deciding, it was best to let their conversation lapse—for it was making her increasingly uneasy—Bree glanced down at the diary she'd just opened. This entry was in late winter, only a moon's turn before The Day of the Hag. And here, finally, there was mention of Cailean mac Brochan.

Mother Gelda called me in to see her today.

A letter has arrived from the High King's chief-enforcer. He wishes for a wife and has asked her to select a suitable woman for him.

She has chosen me!

Apparently, he is too busy to make the trip here to meet me first. Instead, he told her that he wishes for a sweet, obedient woman who will not make too many demands on him.

Mother Gelda thinks I am the perfect choice.

I'm excited, of course … relieved that I've finally been chosen. But there is also a part of me that wonders why he wouldn't make the trip here. Surely, he wants a bride he finds attractive?

Maybe that doesn't matter to him.

I must admit that I'm nervous. The chief-enforcer! The most formidable of all the warrior-druids. The rumors tell of a terrifying brute of a man who is shadowed by a fae hound.

My heart quails at the thought of such a beast. It's said that if it howls thrice, the sound will stop your heart.

However, I must be brave. I will write to my husband-to-be and tell him I am looking forward to becoming his wife. Hopefully, he will write back, and we will establish a relationship of sorts before we meet.

Bree stopped reading and glanced up once more, taking in her husband's sharp profile. She wondered then, what Fia would have made of him, had they met.

22: FLEETING INTIMACY

"THE FIRST THING you must learn are the weak spots of a man's body." Bree faced Mirren in the center of the chief-enforcer's alcove. They'd pushed the table back against the wall to give themselves some space. It was mid-morning, and no one was likely to disturb them for a while.

However, Bree wasn't in the mood for giving lessons. She didn't need to provide mac Brochan with another reason to be suspicious of her. She'd awoken early, tense and ill-tempered, with a nagging sense of failure.

If only there was a way she could spy on the High King and his druidic council. As Mirren had informed her, they met regularly, every four or five days. But every time he called his druids to him, the High King placed guards at the entrance to the hall, forbidding everyone—even servants—entry.

It was impossible to listen in on them.

Mirren nodded before licking her lips nervously. Her handmaid was still worryingly pale, and her face was blotchy this morning—a sign she'd spent most of the night weeping. Bree didn't want to put her through this, yet maybe a distraction would help.

"Target the nose, eyes, throat, just below the breastbone, groin … and knees," she continued. "Don't bother going for anywhere else, especially not with a trained warrior."

Mirren winced. "You make it sound so easy."

"Don't be afraid to let them come close," Bree instructed. "It helps if they think you're weak … but that's when you strike."

Her handmaid's features tightened at these words, something dark moving in the depths of her eyes.

"Of course, preventing a situation is always better than having to fight." Bree paused then, her brow furrowing. "But when you're cornered and forced to defend yourself, there are four basic moves that could save you."

Mirren swallowed. "Show me then."

Bree nodded. "Right … let's start with this one." She mimicked driving the heel of her hand into Mirren's nose. "A broken nose really hurts … and it makes the eyes water, which should give you enough time to get away." Bree repeated the move. "See how I step in close, how I put the weight of my body behind it?"

"Aye."

"Well, it's your turn now. I'm going to grab you … and you're going to hit me in the nose with the back of your hand."

"But won't I hurt you?"

Bree snorted. "Let me worry about that."

A moment later, she leaped at Mirren.

The lass shrieked and lashed out, her palm flashing upward. Bree jerked her head back just in time, to avoid a crushed nose.

"Aye, that's it." Bree's mouth quirked. "You're a quick study."

Mirren's eyes glinted, high spots of color appearing on her pale cheeks. "If I imagine you're one of them … it's easier." There was a hard edge to her voice that Bree hadn't heard before. The sweet, smiling woman who'd laughed with her as they sat mending clothes together was gone.

Bree's breathing grew shallow then. Those bastard enforcers had stolen more than Mirren's innocence; they'd broken something inside her. She was brittle now, a vessel for rage and revenge to fill.

Their gazes met and held before Bree cleared her throat. "Right, next, I'm going to teach you the eye gouge."

Mirren nodded. "Good."

Bree took her handmaid through the first four essential self-defense moves. After showing her how to break a man's nose, and how to drive her fingers into his eyes, she demonstrated how to use her knees and elbows as weapons as well, aiming for the sensitive spots she'd highlighted earlier.

And Mirren's attention never wavered.

Bree was walking across the yard before the broch, returning from accompanying Mirren to the bakehouse, when shouting drew her attention.

Swiveling on her heel, she spied a horse and rider thundering through the gates.

Bree's gaze slid over the newcomer, taking in the dried blood that slicked his side and the sweat coating his ashen face. He pulled up his winded mount a few yards from Bree and attempted to dismount. However, the man was so weak that he collapsed onto the hard-packed dirt and lay there, panting.

Bree closed the distance between them and knelt, helping the man onto his back. It was hard not to wrinkle her nose at the reek of him; the sweet smell of decay warned her that the wounds he carried now festered.

"What happened to you?" she asked.

"The High King," the man rasped, ignoring her question. "I … must … speak to him."

"Fia!" Bree glanced up to see her husband striding across the yard toward her. His scowl warned her to move back from the injured man, but she held her ground. "What are you doing out here?"

"I escorted Mirren to the bakehouse," she replied coolly, holding his eye. "After what happened, she's … understandably … nervous."

Her husband's mouth thinned, although he didn't reprimand her. Instead, he halted and hunkered down next to the prone man. "I'm Cailean mac Brochan, the chief-enforcer," he told the man brusquely. "Name yourself."

Relief flickered across the stranger's face. The High King wasn't before him, but he'd speak to his emissary. "Garth mac Donal," he breathed, his voice weak now. "I'm a tax collector."

His eyes glittered with fever as he met the chief-enforcer's gaze. "We were attacked in the north."

Mac Brochan's brow furrowed, and Bree stilled, excitement fluttering under her ribs. Perhaps she was about to discover something that could help her people, something she could send back to Mor. *Finally.*

She held her breath, waiting for the man to say more, for mac Brochan to question him. However, after a brief pause, her husband glanced her way, his expression stony. "Fetch the healer."

"I'm going away tomorrow." Halfway through the noon meal, mac Brochan broke the silence between them.

Bree glanced up from where she was wrestling with an overcooked piece of roast venison. It was as tough as boiled leather. "Aye?" Of course, after witnessing the arrival of the tax collector that morning, she wasn't surprised by this news.

He gave her a curt nod and reached into the basket between them, helping himself to a slice of oaten bread.

"Are you going north then?" she asked lightly, bracing herself for his stony silence.

To her surprise, he nodded. "To the Uplands … the High King's tax collectors were attacked north of the Goatfell Mountains."

"So, the man this morning was the only survivor?"

Her husband gave a curt nod.

"Did he reveal anything useful?"

"Not much … he died around noon."

Bree took this news in, disappointment rising. Curse it, she'd hoped for something juicier. Nonetheless, now that mac Brochan was talking to her, she'd keep the conversation going.

"Did the Shee attack them?"

He shook his head. "More likely tribespeople." Mac Brochan took a mouthful of bread and chewed slowly before swallowing. "The Overking of Cannich has little control over his people these days … especially the Circines tribe."

It pleased Bree to learn just how unpopular Talorc mac Brude was with his people. The three hill tribes of the Uplands had always been difficult to control, and these days, the chieftains who'd bent the knee to the local overking were unruly.

Nonetheless, there was a vagueness to her husband's response that frustrated her. He knew more than he was letting on. Taxes weren't the only issue with the Uplanders. If the overkings were busy building armies, they'd be drafting local men. She wondered if the Circines had rebelled.

She wanted to ask mac Brochan about this, but—remembering his response last time she'd inquired about the High King's armies—she held her tongue.

"You are to behave yourself in my absence," mac Brochan said then.

Bree couldn't help it, her mouth curved. "Was that a jest, husband?"

His gaze snapped up to meet hers. "No."

Bree pulled a face. "I don't know what trouble you think I'll get up to."

He snorted, and her pulse quickened in response. Of course, after the events of the past days, he'd be keeping an even closer eye on her.

"How long will you be away?" she asked after an awkward pause.

"I'm not sure … although it's likely to be the full turn of a moon."

Bree wasn't sure whether to feel relieved that she'd be spared his company—or frustrated that she'd have to wait longer still to work on building trust between them.

Mac Brochan was even more suspicious of her now.

As such, despite that she wanted to ask him for more details, like the size of his patrol, and the route they'd take north, Bree swallowed the urge.

I have something to send to Mor now though, she reassured herself. It wasn't much, but it would hopefully take the edge off the Raven Queen's impatience. And if she made sure she was up at first light and watching from the walls as the men departed, she'd discover their numbers too.

Bree glanced over at the hearth then, where Skaal was gnawing at a bone. "Will your hound be going with you?"

"Of course … she follows me everywhere."

Bree met her husband's eye once more. "Won't you tell me how Skaal came to be your companion?"

Mac Brochan's mouth pursed, and he leaned back in his chair, studying her under dark brows.

Bree suffered his inspection, even as her breathing grew shallow. Curse the man, he was locked tighter than a tomb. "Forgive me, husband," she muttered, reaching for her cup of wine and taking a sip. "Yet again, I forget my place."

He huffed a humorless laugh. "Why is it that even your apologies are like a fist to the face?"

Wincing, Bree took another sip of wine. It looked as if they were about to pass another silent evening.

"Five winters ago, I was part of a war band in the far north of the Uplands," mac Brochan said then, surprising her. "The world was frozen, the Sharp Billed Wind cutting straight to the marrow. Mid-winter Fire approached, and the High King had sent us to Darkmere, to attack the Shee when they emerged from their barrow at Mid-winter Fire."

Bree fought a scowl. Aye, she remembered that attack and Mor's fury afterward. Mid-winter Fire—the Winter solstice—was a sacred time for both the Shee and the Marav. Despite the cold in the mortal realm, the Shee ventured forth from their barrows, walking between the two worlds, and bringing back offerings from Albia. They collected hawthorn and drualus, as well as blood-red holly berries and the fallen acorns from mighty oaks.

"We thought we'd catch them unawares, especially that far north," the chief-enforcer went on. "We knew fae hounds stalked those mountains, and so we stoppered our ears with soft wax, to protect ourselves from their howls, before we fought them. But their numbers were far greater than we'd anticipated, and they eventually shattered our ranks. Many of our war band fell."

He halted there before he absently raised a hand, his fingertips skimming the left side of his ribcage as if recalling the incident. "I too was injured. A blizzard came upon us, and I was separated from the other enforcers. Weak from the loss of blood, I crawled into a cave … ignorant of the fact that it was a fae hound's den."

Bree's gaze widened. "That was unlucky."

The corners of his mouth lifted in the barest hint of a smile. "The Warrior was looking down on me that day … for the cave was empty when I arrived." He glanced over at Skaal. The hound had stopped chewing at her bone and now sat up, ears pricked, as if listening to the tale.

"In truth, I was too weak, too cold, to pay much attention to my surroundings … I only cared that I'd escaped the blizzard and the Shee," he continued. "I fell asleep, and when I awoke, I found a tiny fae hound pup nestled against me. It was then that I realized where I'd stumbled into." His expression softened slightly as he continued to look at Skaal. "She was alone … I don't know what happened to the rest of her litter."

"Fae hounds don't whelp large litters like wolves or dogs do," Bree answered. "One or two pups per litter is all you get … which is why they're so rare." Her husband's attention snapped back to Bree at this, and heat rushed over her. What was she doing? "Or so I've heard," she added quickly. "Mother Gelda explained such things to us."

The chief-enforcer watched her intently for a moment before nodding. "Aye, well, this pup was alone. The blizzard stretched out, and I lay there in the fae hound's den, too weak to move. I braced myself for the mother to return … but she never did." Something shadowed his eyes then—surely not remorse? "We must have slain her during the battle."

Bree's fingers tightened around her cup of wine. *Of course, you did.*

"I'm surprised you survived to tell the tale." Bree dropped her gaze to her trencher. She didn't want him to see her reaction.

"As was I," he replied. "However, I slaked my thirst on melted snow and ate the dry oatcakes and cheese I carried with me. I shared the cheese in little pieces with the pup."

"I'd have expected you to wring its neck." Bree dug her eating knife into the leathery venison once more. The thought of this man sharing his rations with a fae hound pup was incongruous, to say the least.

He harrumphed, and Bree glanced up to see he was looking at Skaal once more. "I couldn't bring myself to," he admitted with a shake of his head. "And when I was strong enough to walk, I left the cave and brought Skaal with me." His mouth curved into a real smile then. "You've been with me ever since, haven't you, lass?"

Skaal pushed herself up, her heavy fringed tail thumping on the floor.

Something tugged deep within Bree's chest as she observed the bond between them—a complicated emotion, somewhere between jealousy, longing … and *respect.*

Watch it, she warned herself. *Don't you dare think there's any decency in him.* "I don't believe it," she said, unable to stop herself from teasing him. "My ruthless enforcer husband has a heart, after all."

Mac Brochan's gaze cut to her, the softness she'd witnessed upon his face as he looked at his hound disappearing.

Immediately, Bree regretted her sarcasm. Iron choke her, she'd get nothing out of him now.

Her husband's lips parted, as if he was going to answer her, before they compressed tight, swallowing his response. Picking up his cup of wine, he drained it in a long, deep draft. He then slammed the cup down on the table between them, making it clear that their conversation, and the fleeting intimacy that it had brought, was over.

23: SHIELDS

MIST WREATHED THE yard before the broch, drifting like smoke over the spiky wooden ramparts surrounding it and curling around the peaked roof of the broch itself.

Leading his horse out of the stables, Cailean whistled to Skaal. Moments later, the huge dog with a shaggy dark-green coat and glowing golden eyes stalked out of the mist. Skaal carried an aura of Sheehallion magic with her. The Shee were fleet of foot and capable of blending with their surroundings at will when it suited them. It was what made them so difficult to hunt.

Vaulting up onto his stallion's back, Cailean cast a look around the yard, at the company of twenty enforcers who'd join him on this patrol. His brow furrowed as he viewed them. With Drago and Frang gone, their numbers were dwindling. Those two had always been trouble, and he felt no remorse at executing them—even if the High King wasn't pleased with him about it—but they were among his fiercest warriors. He needed to replace them.

Raen was training more enforcers, although the young warrior-druids weren't yet ready to leave the Isle of Arryn and join him. Cailean had left his remaining twenty-two enforcers here, to guard the High King, and when Torran returned from Baldeen, he'd oversee them in the chief-enforcer's absence.

Cailean's frown deepened. Torran was due back soon, and he'd wanted to be here when he returned, for Mother Gelda's answer mattered to him.

These days, he trusted nothing that came out of his wife's mouth.

Jaw tightening, he reined Feannag around and headed toward the gates that led from the broch onto The Thoroughfare. The stallion tossed his head, his bit jangling, and side-stepped. Feannag—so named for his crow-black coat—was eager to be away again.

Seating himself deeply in the saddle, Cailean squeezed with his thighs, keeping the stallion in check. Feannag would be able to stretch his legs as soon as Duncrag was at their backs.

Wordlessly, the enforcers fell in behind their leader, the hollow clip-clop of their horses' hooves, the creak of leather, and the jangle of iron filling the damp air.

As Cailean led the way across the yard, the skin between his shoulder blades prickled.

Someone was watching him.

Twisting in the saddle, he glanced over his shoulder, his gaze lifting to the top of the stone wall that ringed the broch. A woman stood there, watching him go. She wore a blue mantle, her oak-brown hair unbound and spilling over her shoulders.

Sensing his rider's sudden tension, Feannag snorted and bucked. Keeping his seat easily, Cailean stared up at his wife.

Had Fia come outdoors to see him off?

His breathing grew shallow, and it struck him then that seeing her there *pleased* him.

His gut clenched. *Watch yourself.*

The Reaper's cods, he didn't like how she affected him, how his gaze often sought her out. He ignored her most of the time, and only spoke to the woman when he had no other choice—but the truth was, she fascinated him. He'd never known a woman could be so full of contradictions. She had a lush body and a tongue like a whetted blade.

And she could fight.

He'd met female warriors—the High King's guard had a few—although female enforcers were rare. Women tended to display gifts for the other druidic paths. But he couldn't believe a Maid of Albia would be taught such a skill. It made no sense to him.

Gods, the woman vexed him though. He'd told her she wasn't to question him about the High King's business, but she persisted.

Indeed, as Fia's father had noticed in Braewall, mac Brude *did* have his overkings building armies for him. Their recent journey south had been to check on King Dunchadh's progress.

The High King had tried to cloak his plans in secrecy. However, after recent events, he now suspected the Shee knew what he was up to—something that had infused him with urgency.

This next trip had a dual purpose: after investigating the attack on the High King's tax collectors and retrieving the stolen revenue, Cailean had been instructed to travel to Cannich and hurry King Ailean up. He'd been struggling to draft Uplanders, and the High King was displeased with his slow progress.

Fia continued to gaze down at him, and Cailean tore his attention from her.

Her questions weren't the worst thing about her. His wife distracted him. He'd made a mistake the day before, being so candid with her about how Skaal had come to be with him. He regretted it now.

The less his wife knew about him the better.

Urging Feannag through the gates, he made a silent promise that when he returned to Duncrag, his shields would be back in place.

"The broch is still buzzing like a bee's nest after what you did."

Bree glanced up, from where she'd been pouring ground seeds into a leather pouch, to find Lara watching her. The princess's pine-colored eyes were sharp with curiosity, and Bree stifled a sigh.

She'd been expecting this—and had avoided Princess Lara over the last few days.

To Bree's left, Eldra turned from retrieving a clay bottle off a high shelf. "Aye, the servants talk of nothing else at mealtimes." She then favored Bree with a probing look that made her skin prickle.

Eldra had a canny way about her that never failed to put Bree on edge.

Masking her discomfort, Bree gave a soft snort. "They'll move on to other subjects soon enough, I'm sure."

"Maybe." Lara's lips curved. "But it's a rare thing … for a woman to take on two enforcers."

"Mother Gelda at the House of Maids has introduced self-defense as part of our training," Bree replied, repeating the lie that now slipped easily off her tongue. "For my last year there, I had a combat instructor."

She didn't look Eldra's way as she spoke, for she'd already told the healer this story. Nonetheless, she felt the weight of the woman's gaze upon her.

"I believed Maids of Albia were schooled only in how to please their husbands and little else." Lara glanced down at the mortar as she began grinding parsley into a paste. "Although I'm pleased to be proved wrong."

Bree forced a tight smile, wishing they could talk about something else. After watching her husband depart with a band of twenty enforcers earlier, she'd been on her way back to their alcove to retrieve a silver acorn and send a message to Mor, when a servant had intercepted her. The princess requested her presence in the healer's chamber. Seething with irritation, she'd gone downstairs.

"It's fortunate you were nearby when Mirren was attacked, Lady mac Brochan," Eldra said after a pause. "Even so, they brutalized the lass."

Bree glanced the healer's way to see that she was frowning. "Aye, and Mirren is still suffering," she replied. "Although her physical injuries aren't the worst of it."

"I'm glad the chief-enforcer executed them," Princess Lara said then, her voice hard. "Even if father is vexed with him over it."

Eldra's gaze widened at this, while Bree stilled, anger kindling in her belly.

Witnessing their reactions, Lara grimaced. "Enforcers take a long time to train, and these days, the number of young men displaying the gift lessens. Father believes mac Brochan acted rashly."

Bree fought a scowl. It didn't surprise her that the High King would defend rapists. He hunted her kind like vermin and treated his own people with disdain. Nonetheless, the anger simmering in the princess's eyes made it clear she didn't agree with her father.

"Did you hear that Lady mac Brochan's husband challenged her to a fight afterward?" Eldra asked as she handed the princess the clay jar she'd just retrieved. "Just a few drops will do, Your Highness."

"I did," Lara replied, following the healer's instructions, as she cast Bree a veiled look.

"Aye, well … the less that's said about that the better." Tying up the pouch she'd just filled with ground seeds, Bree dusted off her hands.

"I was talking to an enforcer yesterday who witnessed the fight … and he said you held your own admirably," the healer added. Once again, something in her tone put Bree's hackles up.

"Not really," she muttered. "He just toyed with me for a bit before knocking me onto my arse."

Lara lifted her hand to her mouth to hide a laugh while Eldra raised her eyebrows questioningly.

Heat washed over Bree as she remembered the humiliating encounter.

Her pulse fluttered then. She hadn't meant for mac Brochan to see her earlier, as she'd stood upon the walls watching him depart. The impact of their gazes meeting after he'd twisted in the saddle, his stallion dancing under him, had made her heart kick against her ribs. But she'd ridden the discomfort and held his stare.

He'd been the first one to look away.

Afterward, she'd told herself it wasn't a bad thing, to let him think she'd come out to see him off. If he believed that she was forming an attachment to him, it would stroke his male pride. His absence had earned her a reprieve, but Bree was walking on a knife-edge now—one misstep and she'd tumble.

It was mid-afternoon before Bree got any time alone.

Mirren had gone down to retrieve clean clothes from the laundry. The lass would be busy for a while, sorting and folding.

Even so, Bree moved swiftly. Crossing to her trunk, she dug down to the bottom, retrieved her leather pouch, and extracted a silver acorn. These were precious in Sheehallion, for silver oaks were rare. Shee royalty had always used silver acorns to send important, and private, messages.

Seating herself on the closed trunk, she held the acorn in her upturned palm and breathed upon it, whispering the charm. "Open to me, dear one … so that I might tell you my secrets."

A heartbeat passed, and the outer husk of the acorn unfurled, like the wings of a moth, waiting for Bree's message.

"The chief-enforcer rides north to the Goatfell Mountains," she murmured. "He travels with a company of twenty warrior-druids. There has been unrest … it appears the Circines tribe is involved. If you wish to intercept the enforcers, the opportunity is there." Bree paused before adding, "There are fears that the druidic bloodlines are failing … the High King is desperate for all druids to bear offspring, but especially the enforcers."

Her heart skipped a beat then. She wasn't sure what Mor would do with these details, but she was well overdue for her first update. For the moment, it suited Mor that the chief-enforcer lived, so he could give up what he knew to Bree. But, even if he died, would that mean the job was over? Could she go home?

Don't get ahead of yourself. Mac Brochan's widow wouldn't likely be cast from the broch. She could still be the Raven Queen's eyes and ears here.

Her pulse stuttered once more, and Bree's mouth thinned. For some reason, the thought of mac Brochan never returning to Duncrag unsettled her. It shouldn't—she should rejoice. Meanwhile, the silver acorn closed in on itself, sealing her message within.

Ignoring the uneasiness that still pitched within her, Bree rose to her feet, the acorn clasped in her hand, and left the chief-enforcer's alcove.

As she'd done at dawn, she made her way up onto the walls, but, this time, she walked to a scheduled spot on the eastern ramparts, where pigeons cooed, that looked out at where the River Lethe widened as it headed toward the sea. The morning's mist had burned off, and sunlight glittered off the water. Her gaze traveled to the willows growing upon the riverbanks, far below, their foliage bright green with new growth.

The distance was too great, and her mortal eyesight too weak, for Bree to spy anything perched there—yet Mor had assured her that Eagal would sit among the trees during daylight, awaiting news.

Glancing around, Bree made sure that no one was watching her. There were no sentries in this section. She was safe.

She drew in a deep breath then before letting out a low caw. It hurt her throat to make the sound—one that had come so easily to her in her Shee form—but she managed it. The caw carried through the still afternoon air, over the thatched and sod roofs of the cottages that tumbled down the crag below her.

She then waited.

A short while later, a large raven appeared, winging its way from the willows, in a wide arch toward the broch that perched atop the promontory. The raven was bigger than most, its feathers a deep blue-black that gleamed in the sunlight.

Eagal swooped down then, landing lightly atop a post just a few feet from Bree.

Mor's messenger fixed her with a hard, glassy gaze, and despite that she'd seen the bird several times over the years, Bree suppressed a shudder. 'Eagal' meant 'Fear', and he was aptly named. The bird had a way of looking at you that stripped away your defenses.

All the same, Eagal was her first contact with home in well over two turns of the moon.

Bree's eyes fluttered closed for a moment, a heavy weight settling upon her chest as longing for Sheehallion, with its soft air and bright skies, barreled into her.

You can't go home yet … not until you discover something of real use.

The reminder was a sobering one. Pulling herself together, she opened her eyes. Then, glancing around to ensure she wasn't being watched, she stepped forward, offering Eagal the silver acorn upon the palm of her hand.

The raven fixed her with a beady stare for an instant longer before he plucked the acorn up. And then he was airborne once more, swooping east. No doubt, he was flying toward Deeping, the barrow nearest to Duncrag.

Bree watched him go, her pulse racing.

24: SEVEN CROWS

BREE WAS DESCENDING the worn stone steps from the walls when a heavy-set bay horse thundered into the yard, ridden by a lanky man with short blond hair.

Torran.

Bree frowned, melting into the shadows at the base of the stairs lest he see her. Best she was as secretive as possible about her movements.

His horse was lathered, and when he drew it up, a stable hand emerged to take it from the enforcer. "Where have you been these past days?" the older man asked as Torran swung down from the saddle.

"On a brief visit to the House of Maids," Torran replied.

A chill washed over Bree at this admission. *Shit. Shit. Shit!*

"Why is that then?" the nosy stable hand asked. "Buying yourself a bride too, are you?"

Torran's lip curled, although he didn't answer. "Where is the chief-enforcer?"

"He's not here … the High King's sent him north to deal with trouble."

"Aye?"

The man nodded. "The Circines are stirring things up again."

Torran's jaw tightened at this news. Then, giving his horse a gentle slap on the rump, he turned and strode away across the yard toward the broch. Bree followed, grateful for her light sandals, which moved noiselessly across the hard-packed earth.

And as Torran walked, he withdrew a rolled piece of parchment from a pouch at his waist.

Bree's heart kicked hard at the sight.

She should have realized that her husband wouldn't let things be after discovering she could fight. Of course, he wanted to make sure that she wasn't lying to him about Mother Gelda hiring a fighting instructor to teach the Maids of Albia.

Bree started to sweat. Picking up the skirt of her tunic, she followed Torran inside and up the stairs to the first floor, hoping that he'd leave the message in their quarters. Unfortunately, he veered left, instead—nodding to the guard posted on the landing and pushing aside the heavy curtain shielding the chief-enforcer's meeting alcove. Torran then disappeared inside.

The guard glanced her way as Bree appeared. "Good afternoon, Lady mac Brochan."

"Afternoon." Heart pounding, Bree walked past him and dove into the safety of the quarters she and the chief-enforcer shared, where she paced the floor.

She couldn't let mac Brochan read that letter.

It was over for her if he did.

Supper had come and gone when Bree made her way up the stairs, carrying a tray that balanced a heavy stoppered bottle and four pewter goblets studded with garnets.

"Where are you going with that, Lady mac Brochan," a guard greeted her when she reached the first-floor landing and turned left. While he was in residence at the broch, the chief-enforcer didn't post a guard on the landing. However, to her frustration, there was always one there during his absences.

Bree flashed him a bright smile. "The fortified blaeberry wine my husband ordered from Troon has arrived," she informed him. "I'm leaving it in his meeting alcove for when he returns home."

The guard, a coarse-featured man with eyes too close together, frowned before he nodded to the curtained entrance at the other end of the landing. "Why don't you leave it in your quarters?"

"The chief-enforcer prefers to drink in here," she replied sweetly. "So he might share the wine with his men over a few games of dice."

"Aye, but he won't be back for a few days yet."

"No," Bree replied patiently, keeping her smile fixed. "And the wine will be waiting for him when he does."

The guard squinted at her before clearly deciding he couldn't be bothered deciphering the reasonings of a flea-brained woman. He grunted then and gestured to the entrance to the chief-enforcer's private space. "Go on."

Bowing her head so the guard wouldn't see the jubilation in her eyes, Bree stepped forward and shouldered the curtain aside, entering the alcove. She hadn't been inside here since the day of her arrival at Duncrag, and the moment she stepped within, the smell of leather and ash, with a whisper of clove, wrapped itself around her.

Cailean mac Brochan's scent.

Before she realized what she was doing, Bree dragged the smell deep into her lungs. Her chest tightened then, a strange fluttering beginning deep in her belly.

She halted abruptly, her fingers tightening around the edges of the wooden tray.

Iron flay her, she hadn't meant to do that. What had come over her?

All the same, the chief-enforcer's presence permeated this chamber. It was his domain. Everything, from the iron swords and axes that hung on the walls, to the wolfskin rug in front of the hearth, reminded her of the mortal she'd shackled herself to.

It overwhelmed her senses.

Curse this mortal body. It made her weaker, more susceptible to things that wouldn't usually bother her.

Jaw clenching, Bree moved once more, carrying the tray over to the sturdy oaken table that sat at the back of the space. A neat stack of fresh parchment sat upon one corner, together with a stoppered pot of ink. Another pot held a collection of quills. Everything was tidy, reflecting her husband's orderly, military, mind. Mac Brochan controlled everything around him. How frustrating for him that his wife was so unruly.

Setting the tray down on the table, her gaze went to the rolled piece of parchment that waited there.

It bore a wax seal, with the sigil of a holly leaf upon it—the House of Maids.

This was it.

Bree grabbed the message and deftly tucked it into her bodice.

Straightening up, she then cast a glance around the alcove. This was her opportunity to see if her husband had left anything—letters, maps, or hastily scribbled notes—behind that might be useful to Mor. However, a quick survey revealed that every surface was clear.

There was nothing helpful here.

Bree left the wine for mac Brochan's return, turned, and made her way back out onto the landing. The guard nodded to her as she departed, and she flashed him another smile. Yet, all she could think about was returning to the privacy of her quarters. Heart pounding, she forced herself to walk across the landing at a sedate pace. However, once she was alone, Bree deftly unsealed the missive and read it.

And as she did so, her stomach swooped.

Unfortunately, it was as she'd suspected. Mother Gelda confirmed, in just three blunt sentences, that no Maid of Albia had ever been trained to fight.

Bree gnawed at her lower lip. Mac Brochan would discover the truth soon enough—even if he had to ride to Baldeen himself for answers. But in the meantime, she'd stall him.

Crossing to the fire, she threw the letter in, watching as the golden tongues of flame devoured it.

A thought occurred to her then, and ice slithered down her spine. Of course, when mac Brochan returned, Torran would ask the chief-enforcer if he'd gotten his missive. But what if Mother Gelda had spoken to Torran? *What if he knows what the letter contains?*

Bree watched the last of the parchment blacken and shrivel.

Keep your nerve. Mother Gelda had written to the chief-enforcer. Her words were for his eyes only. Instinct told her that Torran didn't know. And with any luck, Mor would play her part. The Shee would attack the chief-enforcer's band, and he'd never return to Duncrag to discover his letter missing.

She had to brazen this out—it was either that or fail Mor as Bryce had.

"Fia," Mirren's voice intruded then, carrying through the curtain shielding the chief-enforcer's quarters from the landing. "Princess Lara requests you join her in the hall, for an evening wine."

Bree clenched her hands by her sides.

Curse it. Over the past moons, she'd developed a reluctant liking and respect for the princess. But now wasn't the time to have a chat over a goblet of wine. Her nerves were as tight as a drum—company was the last thing she was in the mood for. Nonetheless, she wouldn't decline. She couldn't.

"Aye," she called back. "I shall be down shortly."

Princess Lara wasn't alone in the smoky hall. As Bree entered, the High King and the prince glanced up from their game of 'Liar'. The dice game was popular amongst the Marav—indeed,

Mirren had been surprised to discover that her mistress didn't know it.

Bree's skin prickled under the men's inspection.

The High King possessed a quiet menace, while his son brooded. They made an incongruous pair seated there—Talorc's big frame folded into a chair, restless energy bristling off him. The High King was dressed in plain leather, the golden torque about his neck his only concession to his status, while Kennan was clad in a beautifully fitting tunic and breeches with delicately embroidered flourishes. As always, the prince's long jet-black hair was oiled and combed back. Amber-studded rings sparkled upon his long fingers as he picked up the dice pot and shook it.

A few yards away from the High Seat, Queen Teva and her gaggle of ladies had gathered around the largest of the two hearths. They'd been gossiping together when Bree entered, but broke off at her entrance, studying her with interest.

Bree stiffened. Unfortunately, she was still the talk of the broch.

"Fia!" Lara drew her attention then. The princess sat alone upon a stool by the second hearth. She held a distaff in one hand and had a basket of wool upon her lap. Winding wool onto a spindle, readying it for spinning, was a task that Bree still struggled with. However, Lara had likely learned this skill at her mother's knee as a child.

"Good evening, Your Highness."

Lara gestured to the ewer of wine and two cups upon the table next to her. "Pour us some wine and take a seat."

Bree obeyed. Then, cradling her cup of wine, she perched upon the stool opposite the princess.

Taking a sip of wine, Lara met her eye. "I hear Cailean has gone away again."

Bree stiffened. She couldn't get used to the princess calling mac Brochan by his first name. Masking her reaction, she nodded. "I suppose I shall have to get used to it."

"But it feels as if you've barely spent any time together since your handfasting."

Long enough.

"Aye, well, there are many demands on a chief-enforcer's time," she replied, her tone veiled. "It sounds as if things are getting lawless in the north."

The princess glanced over at where the queen consort and her women had returned to their conversation. Meanwhile, the High King and the prince were both focusing on their dicing. "Father has been in a foul mood ever since word arrived about his tax inspectors," she murmured, her brow furrowing. "They took all their coin and then strung the men by their necks from trees."

"Won't it be hard to catch those responsible though?" Bree asked, taking a sip from her own cup. The tart plum wine bit at the back of her throat, but her interest was piqued. Until now, she'd been disappointed about just how little Princess Lara seemed to overhear—but maybe she'd learned something of use now. "I hear the Circines are adept at hiding."

"Aye, they have a young chieftain … Domnall mac Bridei … who is at odds with the local overking. He's quite the troublemaker, and father wants him dealt with."

Bree managed a tight smile. The chieftain's name was useful, certainly, yet she'd hoped for more. "My husband will rise to the task, I'm sure."

The two women fell silent then. The princess put her wine aside and picked up her distaff once more. But her green eyes had clouded, and her features were now strained.

Bree leaned forward. "Is something wrong, Your Highness?"

Lara huffed a sigh. She cut another glance over at the High Seat as if she feared her father could overhear them. Bree doubted he could; even so, she edged closer to catch the princess's next words. "Last night, I dreamed of seven crows sitting on a yew tree."

Bree stared blankly at her, her pulse quickening. Curse her, there were so many Marav superstitions she was ignorant of—this was another one. "And?"

Lara's gaze narrowed, and she made a frustrated sound in the back of her throat. "You know … it's a *portent*," she whispered. "Someone under this roof guards a dangerous secret."

25: DRAWING TOO DEEPLY

"THEY'VE RETURNED!"

Mirren's gasped announcement made Bree glance up from her noon meal. The bread she was swallowing caught in her throat, and she coughed, reaching for a cup of ale to wash it down.

Eyes smarting, she blinked at her handmaid. Mirren stood in the doorway, cheeks flushed from her run up the stairs. "My husband?"

"Aye … and he has a prisoner with him."

Bree's heart kicked hard at this news.

A full moon's turn had passed since mac Brochan had departed with his enforcers. She'd waited for news that they'd been ambushed by the Shee and slaughtered—but none had come. The lengthy silence had been wearying, and as the days passed, Bree had grown frustrated that she still had nothing more to give Mor.

At this rate, she'd be stuck here for years. *If I survive that long.*

But now the enforcers had come home, and they might have brought news.

Pushing back her chair, Bree rose to her feet, her bread and stew forgotten. Leaving Mirren to clear up the remains of her noon meal, she made her way downstairs. But as she approached the heavy oaken doors that would let her out into the yard below, her stomach fluttered.

Iron bite her, she was nervous about seeing him again.

Seven crows in a yew tree.

The princess's dream still haunted her. Lara wasn't a seer, although the vision that had come to her while she slept made Bree feel as if she'd been unmasked.

It had taken all her will to keep the guilt from showing upon her face, and she'd been wary around the princess ever since.

Bree's stomach turned over once more. She wasn't ready to deal with the chief-enforcer. Ever since Torran had returned with that damning missive, all she'd done was kick the stone down the road. Sooner or later, she'd trip over it.

Of course, she could have scribbled a letter of her own, rewriting Mother Gelda's response. Nonetheless, she couldn't have recreated the wax seal easily, and her husband would likely spot a forgery.

She'd dug herself a deep hole and was now stuck at the bottom of it.

Jaw set, Bree strode to the doors and pushed her way through, emerging into a drizzly day. Heavy clouds enshrouded Duncrag this afternoon, the rain falling in a gentle mist. She made her way gingerly down the slippery steps, her gaze traveling across the crowd of men and horses amassed in the center of the yard.

Fewer of them had returned. She now counted fourteen, instead of the twenty who'd ridden out with the chief-enforcer.

The High King had also come out to greet his enforcers and their captive. Talorc stood a few steps below Bree, the prince at his side, his gaze riveted upon the man two brawny enforcers were dragging toward him.

The prisoner was young—no older than twenty winters. Naked to the waist and barefoot, his body streaked with blood and grime, his black hair knotted, the man's dark eyes burned with hate.

Instinctively, Bree knew this was the rabblerousing chieftain.

However, her attention didn't linger on the prisoner. Instead, it shifted to the tall, muscular figure that stood a couple of yards behind him.

Her belly swooped then, and she quashed the ridiculous urge to tidy her hair and smooth her tunic.

Instead, she observed her husband. A moment later, her gaze narrowed. The chief-enforcer might have completed his mission, but he didn't look well. Even from this distance, his skin had an ashen cast, and his face was strained.

At that moment, mac Brochan spied her as well, and his big body stiffened. Across the yard, they stared at each other, and the nervousness that Bree had managed to quell earlier took flight once more. She was suddenly breathless and lightheaded.

"Cailean!" The High King's deep voice boomed across the yard. "Have you brought me Domnall mac Bridei?"

"Aye," the chief-enforcer replied, his voice more gravelly than usual.

"Well done." Talorc moved down the steps, leaving his son looking on behind him, and crossed to where the prisoner struggled between the two enforcers. Like mac Brochan, the other warrior-druids were pale and drawn, and Bree wondered what had befallen them. "I knew you wouldn't fail me."

Mac Brochan bowed his head. "I live to serve, Your Highness."

Bree's jaw clenched. Of course, he did. He was the High King's hound.

"*However*," Talorc went on. "It does vex me to see you've lost enforcers." There was a harsh edge to his voice now. He wasn't half as powerful or wise as the Raven Queen, yet Talorc mac Brude had a core of tempered steel. Like Mor, he wasn't one to accept failure—from anyone.

The chief-enforcer's features tightened at this reprimand, although he didn't offer any excuse.

"We will talk in private about your trip to the north," Talorc said after a pause. "But first, I must know … have you retrieved the coin this wretch stole from me?"

Mac Brochan shook his head. "We could find no trace of it."

"And you never will!" the prisoner shouted, his voice, rough with defiance, ringing across the yard. "Greedy maggot! That coin belongs to my people … you will not bleed us dry! You will not yoke us to your cause like oxen!"

The High King moved swiftly then, with surprising speed for a man of middling age. An instant later, he reached the prisoner and backhanded him across the face. "You are my subject and will kneel before me," he snarled, looming over the chieftain. "Those taxes are mine. Tell me where to find the coin."

A lesser man would have cowered under such wrath, but mac Bridei spat in the High King's face. Despite that Bree had no love for mortals, she felt a grudging admiration for him. The man had balls. "Go rut your mother!"

Bree thought Talorc might lose his temper then and attack the chieftain.

But he didn't.

Instead, the High King drew himself up and wiped the spittle off his face, his expression shuttering. A heavy silence fell over the yard before his gaze shifted to one of his personal guards, who'd stepped up to his side. "Ready a torture chamber in the dungeon."

"Are you unwell, husband?"

Mac Brochan shook his head. "Just drained."

Pouring her husband a cup of ale, Bree crossed to where he sat, slumped in a chair by the fire. Skaal lay at his feet, her fur clumped with dirt and what looked like blood.

Bree wrinkled her nose. The beast reeked. "Drained?"

She handed Mac Brochan a cup. Taking it, the chief-enforcer heaved a sigh. "Summoning druidic power comes at a cost," he replied wearily. "I drew too deeply this time, and I'm paying the price … we all are."

Bree marked the sheen of sweat that covered his face. She'd noticed it outdoors too but had thought it was the rain. But no, the man had a fever. She'd heard that a druid's magic wasn't inexhaustible—and knew they relied on the blood-letting to keep their power strong—but hadn't realized wielding it could weaken them so in the aftermath.

"Hunting the rebels wasn't easy then?"

The chief-enforcer shook his head. "They ambushed us." He lifted the cup to his lips and drained it in just a few gulps. "Somehow, they seemed to know we were coming."

Bree's skin prickled. She wondered if Mor had interfered in Marav affairs—had somehow gotten word to the rebels about the enforcers' imminent arrival. It wouldn't have been the first time she'd used them to do her bidding.

"We were in a pass deep within the Goatfell Mountains," her husband continued, "when a horde of Circine warriors descended upon us."

"A *horde?* How did twenty enforcers fight off such numbers?"

Mac Brochan grunted. "With difficulty."

Bree eyed him. He really did look ill. "Shall I fetch Eldra?"

He shook his head. "What ails me can't be cured by usual means." Mac Brochan drained the last of his ale. "Only a full moon and sacrifice can heal me."

Cold washed over Bree, and she shivered. The Great Raven save her, she'd been dreading this, ever since Princess Lara had described how the blood-letting ritual worked. There was an intimacy to the blood-letting that she feared. And the worry that the ceremony might somehow lay her bare lingered.

Meanwhile, her husband's gaze settled upon her, his already strained features tightening further. It didn't appear as if he was looking forward to partnering with her during the ritual either. "The moon is full tonight ... and I require your help."

Moonlight frosted the world, making Albia look like the realm Bree had left behind. Yet as she walked, barefoot, at the chief-enforcer's side, Bree was only too aware of how far she was from her own people.

Lights flickered in the stand of willows near the river, corpse candles hoping to lure the unwary. A screech echoed through the darkness—an owl perhaps—or something more sinister.

Mac Brochan wasn't the only one climbing the grassy hill behind Duncrag. The shadowy figures of the other enforcers who'd returned from the north surrounded them. And like the chief-enforcer, they hadn't made this journey alone. Women, barefoot and cloaked like Bree, walked at the warrior-druids' sides. The enforcers had all traveled out of the fort before leaving their weapons and boots at the foot of the hill.

Meanwhile, Bree found it increasingly difficult to concentrate over the thunder of her heart. She silently cursed Mor too. Had the queen known that she'd have to take part in blood-letting and let foul druidic magic course through her? It would be an invasion, and she'd have to be careful to ward herself against any probing.

The sacrificers mustn't discover who she really was at her core.

Bree struggled to slow her quick, shallow breathing. Somehow, she knew Mor had known. And she'd deliberately not told her.

A semi-circle of scarlet-robed figures waited at the brow of the hill.

Gregor mac Hume stood among his sacrificers, waiting for the enforcers. The big rawboned man was an intimidating sight, with the moonlight gleaming off his high cheekbones and bald head. His dark gaze gleamed as it fastened upon mac Brochan.

Dizziness swept over Bree as she breathed in the pungent smell of druidic magic. The cool night air was heavy with the scent of pine and campfire ash.

Mac Hume stood at the edge of a large flat stone that had been etched with a woven, circular design. Moonlight gleamed dully off iron then—the chief-sacrificer gripped a knife.

Bree cut a glance at her husband. "I don't like the look of that blade," she hissed.

To her surprise, mac Brochan reached out and took hold of her hand. Despite that his breathing was labored, and his hand damp with sweat, his grip was firm and oddly reassuring. "Don't worry," he said, a rasp to his voice now as he towed her forward. "Gregor isn't going to cut your throat."

26: MOONLIGHT AND SACRIFICE

The chief-sacrificer's voice had a goading edge.

The two men locked gazes. Watching them, it occurred to Bree that they weren't friends. Aye, they were both members of the High King's druidic council, but the animosity that crackled through the air made the fine hair on the back of her arms prickle.

"Aye," the chief-enforcer grunted. "Do it then."

"On your knees … both of you," mac Hume gestured to the flat, carven, stone. "Facing each other." He cast Bree a sharp look then, for the instructions were clearly for her benefit.

Forcing herself not to scowl at him, Bree complied. Meanwhile, the sacrificers standing in a horseshoe around them started to chant.

"Hold your free palm up, above the center of the stone," the chief-sacrificer ordered.

Bree did as bid once more. Meanwhile, her other hand was still locked in mac Brochan's firm grip. She didn't look his way though. Instead, her gaze was fixed upon the chief-sacrificer and the iron blade in his hand.

Her pulse quickened, dizziness sweeping over her. Princess Lara had assured her the blood-letting ceremony wouldn't harm her, yet the sight of iron made her flinch. Loathsome metal, a bane to her kind.

The chief-sacrificer bent over then and drew the blade sharply across mac Brochan's hand.

Her husband's body jolted, his breath hissing between his teeth. "*Fuck*. That was deeper than necessary, Gregor."

"Was it?" mac Hume chuckled before the fingers of his free hand wrapped around Bree's wrist. "Hold still, Lady mac Brochan." He gentled his voice then as if he were speaking to a skittish horse. "This will sting."

Holding her wrist fast, he drew the knife blade across her palm, although much gentler than he had with her husband's.

Stinging pain bloomed, and Bree drew in a sharp breath.

Mac Hume lifted her hand then, pressing the cuts upon her and the chief-enforcer's hands together tightly. A moment later, he began to murmur words, ancient and guttural, of the long-dead tongue that only the druids used. And as he spoke, the tattoos on his neck began to gently glow.

Meanwhile, the gathered sacrificers continued to chant. The air around them stilled, and the smell of pine resin and ash filled Bee's nostrils—so cloying that it stuck in her throat.

She gave a wheezing cough, yet the druids ignored her.

Her husband had bent his head, while the chief-sacrificer's voice rose and fell.

Pain throbbed in the center of Bree's palm, in time with her heartbeat, although as the moments passed, heat started to build there. And then, mac Brochan's tattoos started to glow. Usually, they were woad-blue etchings, swirls, and patterns that had been etched upon his bare arms and chest from his first year of druidic training.

But now they were alive, glowing silver as if starlight illuminated him from within.

Forgetting the pain in her hand and the strange heat that burned where their cut palms pressed together, Bree watched, fascinated.

Part of her was repulsed by this ritual and everything it represented, and yet, she couldn't look away.

And then, she felt it—a strange and savage joy that bloomed under her ribcage.

Her breathing hitched, and the sensation spread, filling her body and causing her limbs to tingle. Warmth followed, swirling through her belly.

The Great Raven forgive her, she liked this. Lara hadn't lied, the experience was … intense. It was as if every burden she'd ever carried, every worry, every guilty secret, dissolved—and for a short while, she was reborn. For a few blessed instants, she gave up control. She was supposed to keep her thoughts and feelings warded, but the sensation of release was overwhelming. It swept her away.

Bree's eyes fluttered, her breathing slowing and deepening.

Meanwhile, mac Brochan's tattoos continued to glow. Some of them even rippled, as if something pulsed through them, until eventually, they faded once more, returning to dark patterns upon the chief-enforcer's skin.

And the joy and warmth fled Bree's body. She couldn't help it—she sagged in disappointment.

Her husband lifted his head. His gaze was glazed, slightly unfocused.

However, the chief-sacrificer's eyes were sharp, probing. He was staring at Bree with a keen look that made her skin prickle in warning.

Iron smite her, she hoped she hadn't revealed any of her true self. Surely, her Marav body and blood had fooled him.

Moments passed, and then mac Hume stepped back, his expression veiling. "It's done." The chief-sacrificer made a dismissive motion with his hand. "Take him home, and put him to bed … he'll be himself in the morning."

Bree slid her hand from mac Brochan's before she turned her palm over and inspected it. The cut had sealed. There was nothing more than a puckered line of pink skin, and the wound upon the chief-enforcer's palm was similarly healed.

Her breathing quickened. Druidic magic was dangerous to her kind, and yet she'd reveled in the feel of it surging through her veins. And it had healed her.

"Help me up, Fia," mac Brochan's voice was even rougher than earlier.

Wordlessly, she stepped into him and let him use her to pull himself to his feet. Then, to her surprise, he wrapped a heavy arm about her shoulders, leaning upon her, as they moved off the sacrifice stone, letting the next couple take their place.

Together, Bree and the chief-enforcer made their way down the hill, to where they'd left their boots by the banks of the River Lethe.

"Are you strong enough to climb back up to the broch?" Bree asked, handing her husband his boots. "Or shall I fetch your horse?"

"I'll be fine," mac Brochan rasped. "I'll just take it slowly."

Bree's lips pursed as she took in his sweaty face and strained features. "Are you sure about that?"

He nodded. "I'll need your help again though."

Putting their boots on, they walked down to the causeway that led into Duncrag, passing the guards at the gate, who let them through without a word. Of course, they were used to these rituals.

She then glanced at the chief-enforcer's face. It looked even paler than before. "Lean more of your weight on me," she instructed. "I won't break."

He pulled a face. "I'm heavy."

"And I'm stronger than I look."

Her husband snorted. "I'll not argue with that." A moment later, he did lean on her more, and Bree set her jaw as they crossed the open space beyond the gates and began the long climb up The Thoroughfare.

"Gregor doesn't like you much," she said, slightly out of breath now.

He gave a soft snort. "No … the feeling is mutual though."

"Why?"

Mac Brochan's mouth pursed. "We're both ambitious and have always been … rivals."

Bree waited for him to elaborate, but he didn't. It was likely more than that—but her husband wasn't going to tell her. "Why do you need a woman's blood for the ritual?" she asked after a few moments.

"Female blood heals, energizes," he grunted, leaning on her even more heavily now as the way grew steeper. "It gives a man back what he's lost." He paused then, his breathing labored, and cut her a look. "Thank you, Fia."

Bree didn't answer. His response caught her off-guard, and she didn't know what to say. She didn't want his thanks, and yet at the same time, his words made a distracting warmth spread under her ribs—not unlike what she'd felt during the ceremony.

"Princess Lara told me she has partnered with you previously?" she said, deliberately casual.

She could have sworn the ghost of a smile curved his lips at her comment. "Aye."

That was all he had to say about Lara though, and the warmth under Bree's ribs deepened to a burn, a reaction that vexed her. No, she wasn't jealous. She didn't care whom this brute shared blood with. All the same, the intimacy of the blood-letting wasn't something Bree had been prepared for; in the aftermath, an unwelcome sense of closeness to her husband had settled over her.

By the time they reached the broch and made their way to the chief-enforcer's quarters, mac Brochan was staggering.

Bree groaned with relief as he let go of her and collapsed into the sleeping nook, rolling onto the furs and stretching out on his back. He closed his eyes then, his chest rising and falling sharply.

He still wore his leather breeches and heavy boots, although Bree guessed he was too exhausted to take them off. As such, once she'd removed her cloak and hung it up, Bree unlaced his boots and drew them off his feet for him, setting them down by the wall.

Meanwhile, Skaal got up from her place near the fire and padded across to the sleeping nook. Usually, the fae hound ignored Bree, yet tonight, she nudged her hand with a wet nose and licked the recently healed wound upon her palm.

Stiffening, Bree looked down at the huge dog.

Ever since her arrival, she'd been wary of Skaal. Fae hounds were perceptive creatures, and she'd worried that despite her transformation, Skaal might be able to sniff out the truth. "I'm all right," she murmured as Skaal licked her palm once more. She then nodded to mac Brochan. "And so is he … I think." She cleared her throat, her gaze focusing on the man lying on the furs. "Do you want some water, husband?"

"Aye," he replied weakly.

Patting Skaal lightly on the head and wrinkling her nose, for the dog was in desperate need of a bath, Bree moved around the fae hound and went to the table, where she poured a large cup of cooled boiled water. She then climbed onto the furs, next to the chief-enforcer. "Here."

His eyes flickered open, and with a groan, he propped himself upon an elbow before draining the cup. He then sank back down onto the furs. "That's better."

Meanwhile, Skaal lowered her large body to the wooden floor at the foot of the nook and curled up. It looked as if she'd be sleeping there tonight.

Silence fell in the alcove, and Bree stretched out in her usual place. She still wore an ankle-length, sleeveless tunic, but she couldn't be bothered taking it off this eve. Instead, she rolled onto her side and observed the man lying just a couple of feet from her.

Mac Brochan had closed his eyes once more. Fading firelight kissed his tattooed skin. The chief-enforcer's arms and torso were hard, sculpted muscle, and she found herself wanting to trail her fingertips across his skin. Even weakened like this, mac Brochan's raw masculinity sucked the air out of the room.

Bree's belly clenched then. *Enough of this*, she reprimanded herself. *You're running out of time.*

Aye, her husband wouldn't let her this close to him again. Soon Torran would ask the chief-enforcer if he'd gotten the missive he'd left for him.

She needed to find out something useful and send word to Mor before he did.

27: KEEPING SECRETS

DRAWING IN A deep, steadying breath, Bree reached out and boldly trailed a fingertip down his muscular bicep, following the swirl of the woad tattoos that curved across his skin. "These don't *feel* like they were etched by magic," she murmured.

He harrumphed softly, his eyes slowly opening. "Aye, well, each one hurt like The Reaper's blade."

Bree's fingertips traced the marking that wound around his bicep, just above the elbow—a serpent devouring itself. "It must have taken years to have all these done."

"It did … I was fourteen when I received my first. A sacrificer worked on me upon a bloodstone in the moonlight, calling upon The Warrior's strength as she carved out the design and stained the skin with woad."

"Which one was your first?"

His eyes glinted in the half-light before he lifted his hand to the center of his chest. "This one."

Bree peered at the wolf's head, and her mouth curved. "It's fitting … since you're now shadowed by a fae hound." Boldly, she reached out and slid a finger down his chest, gently following the tattooed swirls and symbols she found there. Mac Brochan's breathing hitched, his gaze hooded now, but she pretended not to notice. "These are beautiful," she murmured—and they were, even if their beauty was deadly to her people.

His mouth quirked. "Thank you, wife … although, as you've seen, using them comes at a cost."

Bree raised her gaze to his once more. "So, you wield The Warrior's strength when you fight?"

"Aye … one of the first things a druid learns when they take the enforcer's path is how to draw on their power, their courage." His mouth quirked. "Unlike the other paths though, our strength is purely physical. I can't wield wisdom or insight like a seer or a counselor, nor can I commune directly with the Gods like a sacrificer, or weave sagas like a bard. Enforcers are weapons … savages."

Bree inclined her head at his blunt words. There was no bitterness in them though; he was merely stating a fact. This was her opening to deepen their conversation, and she'd take it.

"Why were you so set against taking a wife?"

Her husband's eyes darkened at her question, something moving in their depths.

Bree's breathing grew shallow. Aye, there was something there—a reason why this man kept himself walled off from others. She sensed a deep well of loneliness in him, and she wished to peer into it. She was pushing things now, deliberately. If she could get him to talk about himself, to trust her, he might divulge other details as well.

But a moment later, he blinked, and his gaze veiled. "It doesn't matter," he replied, his tone gruff now.

"I think it does," she replied softly, holding his eye. "What happened to your family, Cailean?" Her pulse lurched then; it felt far too intimate to use his first name, but she was desperate now. She couldn't let him retreat.

It was too late though. As their stare drew out, mac Brochan's face hardened.

Iron smite her, she'd just hit another wall.

"Leave it alone, wife." There was a warning edge in his voice now.

"I left the letter … sealed with wax … on your table. It should still be there, awaiting you."

Cailean shot another look across the tidy surface, his gaze taking in the tray with a stoppered clay bottle and pewter goblets. "Did you bring this in too?"

Torran snorted. "No … do I look like your servant?"

Cailean scowled. Only his second could get away with such a response.

It was late afternoon of the day after Cailean's return to Duncrag. He'd meant to check his meeting alcove earlier, but the blood-letting had drained him. He'd slept later than was his habit, and then the High King had summoned him for a debrief. Their meeting had dragged on, and Cailean had ended up eating his noon meal with his liege rather than with his wife. Afterward, Talorc had summoned the rest of the druidic council, and they'd had a lengthy meeting that had stretched on all afternoon.

Finally, as supper approached, Cailean had gone to his meeting alcove. But the letter he'd expected to find was nowhere to be seen. Torran had come looking for him shortly after.

Moving to the table, Cailean picked up the bottle and pulled out the cork, sniffing the contents. It was fruity and cloying.

"Blaeberry," he muttered. He couldn't stand blaeberry wine, especially the fortified variety—something most of the servants here knew.

Setting down the bottle, he glanced Torran's way once more. A deep groove had cut between the enforcer's tawny brows, and he'd folded his arms across his chest.

"So, you haven't been back in here since leaving the letter?" Cailean asked.

Torran shook his head, his jaw tensing. "And the guards don't let anyone into this alcove."

Cailean growled a curse. Aye, they didn't. However, there was one person who might have been able to persuade them to break the rules. *Devious bitch.* Heat ignited in his gut, anger flaring. Banking it, he tried to keep his focus. "I don't suppose Mother Gelda told you what her response contained?"

Torran shook his head, and Cailean dragged a hand down his face as the heat in his stomach started to pulse.

"She did tell me something worrying though," Torran admitted then. The groove between his eyebrows deepened into a scowl. "Your bride's escort never returned to Baldeen."

Cailean stilled, the fire in his belly dousing. "What?"

"Four men were hired to ensure she reached Duncrag safely ... but they've gone missing." Torran's gaze glinted. "And a search has yielded nothing ... not even bodies."

Silence followed these words, while a chill crawled down Cailean's spine.

"I fear your wife is keeping secrets, Cailean," Torran said quietly, holding his eye.

"She is." Cailean turned on his heel and stalked toward the landing, Skaal shadowing him. "And it's time I got some answers."

"Don't hesitate. I could have crushed your windpipe by now."

"But I don't want to hurt you."

"You won't." Bree released her grip on the handmaid's arms and stepped back.

Mirren glanced over her shoulder, her brow furrowing. "Very well," she muttered. "Shall we go again?"

Bree nodded. "Ready?"

Mirren faced forward once more. "Aye."

The two women stood in the middle of the chief-enforcer's alcove. It was risky teaching Mirren when her husband was in residence. However, mac Brochan was caught up in meetings this afternoon, and training her handmaid was a welcome distraction.

Bree had been on edge all day, waiting for the chief-enforcer to talk to his second-in-command, to learn that Torran had brought back a letter from the House of Maids, and that it had gone missing.

In the meantime, it pleased her to be able to teach Mirren some new skills. Her handmaid had proved to be an eager student, although the lass hadn't been herself since the attack. She rarely smiled these days, and there was a cynical edge to her now. She'd also taken to carrying a boning knife tucked into her belt, just in case another brute inside the broch cornered her.

Mirren's transformation had saddened Bree a little before she reminded herself that it was a harsh world, and only the tough survived.

Stepping into her, she threw her arms around Mirren's chest.

The lass jolted in her grip, and arched back, the back of her head smacking Bree's nose. Cursing, Bree let go of her and staggered away. Her hand lifted to her nose and came away bloodied.

"The Mother forgive me!" Mirren whipped around, her expression horrified. "What have I done?"

Eyes smarting, Bree wiped away the blood and grinned. "Nice move!"

"But I *hurt* you!"

Bree snorted and walked to the washbasin, picking up a damp cloth and cleaning her nose. It hurt, although luckily, Mirren hadn't broken it. "Serves me right for underestimating you." It was true—she'd expected her maid to jab at her ribs with her elbow. Instead, she'd headbutted her.

She cast her handmaid a sidelong look, to see a slight smile tugging at her mouth. "You did?"

"Aye ... you're fast."

At that moment, the chief-enforcer stormed into the alcove.

Bree put down the washcloth and turned to face him. But one look at his thunderous face told her that the game was up.

After all the waiting, it was almost a relief.

"Leave us." Mac Brochan's voice cracked across the chamber like a whip.

Mirren's gaze flicked between husband and wife, her blue eyes shadowing. Then, she ducked her head and scurried from their quarters, the heavy hanging swishing shut behind her.

Skaal, who'd followed mac Brochan inside, sat down near the entrance, silently barring the way out. Meanwhile, the chief-enforcer advanced on Bree.

She held her ground, even as her pulse went wild. "Why the foul temper, husband?"

"Enough with this fucking mummery," mac Brochan ground out. He skirted the edge of the table and crowded her. "What did you do with the letter?"

And despite that she wasn't afraid of him, Bree backed up. Lifting her chin, she met his narrowed gaze. She had no choice but to brazen this out. "What are you talking about?"

"So, you want to play a game, do you?" The menace in his throat did make a frisson of fear skate down her spine then.

"No … I just—"

"The letter that came from the House of Maids." He continued to advance on her, stalking her now. "I didn't believe your tale about learning to fight … and so I sent a missive to Baldeen, asking Mother Gelda to confirm my suspicions. She responded, and her letter was left in my meeting alcove."

"I only left you some wine." Bree's spine hit the wall. There was nowhere to go; the bastard had her bailed up, and her pulse leaped into a canter. "I thought you might appreciate it upon your return. I didn't see any letter."

He leaned in, placing his hands on either side of her, caging her in. "Liar. What did you do with it?"

"Nothing." Bree leaned her head back against the wall, craning her neck now to maintain eye contact.

His fury blazed. This close, she could taste it.

And her anger answered its call, expanding like an unfurling fern in her chest. How she wanted to lash out at this enforcer, to drive her knee up into his groin, and to slam the heel of her hand into his nose as she'd shown Mirren.

She was done for, yet she'd go down fighting.

"While he was at the House of Maids, Torran discovered that your escort never returned home," he growled. "What do you have to say about that?"

Bree's stomach dropped like a stone.

Shit. Of course, they'd wonder what happened to the men Gavyn and his Ravens had slain. She should have expected this.

"The roads are dangerous," she replied, her mouth suddenly dry. "Perhaps they fell foul of the Shee."

The chief-enforcer leaned in closer, his scent crowding her senses. Damn him, he was too close. Their bodies were almost touching, and his heat engulfed her. "Another falsehood."

"I don't know what happened to my escort," she gasped, her pulse thundering now.

"Lie after lie," he bit out, his blue eyes drilling into her. "And all the while, you constantly push me."

Bree flushed hot. "I seek to form a bond with my *husband*," she shot back. "Is that wrong?"

"I made our arrangement clear … but it appears you have a purpose of your own."

Bree started to sweat. "You tricked me!" She threw the accusation at him. "I wouldn't have accepted your proposal if I'd known our marriage was to be a ruse."

The chief-enforcer's lip curled. "Don't try and make this about me." His eyes hardened. "Your lying ends here. Tell me the truth, woman. All of it."

Bree glared up at him, her fingers curling into fists at her sides. Her limbs tingled now, and heat washed over her. Things were about to get ugly.

"Mac Brochan," a gruff male voice intruded then, carrying through the curtain in the doorway. "The High King summons you to supper."

"What?" the chief-enforcer snapped, yet his attention never strayed from Bree's face. "*Now?*"

"Aye. All the druidic council have been called."

"*Again?*" Mac Brochan swore softly, his face twisting, before he answered, "I'll be there shortly."

The guard on the other side of the curtain cleared his throat apologetically. "The High King requires your wife to join you."

28: ON BORROWED TIME

BREE'S BELLY PITCHED as she lowered herself onto the bench seat next to her husband.

In other circumstances, an invitation to supper by the High King and the opportunity to observe his druidic council would have excited her—finally, a chance to learn something of value—but not this evening.

At present, she felt sick.

You're on borrowed time now, she reminded herself as she smoothed her sweaty palms upon the skirt of her tunic. She'd recently picked the new garment up from the seamstress; it was a deep woad-blue with gold ribbon sewn into the hem and around the neck. Her bronze arm ring set off the tunic's rich color.

Ever since her arrival at Duncrag, she'd watched her husband disappear in the evenings to the High King's councils, only to return a long while later, often when she'd already retired to the furs. And, of course, mac Brochan never spoke of what was discussed at these private meetings.

But this eve was a break with routine.

Thank the Ancestors.

They'd been close to the point of no return earlier, and when her husband had stepped back from her, fury had simmered in his eyes. "We'll continue this after supper," he'd told her, not hiding the threat from his voice.

Bree's pulse spiked at the memory. They couldn't be alone again. She was done here. As soon as supper was over, she needed to find a way out of Duncrag. Mor would be angry, but she'd face her wrath.

Somehow, she'd find a way to appease the Raven Queen.

Cold washed over Bree then. Curse it, her pouch of silver acorns was still upstairs. She had to retrieve them. They were her only way to communicate with Mor, should Eagal find her.

However, even while her mind scrabbled, Bree was only too aware of the chief-enforcer's nearness as he slid onto the bench seat next to her, and the heat of his thigh as it brushed against hers.

Her stomach pitched once more—yet not from panic this time.

Iron brand her, this was the last thing she needed.

His nearness earlier as he caged her in against the wall, the scent of him, his heat and strength, had confirmed the attraction between them—one that had sparked right from the beginning.

She was in mortal danger, but his proximity had roused more than panic. It had awoken a wild hunger within her.

Dizziness assailed her, and she gripped the edge of the table to steady herself.

This wasn't part of the plan. She was supposed to gain his trust, to deceive him—but the realization of just how much she *wanted* him horrified her. He was one of the hated enforcers—an enemy of the Shee. If he knew who she really was, he wouldn't hesitate to plunge a blade through her heart.

Bree understood all of that, yet her breathing still grew shallow as his hand accidentally brushed hers when they both reached for the same cup of wine.

She cut mac Brochan a veiled look then and caught him watching her.

Hostility and distrust burned in his blue eyes—and something else too.

Heart pounding, Bree tore her gaze from his. She had to keep her nerve. *He's just a man*, she repeated the phrase that had anchored her ever since her arrival at Duncrag. *No match for you.*

The words now sounded hollow though. Her husband had already shown himself to be a formidable opponent, and he was close to besting her.

Trying her best to slow her breathing and find her equilibrium, Bree shifted her attention from mac Brochan. Instead, she surveyed those seated at the tables that had been arranged in a square around the smallest of the hearths. It was an intimate gathering this eve, in contrast to a hall full of warriors who'd gathered for the chief-enforcer's wedding feast.

The queen consort and the princess were both absent, although Prince Kennan sat at his father's right hand. Both men were striking in black leather, their dark hair combed back and golden torques gleaming at their throats. However, the High King's presence dominated his son's.

Around the table sat five druids, all clad in different colored robes. Each member of the druidic council sat with their spouse.

Directly across the table, Gregor mac Hume was watching her husband with a hooded gaze, a thin smile playing upon his lips.

Bree's tension wound tighter. She didn't like that smile.

Mac Hume caught her watching him then, and his eyes glinted.

Pulse thudding in her ears, she tore her gaze away. Mac Hume's expression reminded her of the look he'd given her after the blood-letting ceremony.

It was as if they shared a secret.

Staring down at the trencher before her, Bree focused on keeping her breathing steady.

Just get through this supper.

Servants appeared then, bearing platters of breads studded with hazelnuts and walnuts, rich venison stew, braised kale, and wheels of aged goat's cheese. As always, the food here was pungent, overpowering—causing Bree's already tense stomach to clench.

Shades, how was she supposed to force any of this down?

Having served the table, the servants departed, leaving the High King and his supper guests alone.

"It's a pleasure to see my chief druids … and their spouses … gathered here this evening," the High King spoke up then, his powerful voice rumbling across the now silent hall. However, his expression contradicted his words. A frown creased his brow, and his mouth was turned down at the edges.

He picked up the gem-encrusted goblet before him and took a measured sip. "Druidic gifts are only passed through certain bloodlines … and the gifts you bear grow rarer."

Queasiness washed over Bree once more. There would be a reason why the High King was reminding them of something all his council would have been aware of.

"Aye, Your Highness," the chief-sacrificer said with a nod. "That is why Beatha carries our fourth child." His gaze swept around the table, while beside him, his wife gave a smug smile. "The rest of you are slow to produce."

This comment brought tight lips and scowls from some of those around the table. None of them liked being reminded of their childlessness. Bree cast her husband a sidelong glance then, noting that his expression remained shuttered. If the chief-sacrificer's comment vexed him, he hid it well.

"Of course," mac Hume drawled, not yet finished. "Some of you are trying, at least." His gaze fell upon the chief-enforcer. "While *others* make no effort at all."

Silence settled at the table.

Bree started to sweat. Next to her, mac Brochan stilled.

"Indeed," The High King leaned forward in his carven chair, his hatchet face tightening as he fixed his chief-enforcer in a gimlet stare. "Gregor informs me that during the blood-letting ceremony, he discovered that you and your wife have not been … *intimate*."

Bree's already fast pulse took off, while across the table, Gregor smirked.

She should be relieved, for she'd worried he'd somehow delved into her soul and learned that she'd once been Shee. But this wasn't good news either.

"Aye," the chief-sacrificer replied when mac Brochan remained stubbornly silent. "Usually, when wedded couples perform the rite, I can sense a 'melding' between them that comes from having joined physically. But not between these two."

With a sinking belly, Bree waited for the High King's judgment.

However, her husband responded first.

"Gregor lies," he growled.

The High King's dark gaze glittered. "And why would he do that?"

"Because he's a shit-stirring bastard who's never liked me."

Talorc snorted. He then glanced across at a slender, sharp-featured man robed in green: the chief-seer. "What say you, Allaster? Has mac Brochan plowed his wife?"

Silence fell once more, all gazes settling upon Allaster mac Coll. Moments passed, and the druid's lean face tightened, before the tattoos on his neck started to glow faintly.

Bree's heart kicked against her ribs. Quickly, she raised her mental wards, hoping that her husband had done the same. Seers weren't just masters of divination; they could also touch minds—just as the arch-druid had attempted to do on the day of her and mac Brochan's handfasting.

The chief-seer's eyes narrowed as he stared her down. Aye, he'd met resistance, and it surprised him. After a few moments, his attention shifted to the chief-enforcer. Eventually, mac Coll pursed his lips and looked at the High King. "I'd say not, Your Highness."

"What have you seen?"

"Mac Coll has *seen* nothing," mac Brochan ground out, his lip curling.

Relief fluttered through Bree. Of course, his mental wards would also be strong. He wouldn't allow any seer to touch his thoughts.

Unfortunately, her relief was short-lived.

"I may not be able to touch *either* of their minds," mac Coll replied, undaunted by the chief-enforcer's aggression. "But there is hostility and distrust between them … and I suspect there has been no carnal intimacy."

Bree's heart kicked like a pony against her ribs, sweat trickling under her arms now. She chanced another glance at her husband then—her belly swooping at the cold anger she spied on his face. Mac Brochan's face got a hawkish look when his temper rose. Tension crackled through the air in the hall.

"You disappoint me, Cailean." The High King's voice splintered the silence, low and hard. Next to him, Prince Kennan looked on, a frown marring his brow as he viewed the chief-enforcer. Likewise, all gazes were riveted upon mac Brochan. "You promised you would fulfill *all* your obligations."

The chief-enforcer didn't reply.

"Don't bother trying to lie your way out of this," Talorc went on, a vicious edge creeping into his tone now. "For I see that Gregor is telling the truth." The High King looked at Bree then, and the sweat bathing her skin turned cold. "What is wrong with the woman? She's fair of face and has a ripe body." His mouth pursed then. "Don't tell me you have the same tastes as my son?"

Next to the High King, Kennan jerked as if his father had just elbowed him in the ribs. An instant later, the prince's handsome face hardened. Nonetheless, he held his tongue.

As did the chief-enforcer.

"Unfortunately for him, the prince has duties he must fulfill… and so do you." Talorc leaned forward further still, his strong, ring-encrusted hands gripping the armrests of his chair. "I care not where you'd *prefer* to stick your prick … but my realm needs more enforcers, and that means you *will* fill your wife's belly with your sons. Is. That. Clear?"

The threat in the High King's voice shivered across the hall.

Silence followed before mac Brochan finally answered. "Aye, Sire." The words fell like ax blows.

The two men locked gazes for a heartbeat before Talorc mac Brude sank back into his chair. "Good … I'm glad we've cleared that up." His expression turned severe once more. "I'm giving you a second chance, but there won't be a third."

29: TRAPPED

BREE HAD NO APPETITE. Nonetheless, she forced each mouthful of her supper down, focusing on chewing and swallowing. The wine was so strong it made her eyes water. She drank sparingly anyway; she needed to keep herself sharp this evening.

Ever since the High King's harsh words to the chief-enforcer, her husband had retreated into stony silence. Meanwhile, conversation rose and fell around the table, as those of the druidic council discussed general matters.

Bree listened carefully, her ears straining for any details that could aid her people. However, most of what she heard was frustratingly mundane. It looked as if she'd have nothing to bring back to Mor—nothing to soften her failure.

That was—until the chief-sacrificer asked after the High King's new prisoner. "How fares mac Bridei, Sire?"

Talorc's face screwed up, and he sank back in his chair, steepling his hands before him. "He's dead."

Mac Hume murmured a curse at this, and the High King cut him a warning look at the implied criticism. "For all his bluster, the Circines chieftain didn't hold up under my interrogations. He failed to yield the location of my taxes before he threw himself onto the blade that I was using to slowly carve him apart."

The sudden silkiness in the High King's voice showed how much he'd enjoyed torturing his enemy, although the groove between his brows revealed his displeasure that his prisoner had died so soon.

Disgust soured Bree's mouth. Torture was for cowards. Usually, someone of his rank wouldn't lower himself to bloodying his hands in a torture chamber.

"I suggest we send more enforcers north, Your Highness," The chief-counselor spoke up then, her expression grave. "The tribespeople will likely talk once they know their chieftain is dead."

The High King nodded, even as his heavy brows knitted together. "That is my plan, Annis … eventually."

The chief-counselor's mouth pursed. "Sire, if I may be so bold … it's best to strike now, while they are scattered and leaderless."

"Wise advice, as always … but the Circine problem will need to wait until autumn to be resolved. I need my enforcers for something *else* this summer." Talorc paused, his eyes glinting. "After I met with you all this afternoon, I paid a visit to another prisoner … and am pleased to announce we've had a breakthrough."

The tightness in the High King's voice betrayed his excitement, and something deep inside Bree's chest clenched.

A hush fell while everyone at the table waited for Talorc to continue.

"Damhan has finally spoken," he said.

Bree's heart jolted. Her predecessor, Bryce, was still here at Duncrag—and was the High King's prisoner, after all. Next to her, mac Brochan leaned forward. "The healer is still alive?"

Talorc's smile hardened. "Aye … unlike mac Bridei, he has proved remarkably resistant to torture."

Bree's breathing grew shallow. The gloating look on the High King's face warned her that Bryce had compromised them. She waited for him to continue, to reveal the extent of the damage. Instead, he leaned farther back in his chair and cast a dispassionate look around the table. "Druids, bid your spouses good eve," he murmured. "Some things are for your ears only."

Fuck.

Disappointment was a stone on Bree's chest. Around her, the men and women who'd accompanied the druids to supper rose to their feet and headed toward the doors of the hall. She followed suit, her mind already racing ahead.

This was her chance. While the chief-enforcer was busy, she'd go down to the dungeon and find out what Bryce had told the High King, and deal with him. After that, she'd get out of the broch.

She was leaving Duncrag tonight.

But to her consternation, her husband also stood up, and with a nod to the High King, accompanied her out of the hall. In the entrance area beyond, he motioned to two fort guards standing nearby. "Take my wife upstairs to our alcove, and ensure she stays there."

Heat ignited under Bree's ribcage, and she spun around to glare at the chief-enforcer. "What? Am I a prisoner now?"

He didn't reply, although his stony expression told her she was. Meanwhile, the guards moved toward her, and the other spouses who'd left the hall cast her curious looks. Ignoring them, Bree raised her chin and turned away from her husband, heading toward the stairs, even as panic clawed up her throat.

Iron cage her, she was trapped.

Stepping inside the alcove she and mac Brochan shared, Bree let the curtain swish closed behind her before squeezing her eyes shut.

Her breathing came fast and shallow, and she struggled to slow it.

Her throat and chest were so constricted, that it was difficult to draw breath at all.

It's over.

Crossing to the table, Bree poured herself a cup of water and gulped it down. Her panic took a while to subside, but eventually, her breathing slowed, and she could think clearly once more.

This mission had been ill-fated from the beginning, and now she was about to face the same end as Bryce. Imprisoned. Tortured.

Bree clenched her jaw and slammed the wooden cup down on the table.

No. She'd fight Cailean mac Brochan to the death before she allowed him to drag her down to the dungeon, to become the High King's plaything.

She paced the alcove then, her bare feet whispering on stone. And as she circled, her mind churned.

You must escape. Now.

Aye, there were two guards outside the alcove, but she could take them on. Bree halted then, her gaze flicking to the wall where a long-bladed dagger hung. Could she risk going down to the dungeon to look for Bryce?

Her pulse started to thunder in her ears.

Aye, she'd talk fast when she saw Mor again. However, if she returned to Sheehallion with *nothing* to give her queen, she wouldn't be popular. And if she caught Mor in the wrong mood, she might even end up in 'the pit'—a deep cavern under Caisteal Gealaich, where a wyrm, a hungry serpent, lived.

None who were cast into that foul place ever emerged.

No, she couldn't leave without seeking Bryce out first. Mid-Summer Fire was around six days away now. Once she fled Duncrag, she'd make her way back to The Ring of Caith and ready herself to pass through the stones once more.

One thing at a time though. Getting out of this fort wouldn't be easy.

Halting, Bree's gaze flicked to her wooden trunk by the sleeping nook. First, she needed her silver acorns, and next, she'd pull on some boots and her cloak and help herself to some of the chief-enforcer's weapons.

It was time to drop her spy's identity.

Time for the assassin to show her claws.

However, she was about to move toward the trunk when the curtain swung open, and her husband stepped into the alcove. Skaal slipped in behind him, her golden eyes glowing dangerously.

The fae hound sat down then, her hairy bulk blocking the only exit again.

30: UNDER MY SKIN

THE CHIEF-ENFORCER HALTED, his gaze raking over Bree.

Staring back at him, she swallowed a scream of frustration. Everywhere she turned, this whoreson was always there, thwarting her. How she longed to thrust a blade between his ribs.

Pushing down her rage, Bree sucked in a deep breath before letting it out slowly. "That was a brief meeting, husband," she said, surprised at how calm she sounded.

His mouth pursed. "Fast but decisive … I'm riding out with my enforcers and a host of warriors at first light."

Bree went cold. Ancestors, what had he learned? "Is the High King going with you?"

"No, Prince Kennan has that privilege."

"Where are you going?"

"I'm not telling you that, wife." Mac Brochan advanced on her then, yet unlike earlier, Bree didn't back away. "Such information is privileged. I wouldn't tell you, even if I trusted you … which I don't."

She held his eye, even as the blood roared in her ears. *Kill him!*

However, taking down two unsuspecting guards who had their backs to her was one thing—fighting the chief-enforcer and his fae hound was another. Bree had the wits to know when she was outmatched.

"We have much to discuss," he said then.

"Do we?" Bree put her hands on her hips and raised her chin.

"Aye … you were about to tell me how you *really* learned your fighting skills … and about what happened to your escort."

"I've already responded to both questions."

"You lied." He loomed over her now, his eyes stormy, a muscle working in his jaw. "I want the *truth*."

"And if I don't give you the right answer?" she shot back, unable to stop herself from goading him now. "What will you do? Torture me?"

His mouth twisted. "That's our High King's pleasure, not mine."

Bree snorted. "Really? You mean you don't enjoy spilling a little blood … watching fear bloom in your victim's eyes?"

"When they truly vex me, aye," he growled back.

Heat pulsed in Bree's gut now. "And do *I* vex you?"

His gaze narrowed. "I know what you're doing, Fia … and it won't work."

"What am I doing?" She shoved him in the chest. Ancestors, it was like smacking a boulder.

"Trying to draw my attention from the matter at hand."

Snarling a curse, she lashed out at him then, aiming for his jaw. Aye, she was outmatched, but she could still do some damage.

Mac Brochan caught her wrist, and she struck at him with her other fist. He caught that one too, and she lunged toward him, bringing her knee up to drive it into his cods. However, moving at breathtaking speed, he spun her around and shoved her forward.

One moment they were standing in the center of the alcove, the next Bree found the front of her body flattened against the stone wall on the far side. Her husband held her fast, while his hands pinned her wrists at her sides.

Behind them, Skaal growled. The low, threatening rumble carried across the alcove.

"Brute," Bree gasped, struggling in his hold. It was impossible to budge him though. Curse it, she was so weak in this body.

"Aye." His breath whispered against her ear. "But this is the side of me you constantly try to provoke, isn't it?"

Heat pulsed traitorously low in her stomach at these words. Aye, this arrogant bastard sparked something wild inside her. She became keenly aware then of the hardness and warmth of the body pressed full length against hers.

"Let me go," she wheezed.

"Tell me who taught you to fight, and I might."

"My father."

That wasn't a lie. Her father, one of Mor's best warriors, had taught her and Gil a few moves before they both had formal instructors. He'd been hard on them both too—his criticism harsh.

"And why would he do that?"

"It's how things are done in my family."

Mac Brochan leaned harder against her, his hold on her wrists tightening. "Try another, less flippant, answer."

Bree gasped, even as his heat, his scent made her senses reel. "I come from a line of warrior women," she eventually conceded. Again, it was the truth. "He wanted to continue the tradition."

"Is that another lie?" His hot breath caressed her neck.

"No." To Bree's horror, her answer had come out as a sigh. The Great Raven forgive her, this man's presence was overwhelming. Her eyes fluttered shut, and, unable to stop herself, she found herself softening her body and sinking back against him.

Moments passed, something shifting between them—a mutual awareness that couldn't be denied.

When the chief-enforcer spoke, his voice was strained. "Why do you get under my skin?"

"Because I challenge you," she whispered back. "And you like it."

Mac Brochan made a rough sound in the back of his throat, tension rippling through his big body.

An instant later, he spun her around to face him once more.

And then, his mouth crashed down upon hers.

The suddenness of it made her gasp, her body stiffening against his, before hunger snapped through her like a bullwhip, and her lips parted to receive him.

They kissed hungrily, violently, tongues tanging and teeth clashing.

Bree bit down on his lower lip and tasted blood.

Mac Brochan grunted a curse against her mouth, hauling her hard against him. Bree answered by wrapping her arms around his neck, her body melting into his as she soothed his lower lip with the tip of her tongue.

And in response, her husband tangled his hands through her hair and deepened the kiss. Bree couldn't help it—she moaned. His embrace was dominant; it utterly undid her.

She felt it then, the thick column of his arousal, straining against his breeches, and pressing into her belly—and the lust that had caught fire in her veins roared into an inferno.

Iron consume her, she needed this, needed *him*. It was wrong. It was dangerous. And yet at that moment, she didn't care.

Her hands slid down to the broad expanse of his chest, her fingers fumbling as she clawed at his vest. She had to get this off, had to touch his hot skin.

Breathing hard, he broke off the kiss and helped her, tearing off the leather vest and tossing it aside.

Bree lowered her gaze then, her mouth going dry at the sight of the magnificent bulge in his breeches. Suddenly, she ached to free his rod from its leather prison. The wild urge to sink to her knees before him, to take him deep into her mouth and listen to his groans fill the alcove, swept over her.

Sighing, she reached for the laces of his breeches, yet to her surprise, he brushed her hands aside. Before she could protest, he bent down, caught the skirt of her tunic, and lifted it, drawing the garment up and working it over the swell of her hips and bust, before pulling it over her head.

And when she stood before him, naked save her bronze arm ring, mac Brochan's gaze devoured her. His lips parted, and his blue eyes darkened to black.

A faint flush had risen to his cheekbones, and his gaze glittered with such hunger that dizziness swept over Bree. No one had *ever* looked at her like that. He gazed upon her as if she were The Maiden herself.

Whispering an oath under his breath, mac Brochan yanked her into his arms again, his mouth capturing hers for another hot, greedy kiss. His tongue stroked hers with a sensual determination that made Bree writhe against him, while his big hands claimed her body. The feel of his callouses against her smooth skin, the heat of him that enveloped her like a furnace, made it difficult for her to form a coherent thought.

She was greedy for him too. For this brief moment in time, the heat between them incinerated the lie she'd woven.

Tearing his mouth from hers, her husband sank down before her, his palms sliding across the sensitive skin of her breasts as he lifted and pushed them together. He then bent his head and drew a nipple deep into the hot cavern of his mouth.

Bree gasped, wet heat pulsing between her thighs. Reaching up, she slid her fingers through his short hair, pushing him against her, demanding more. And he delivered, sucking hard enough to make her sag against him. And then, when that nipple was swollen and aching, he shifted his attention to its twin.

Her eyes fluttered shut, and she let her head settle back against the rough stone wall, giving herself up to sensation.

Meanwhile, his hands continued their exploration of her body, and when they parted her trembling thighs and slid between them, her gasp filled the alcove.

A groan rumbled in his throat, and he ripped his mouth from her breast. "Fuck … you're so wet."

Bree whimpered. There was no denying it.

Stroking her with a tenderness that made an ache rise in her chest, he then spread her legs wide, hooking one over his shoulder so that he exposed the tender skin between her thighs to him.

The warmth of his breath feathered over her most intimate place, and Bree steadied herself against the wall with her hands, her fingertips digging into the stone. And just as well too, for an instant later, his mouth found her—and as his tongue flicked, lapped, and circled, Bree bit down on her bottom lip. Pleasure coiled and pulsed between her thighs.

His grip on Bree tightened, and he opened her wider, lifting her against his mouth. Shades, he was relentless, pleasuring her as if it were his life's purpose. She couldn't believe they were doing this—and that nothing had ever felt so right. And if his questing tongue wasn't enough to drive her insane, he sucked her as he had her breasts, before grazing the sensitive pearl of flesh nestled within the petals of her sex with his teeth.

Bree choked back a cry, molten pleasure flooding and twisting through her lower belly and loins as she bucked uncontrollably against him. He continued to lick and suck her through her climax, until she sagged against him, panting.

Breathing hard, mac Brochan released her and climbed to his feet. And as he did, their gazes met once more. The intimacy of the moment made the ache rising under her breastbone intensify. It was too intense to look at him like this, to stare into the depths of his woad-blue eyes and see her own hunger reflected back at her.

Still struggling to catch her breath, she lowered her gaze, taking in every hard-muscled inch of him until her attention settled upon the huge bulge in his breeches.

Whispering an oath, she reached between them with unsteady hands and stroked the length of it, and when mac Brochan groaned, stepping back so she could touch him properly, hunger clenched low in her belly. Without stopping to consider her actions, she sank down before him and unlaced his breeches.

And this time, he didn't stop her.

31: BREAKING THE SPELL

DEFTLY, BREE RELEASED his rod from its leather prison. The sight of his shaft, long and thick, straining toward her from a nest of dark hair made need twist deep inside her.

An instant later, she wrapped her fingers around the base of his rod, her other hand cradling his bollocks.

Mac Brochan gave a deep, sensual groan, and encouraged, Bree leaned in, capturing the swollen head of his shaft in her mouth. She then drew him in deep, sucking him enthusiastically.

The chief-enforcer cursed, his voice choked as he tangled his fingers in her hair, urging her on.

Molten heat flared between Bree's thighs as she worked him, drawing him so deep that he hit the back of her throat. And she'd have taken him over the edge, let him spill in her mouth, if he hadn't yanked himself back.

"Not yet." Mac Brochan's face was all savage angles now, his chest rising and falling sharply. Pulling Bree to her feet, he threw her onto the furs.

Sprawled there, her breathing now coming in ragged gasps, Bree watched her husband heel off his boots and yank down his breeches before kicking them onto the floor.

His shaft, gleaming in the firelight, thrust up proudly before him.

Bree swallowed a groan. The night of their handfasting, when she'd first set eyes on his rod, his size had cowed her. But now, the Ancestors forgive her, she wanted *that* inside her.

Later, they'd be enemies once more, but right now, she wanted to be his lover—to forget they were on opposite sides and that this could never happen again.

Crawling onto the furs, mac Brochan spread her thighs wide. He then caught her by the knees and pushed her legs back so that her torso was bent double, exposing her fully as he nestled the head of his swollen rod at her slick entrance.

And then, inch by inch, he sank into her.

As he did so, mac Brochan's eyelids flickered, the muscle in his jaw flexing, before he ground out a curse.

Bree whimpered in response as he sank deeper, filling her, stretching her, until he was buried deep inside. Her husband stilled, his chest breathing hard, his heavily muscled, tattooed torso gleaming in the firelight.

Bree gazed up at him. He was quite simply beautiful, and until the end of her days, she'd never forget how good it had felt to have him buried to the hilt in her. And the fact that it would never be repeated made this moment even more vivid.

He rolled his hips then, and she lost all coherent thought.

Tension coiled in the cradle of her hips once more, although it started deep inside her womb this time. With each slow, sensual thrust, she angled her hips to meet him, opening herself up to him. Bree heard her own desperate groans now, echoing through the chamber, but didn't—couldn't—stop herself from making them.

This felt so good.

And then, to her disappointment, mac Brochan withdrew from her.

She cried out, clutching for him, but he merely turned her over, pulling Bree onto all fours—before he thrust into her from behind.

Bree whimpered. *Oh, fuck*. This angle was so different from the first, yet even more intense.

As before, he took her in deep, controlled thrusts. Leaning over her, his slick skin sliding against hers, he reached between her trembling thighs, opening her up with his fingers, and stroking her as he had earlier.

Bree gave a choked cry, her body shuddering now.

His touch destroyed her. She wasn't used to coupling being this … *raw*. In the past, her encounters, although pleasurable, were a purely physical release. However, something about this man heightened everything.

He turned her inside out. He made her want the forbidden.

Bree tried to claw herself back from the edge—from giving in to sensation completely. It was dangerous; this coupling was a mistake. But right now, she welcomed the wrongness of it.

Mac Brochan slid his hand from between her slippery thighs then, and she whimpered in disappointment. But when he wove his fingers through her hair and drew her head back, causing her spine to arch, and pressing her core up against him, the whimper turned into a gasp. "Cailean!"

"Aye, *wife*," he ground out. He grabbed her hip with his free hand, and drove into her, so much harder now.

Hot, wet pleasure crested deep inside Bree. Shuddering and gasping, she bucked against him, enjoying how his hold on her hair tightened to the point of pain, and the dominance of his thrusts. He was making her his, and something deep in her soul sang for it.

Later, she'd regret this, would berate herself for letting lust turn her into a fool. But for the moment, there was only pleasure, only this wild need that wouldn't be sated.

And with a sob, she gave herself up to it.

They didn't speak for a while afterward.

To shatter the silence would be to break the spell.

Bree enjoyed the reprieve yet knew it couldn't last. And as they lay there, she tried to put herself back together, to gather her wits and let the rawness of their encounter fade. Nonetheless, as she lay spooned against her husband in the flickering light of the dying hearth, the sweat finally cooling on their bodies, she relived their wild tumble, committing every detail to memory.

Surely, coupling isn't always like this for the Marav?

It couldn't be. If it were, they wouldn't get anything done—instead, they'd spend all their time having orgies in the furs.

No, Shee or Marav, what she'd just experienced was special.

Don't—she cut her thoughts off then—*He's the enemy.*

Bree's throat constricted. Aye, this didn't change anything.

Before things had gotten out of control, he'd been questioning her—and he'd do so again. And when she continued to lie, for the truth could never be told, he'd drag her down to the dungeon and lock her up, leaving her to the High King.

Bree's eyes fluttered shut. She'd been Mor's best, but she'd made a mess of this job. The Raven Queen had made a mistake in sending an assassin to do a spy's work. Bree hadn't been prepared for Cailean mac Brochan. Right from the first moment she'd locked eyes with the chief-enforcer, she'd been doomed.

Behind her, her husband's breathing was slow and even, yet she sensed that, like her, he hadn't fallen asleep. He too was trying to keep hold of something impossible.

His arm looped over her ribcage, cradling her possessively, and Bree tried to ignore the tug deep in her chest. She didn't want to like the feeling of belonging to him. It was an illusion. A lie, just like the rest of it. Their marriage was woven with gossamer threads.

Eventually, he pulled away from her, rolling across the furs and out of the sleeping nook.

Steeling herself, Bree pushed herself up into the sitting position, her heart thumping against her breastbone as she watched him silently dress.

This was it.

She could resist him, yet it was pointless. She would only be delaying the inevitable. And after what they'd just done, all the fight had gone out of her. A strange fatalism settled over her, a sensation that she'd never experienced before.

Swallowing, to loosen the tightness in her throat, she waited for the ax to fall.

Eventually, the chief-enforcer met her eye. His expression was veiled now, his gaze shuttered; it was impossible to guess what he was thinking or feeling. "I won't be back tonight," he said gruffly. "So … this is goodbye."

Bree stiffened, confusion wreathing up. "Excuse me?" Her voice didn't sound like her own; it was softer, huskier.

A nerve flickered in his cheek as he stared back at her. "It'll take me until dawn to ensure everything is ready for departure," he replied. "I'll be away half the turn of the moon, at least … but when I return, *you* won't be here."

Their gazes fused, and as the moment drew out, realization dawned.

Bree's heart kicked violently against her ribs. Shades, he was letting her go.

"You want me to *leave*?" she asked, making sure she hadn't misunderstood.

He nodded.

"You won't come after me?"

"No."

Bree's breathing grew shallow. She wanted to ask him why, but something held her back. There was a glint in his eye now, a warning not to push any further. The chief-enforcer knew she was a liar and that she couldn't be trusted—but he was prepared to look the other way.

This once.

He was offering her freedom, and she'd be a fool not to take it.

Swallowing the lump that now rose in her throat, Bree silently nodded.

32: A LIGHT IN THE DARKNESS

HE WAS A fucking idiot.

If Cailean had been thinking straight, he'd haul that lying bitch down to the dungeons and interrogate her himself. He'd show her that he wasn't averse to torture—that, when necessary, he could be just as cruel as the High King.

But he hadn't.

Instead, he'd plowed the woman and then, to compound his mistake, opened the door to her cage.

He should go back upstairs and have his reckoning with her, but he wouldn't.

He'd let her go.

This is Talorc's fault, the bastard. Aye, the High King had cornered him, threatened him. Rage had pulsed within Cailean as he'd suffered being humiliated before his peers, and he'd stormed upstairs when the meeting ended, looking for someone to unleash his fury upon. Maybe he wouldn't have acted so rashly if he'd been thinking straight.

Cailean descended the steps before the fog-shrouded yard outside the broch. Halting at the bottom, he surveyed the large company of enforcers and warriors that filled the wide space, readying their horses to ride out.

Dawn was close to breaking, although the enshrouding mist would block out the sunrise. This summer had been cool and damp so far, the light dim. The sun had shown its face rarely over the last moon, and it looked like this journey would be another bleak one.

Cailean's mouth pursed. Their departure was at short notice indeed. Nonetheless, it was the High King's will. They had a decent ride before them and needed to reach their destination before Mid-Summer Fire. They couldn't delay, and so Cailean had spent the night marshaling the men and organizing supplies.

Glancing up at the sky, he let the misty rain kiss his skin. A sleepless night had left him exhausted. Nevertheless, he welcomed the fatigue; it blunted the edges of unwelcome emotions and uncomfortable thoughts.

Lowering his gaze, he surveyed the yard once more. He spied Prince Kennan then, leading his horse from the stables. The prince wore a pinched expression this morning. The eve before, he'd tried to get out of leading this attack.

"Are you sure, father?" he'd asked woodenly when the High King had made his announcement. "Don't you want to claim this victory as your own?"

"I'm getting too old for combat … but you will do me proud," Talorc had replied with a hard smile. "And since it was *you* who unveiled the traitor in our midst, I shall give you this triumph, my son."

But the prince hadn't looked overjoyed about the gesture—and he still didn't.

"There you are." A tall, lanky enforcer strode toward Cailean then. Torran wore a grim expression this morning. "I thought the High King had hauled you in for another meeting."

Cailean grimaced. "No, thank the Gods. I just had to check that our supply wagons were properly equipped." He met Torran's eye then. "As always, I leave the enforcers here under your charge."

Torran nodded, even as his brow furrowed. "Are you sure you don't want me with you on this campaign?"

In truth, Cailean could have done with his assistance. Torran was his best fighter, and they'd always worked well together. However, he didn't trust any of the other enforcers he was leaving behind to look after things in his absence. "No, Torran … I need you here."

One of the stable hands approached then, leading Feannag. Cailean nodded to the man and took the stallion's reins, deftly checking that the girth was tight enough and the stirrups were the right length. He then set about looking over the contents of his saddle bags.

He was armed with enough iron to bring down the Raven Queen herself, with a double-edged broad sword strapped across his back and full sets of daggers and knives; yet with such a swift departure, he worried he'd overlook something.

Especially since thoughts of his wife kept distracting him.

He'd never lost control of himself like that. The sight of Fia sitting naked amongst the nest of furs, her oaken hair tumbling over her bare shoulders, had made him ache to return to their sleeping nook, to plow her until they both collapsed from exhaustion.

It had taken all his will to put on his clothes and leave.

The woman was full of surprises. A Maid of Albia was supposed to be unsullied, yet Fia was no blushing virgin. He hadn't cared though. Cailean liked a woman who owned her pleasure.

Tension rippled through him then as he reminded himself that this was just another lie, another secret. His wife had layers of them. He couldn't believe he was letting this be. The woman could be a spy like Damhan. Lust had robbed him of his wits.

Skaal padded up to him then, waiting next to Feannag.

Shoving aside the suspicions that screamed at him now, he swung up onto the stallion's back and gathered the reins. He then met Torran's gaze once more.

His second's smoke-grey eyes glinted. "May the Gods be with you."

Cailean grunted. "They'd better be."

As he made his way onto The Thoroughfare, riding at Prince Kennan's side, Cailean made the mistake of glancing up at the walls.

The last time he'd ridden out of Duncrag, he'd seen his wife standing there, watching him go. But Fia hadn't come out to see him off this morning. He hadn't expected to catch a glimpse of her, and yet something tightened deep inside his chest at her absence.

Dragging his gaze from the wall, he clenched his jaw. The Reaper's scythe, he needed to tear himself free of this *weakness*.

Curse the High King. This was all his doing. He'd never wanted a wife. Fia had been trouble from the beginning, challenging him and chipping away at his defenses. He'd managed to avoid speaking of his past—for it was a locked vault he refused to open—but she'd somehow pierced his armor, all the same. And his hunger for her, a need that still pulsed like an ember in his gut, would be his undoing if he let it.

Cailean urged Feannag down The Thoroughfare, past turf-roofed cottages that lay in darkness.

A raven's caw echoed through the mist then. A storm bird, reminding him of what lay ahead. Misgiving stirred in his gut. Over the years, he'd always done the High King's bidding without question, had hunted and slain the Shee without mercy.

But this mission was different. This time, it would start a war between two races. Finally, Talorc mac Brude would have the revenge he craved.

Cailean didn't share the High King's excitement though. Instead, thinking of the conflict to come made a heaviness sink into his bones.

"Can you take the washing down to the laundry?" Bree asked casually, motioning to the wicker basket in the corner.

Mirren stopped sweeping and glanced up. "I washed the clothes yesterday."

"Aye … but I spilled wine on my tunic yestereve, so it'll need a good scrub." Indeed, Bree had deliberately marked the garment before her handmaid arrived.

Mirren nodded, putting aside her broom and heading toward the laundry basket. "I'll get onto it now."

Bree watched her handmaid cross the alcove, pressure building in her chest. "Thank you, Mirren," she murmured, hoping she didn't hear the emotion in her voice. "I appreciate everything you've done for me … it's been good to have a friend here."

Mirren halted before casting her an embarrassed smile. "I'm glad you came to live at Duncrag," she replied. Her expression sobered then, her sky-blue eyes shadowing. "You've been a light in the darkness."

Bree swallowed at these words, at a loss for how to respond. Meanwhile, Mirren observed her silently for a few moments. "Is everything well … between you and the chief-enforcer?"

Bree's stomach clenched. Following the evening before, she wasn't surprised her handmaid was concerned—especially after mac Brochan had stormed into their alcove. Letting out a slow breath, she forced a tight smile. "It is now … we just had a misunderstanding, that's all."

A groove formed between Mirren's eyebrows, and Bree suspected she didn't believe her. However, she didn't push the matter. Their gazes held for a few moments longer, and then Mirren turned away, grabbed the laundry basket, and departed.

Alone in the chamber, Bree drew a deep breath.

Enough wallowing in emotion. Her husband had told her to leave, and she would. His merciful mood wouldn't last forever. She needed to disappear before he had second thoughts and sent someone back to deal with her.

Not wasting any time now, Bree pulled on a pair of woolen leggings under her dark-blue tunic. She'd chosen her dress carefully at dawn, for this one had slits at the sides, allowing for ease of movement and riding. Instead of the sandals she usually wore, she pulled on the ankle boots she'd arrived at Duncrag in.

She'd already decided that she'd track the company of enforcers and men. The glint in the High King's eye the previous evening—before he dismissed his druids' spouses from the hall—had warned her that wherever he was sending them would be of interest to Mor. As an assassin, Bree was an expert tracker, although a company of that size would be easy enough to follow.

She'd find out where those bastards were going—but before she set off after them, she had to find Bryce.

She crossed to where mac Brochan's weapons hung on the wall, helping herself to a dagger, which she fastened around her hips. After a moment's hesitation, she also took down his spare knife belt and strapped it across her chest.

Wearing so much iron made her skin crawl, and she'd need to cast the weapons aside before returning through the stones; nonetheless, she wasn't about to travel unarmed. The High King's warriors and enforcers aside, Albia was filled with many dangers. The iron wasn't just to fight with, but to ward off the creatures and wayward spirits that stalked the land.

Bree pulled on Fia's blue cloak. She then dug a few items out of her trunk and stuffed them into a leather pack. Among them were a small coin purse, her pouch of silver acorns, and Fia's diary. She wasn't sure why she brought the journal—only that she couldn't bring herself to leave it behind.

Bree's jaw tightened. Ancestors, she'd gone soft.

She focused then on provisions. Retrieving food and drink from the kitchen would attract too much attention. She'd need to make a stop somewhere before leaving Duncrag.

Plotting her way out of the fort, Bree drew her cloak around her and fastened it with a girdle. She didn't want it gaping open on the way out and giving the guards at the gate an eyeful of iron. She then pushed the small pack into a wicker shopping basket and covered it with a square of cloth.

If anyone asked, she was off to do some shopping.

Emerging from the chief-enforcer's quarters, she walked confidently across the landing, past the guard stationed there, and descended the steps to the wide entrance hall. She'd picked the moment of her leaving well, for the unexpected departure of the chief-enforcer, the prince, and a number of enforcers and warriors, had thrown the broch out of its usual routine. As such, there weren't any guards lingering in the entrance hall as Bree crossed to the stone stairwell leading underground.

Remaining here was risky, and a wiser individual would have stridden from the broch without looking back, but Bree couldn't go without finding Bryce Elmsong first.

Assassins never left loose ends behind. And yet, she was conflicted.

Mor had instructed her to kill Bryce once she'd spoken to him, but couldn't she just take her predecessor with her?

Lips thinning, she shook her head to clear it of such foolish thoughts. After months as the High King's prisoner, her predecessor was likely to be in a terrible physical state. Killing him would be a kindness.

Bree descended the stairs quickly, her boots whispering on the damp stone. She didn't bother to help herself to a torch, for it was best she kept to the shadows down here. Reaching the entrance to the dungeons, she veered left, plunging into the dank stairwell that took her deep into the earth.

Halfway down, she set her basket against the wall and drew the dagger at her side. If she stumbled on Torran again, she'd have to kill him. Her senses were sharp. Aye, she was slower and weaker in this mortal body, yet she was still an assassin. She moved like one now, careful not to warn anyone of her approach.

Bree's fingers flexed around the bone hilt of her knife. She didn't know how many guards kept watch down here at any given time, but she'd deal with them.

Reaching the bottom of the stairs, she crept along a dimly lit passage where cressets flickered against wet walls. The musty smell of damp, mixed with far fouler odors, made her breathe shallowly. Of course, it was a dungeon—she hadn't expected it to smell like lilacs down here.

A few yards farther, she discovered two warriors playing 'Liar' in the guard room. A pile of bronze coins lay on the table between them. However, Bree didn't focus on the coins, but on the heavy ring of iron keys that hung on the wall next to the table.

Her mouth thinned as she watched the guards.

One of them rattled his wooden cup and peered at the dice inside. "Two sixes," he announced with a smirk.

"Liar." His companion snatched the cup from him. He then growled a curse. "What's this ... three double-sixes in a row? You must be cheating."

The warrior opposite snorted. "No, but you're a poor loser. That's all three of your lives gone ... I win." Reaching out, he went to gather the coins. However, the loser's hand snapped out, fastening around his wrist. "Not so fast, shitweasel."

Bree struck.

She killed the winner first, drawing her dagger blade swiftly across his gullet in a practiced swipe.

The second guard's mouth gaped in shock. But he didn't have time to react before Bree was on him, and he too suffered the same fate.

Leaving their bodies slumped across the table, their blood spilling over the pitted surface, Bree grabbed the ring of keys and hurried from the guard room.

The dungeon wasn't large, just a collection of dank alcoves with iron bars that led off one passage. And most of them were unoccupied. Bree passed two prisoners—one a bald man with a thug's face who sat hunched against the wall, and a wild-haired woman who hissed at Bree as she stalked by.

Reaching the end of the passage, Bree halted before the last alcove. Her attention settled upon where a slender figure shivered under a blanket. She then dropped to a crouch, peering into the darkness, and whispered, "Bryce?"

33: MERCY

THE SHIVERING STOPPED, and a head rose. A single eye glinted in the shadowy darkness before a voice rasped. "Who are you?"

"My name's Bree Fellshadow … Mor sent me."

"Mor's assassin?"

"Aye."

He made a choked sound that might have been a sob.

Sheathing her dagger, Bree began trying keys in the lock then, moving deftly, and the third one released the door. Yanking it open, she rushed inside, going to the prisoner's side.

The stench in here was eyewatering. They'd left him to lie in his filth.

Heat ignited in her gut. *Bastards.*

Shoving aside her disgust, she sank down on her knees next to him.

An emaciated man with pale hair that was clumped with filth and dried blood stared up at Bree. The High King had torn out his right eye, and only an oozing socket remained. But the left eye—the color of slate—was fever bright.

"Iron," she whispered. "What have they done to you?"

"The High King … is … creative," Bryce Elmsong said hoarsely, a cracked tongue wetting ruined lips. "There isn't a part of me that isn't broken." He made a wheezing sound then. "But they don't know I was once Shee—they're still not aware we can pass through the stones. Talorc thinks I'm a Marav traitor."

Bree nodded. That was a relief she supposed. Nonetheless, it was hard to concentrate, what with the foul stench in here and the sight of this pitiful creature.

Bryce's hand—filthy and trembling, his fingers twisted—emerged from the blanket then and rested upon her wrist. His touch was surprisingly firm. "Are you here to kill me?"

Bree decided not to answer that question. "When you disappeared, Mor sent me to discover the High King's plans," she murmured. "I posed as a Maid of Albia and wed the chief-enforcer."

Bryce's single eye widened. "You're mac Brochan's *wife?*"

"Aye." Her mouth pinched then. "Did he take part in torturing you?"

She wasn't sure why it mattered, but it did.

"No." The word was barely a sigh. "I've not seen him since the High King's men dragged me down here."

Their gazes fused for a heartbeat before Bree placed her hand over his. It was scalding to touch. Indeed, a fever had him in its grip. "How did Talorc unmask you?" she whispered.

Bryce's cracked lips twisted. "I was careless."

Silence fell then, and Bree waited for him to continue. Eventually, he did. "The prince and I were lovers." His throat bobbed. "One night … after we'd lain together … he told me that Talorc's overkings are building him three great armies with one single purpose … to take on the Shee." Bryce paused there, his breathing labored as if even speaking taxed him heavily. "At dawn, I rose early and rushed up onto the wall with a silver acorn. But I'd just handed it to Eagal, and was watching him fly away, when Kennan stepped up next to me."

Bree stilled. "He saw the silver acorn?"

"Aye … and he betrayed me to the king." Pain flared in Bryce's gaze, and his grip on her wrist tightened then. "You should flee this place. Mac Brude enjoys torture. If he ever discovers … who you really are …" His voice choked off, his body going rigid.

"Don't worry … I'm going." Bree paused, leaning closer to him. Her chest constricted then. Bryce was in a pitiful state, and yet he was worrying about her welfare. "But first, I need to know what you told the High King."

Silence followed her question.

"Bryce." Her hand squeezed his. "After interrogating you yesterday, he's mobilized a war band. They set out at dawn. Where?"

His breathing hitched, despair flaring in his single eye. "I told them that at mid-summer, we gather outside Dunmorth Barrow to dance under the Strawberry Moon." His breathing hitched then, his chest rising and falling sharply. "I withstood him for so long … but in the end … he broke me." Bryce's thin throat convulsed. "I'm sorry."

Bree's heart lurched, alarm eclipsing the pity that stirred deep in her chest. Aye, he was sorry, but Bryce had told the High King where their people celebrated Sheathan. The festival took place the eve after the Marav observed Mid-Summer Fire. Dunmorth Barrow lay to the north, in the heart of the Hallow Woods—an area the Marav avoided. At Sheathan, the Shee, including the Raven Queen herself, emerged from the ancient barrow, bringing with them offerings of sweet mead and summer fruit. They then spent the night feasting and dancing in their sacred place.

So, this was where mac Brochan had been sent.

In six days, there would be a slaughter.

"You must let our queen know," Bryce rasped.

"I will," she replied firmly. Her gaze held his then. What was she going to do about him? On her way down to the dungeon, she'd flirted with the idea of rescuing her predecessor. But it was foolish to even consider it. No, she couldn't take Bryce with her—and Mor's instructions had been clear. They couldn't risk letting the High King extract more details out of him.

As if reading her thoughts, the prisoner moved his hand from under hers and gripped the edge of the blanket. He then drew it back to reveal the ruin beneath. Oozing sores and cuts covered Bryce's naked body, some so deep she could see bone. His guts bulged from a hole in his abdomen.

Bile stung the back of Bree's throat. How was he still alive?

"Don't give him another chance to play with me," Bryce whispered, a plea in his voice. "I don't want to give him anything else."

Drawing in a deep breath, Bree nodded. "You wish for mercy then?"

He let out a deep sigh. "Aye."

"Then you shall have it." She drew her dagger.

Bree watched Eagal take flight, winging his way into the enshrouding mist.

She then exhaled sharply. *It's done.*

Aye, it was, and she should have felt a heady rush of relief. But she didn't. Instead, she felt sick.

Curse her Marav woman's body and its unruly mind.

It had made her weak.

Bree turned from the wall and made her way toward the nearest set of stairs. And as she did so, her pulse stuttered.

Once Mor received word of what the High King was plotting, she'd move swiftly. And when Prince Kennan, the chief-enforcer, and their band of enforcers and warriors converged on Dunmorth Barrow, carnage would follow. Only, it wouldn't be the Shee who fell, but the Marav.

Cailean mac Brochan would die.

Bree's heart kicked hard against her ribs, and she yanked her cloak close.

He spared you, and this is how you repay him?

She clenched her jaw so tightly that pain darted through her ears. No, this was the way it had to be. She'd been sent to use him. She shouldn't care about his fate.

But that was before last night. Before they'd lain together. Before he'd let her go.

Reaching the yard below, Bree struck out toward the gates, basket looped over one arm. She greeted the guards as she passed through, flashing them a smile, even as nausea churned in her belly.

She had to keep moving. She couldn't let her conscience bother her. In all her years as the Raven Queen's assassin, she'd never struggled with remorse.

Until now.

Aye, she needed to remind herself that the High King was planning an unprovoked assault on her people, and that Cailean was his weapon. From now on, she'd be a fool to think about the chief-enforcer with anything but hatred.

She'd changed her plans though. There was no need to track the High King's enforcers and warriors. She knew where they were going. North, like her. The Hallow Woods lay just a short ride beyond The Ring of Caith.

But Bree was done with the Marav now. She had to focus on getting back to the stones in time for the morning of Midsummer so she could go home.

Home.

Her already churning stomach clenched then. What was waiting for her there? A brother who disliked her. A queen who would need to be appeased. The silver acorn Bree had just given to Eagal would please Mor greatly. Nonetheless, Bree wasn't supposed to return home yet.

Mor had made it clear her spy was to remain at Duncrag until *she* decided otherwise.

Bree walked briskly down The Thoroughfare, weaving her way through a flock of unruly goats that a shepherd was attempting to drive up the road. Farther down, she passed the open doors of ironsmiths. Steam billowed from the forges, and the acrid tang of forging metal greeted her, mingled with the reek of open drains nearby.

Screwing her nose up, Bree hurried on. Even after nearly three moons living at Duncrag, the smells inside the fort were an assault on the senses.

Halfway down the hill, she stopped at a stall and bought some bread rolls, along with some cheese and dried plums. A few yards on, she purchased a skin of ale and then a pouch of salt.

Bree had taken note of Mirren's use of salt to ward off malevolent spirits. Her journey north would take five days, and this time, she didn't have a Shee escort to protect her. She needed to prepare herself.

Reaching the bottom of The Thoroughfare, she ducked into the stables behind an ale-hall. There, she surprised a lad who was mucking out stalls and clubbed him over the back of the neck with a broom. He crumpled onto the straw-strewn floor, and she dragged him into an empty stall. She hadn't killed him, although the lad would eventually awaken with a splitting headache.

Moving quickly now, Bree tossed her basket into the back of an empty stall and shouldered her pack. She then saddled the only pony stabled here: a stocky, feather-footed garron.

They rode out onto The Thoroughfare, and she pulled up her hood, just in case anyone recognized her. They'd surely wonder what the chief-enforcer's wife was doing, dressed for travel and riding a garron.

Pony and rider crossed the wide dirt-packed clearing at the bottom of the hill, and Bree urged her mount toward the gates. Moments later, they were past the guards and trotting down the causeway, to where a wooden bridge spanned the River Lethe.

Exhilaration swooped through her then, like a diving swallow.

She'd made it.

Bree had come close to failing numerous times since adopting her new identity. Making a living as an assassin wasn't easy, yet the life of a spy had turned out to be a far greater challenge.

She'd always thought she had nerves of steel. Now, she wasn't so sure. Aye, Mor wouldn't be happy to see her back so soon, but Bree had still managed to deliver vital information to her queen.

It had to be enough.

It *would* be enough.

Duncrag was now behind her, and Bree didn't look back.

34: A CHAFING CONSCIENCE

THE MISTY RAIN was still falling when Bree urged her pony into the woods. The day's end was near. They'd ridden northwest, keeping to the road for the most part. However, as the gloaming settled, she decided to look for a safe place to rest overnight.

In truth, she was concerned someone would come after her and had spent most of the day glancing over her shoulder. The two dead guards in the dungeon, a prisoner with his throat cut, *and* the disappearance of the chief-enforcer's wife would cause a stir. And sooner or later, they'd learn that a pony had been stolen.

Suspicion would likely fall upon her.

Luckily though, the first day's journey hadn't given Bree any unpleasant surprises. The only faery creature she'd spotted was a skulking wulver in the shadows of coppicing limes where she'd stopped at noon. She'd been watering her pony in the burn by the road when she spied the creature.

Wulvers were shy. Indeed, this one—a wolf's head upon a gangly body clad in filthy rags—loped away as soon as it saw her.

Nonetheless, Bree had kept an eye out as she consumed a meal of bread and cheese, and she was relieved not to encounter anything else as the day drew on.

When she left Duncrag, she'd been giddy with relief at her success. She'd discovered valuable information and managed to get out of the fort alive. But, as the day wore on, her mood darkened, and she started to feel hollow.

If her husband hadn't shown her mercy, she wouldn't have made it out.

Cailean mac Brochan had saved her life, and in return, she'd let him ride to his death.

The light was fading when the oakwood opened up before Bree, revealing a small grassy glade with a dark wall of brambles and blackthorn at its western edge. Glancing around, she decided this spot would do for the night.

Sliding down from the pony's back, she removed his saddlery and then rubbed the beast down. "We're going to be traveling together for a few days, lad," she murmured, stroking his damp neck, "so you'll need a name." Her mouth curved then. "How about Flint?" It wasn't original, but since the garron's coat was dark-grey, it suited him.

The garron whickered and nuzzled her.

"You approve then?" Bree combed her fingers through his thick mane. If she were in Shee form, she'd be able to touch minds with the gelding. It would have helped pass the time and made her feel a little less alone, like when she traveled with Tivesheh. Yet despite the limitations of her Marav body, she felt a kinship with the hardy pony all the same.

Leaving Flint to graze nearby, Bree lowered herself down in front of a twisted oak. And then, heaving a deep sigh, she leaned her head back against the rough trunk.

Moments later, her thoughts returned to Cailean—and guilt clutched at her belly. She'd been hungry at noon, yet her appetite was poor again this evening. Curse it, she couldn't let this churning remorse go.

"Put him from your mind," she muttered, unstoppering her skin of ale and lifting it to her lips, drinking thirstily. There was a village just north of here, and she would replenish her supplies at first light before continuing her journey. "Don't you dare start pining for an *enforcer*. His kind are scum."

Her words fell heavily in the silent clearing, although they had a brittle ring to them, as if she was merely trying to convince herself.

Taking another gulp of ale, Bree shifted position on the mossy ground. Her muscles ached after a day in the saddle, yet she welcomed the discomfort. Nearly three moons at Duncrag had turned her soft.

Dragging in a deep breath, she savored the sweetness of the woodland air. It was nectar after the reek in Duncrag. The oakwood was peaceful, with the patter of the rain above her and the chirp of song thrushes nearby. The lush green of her surroundings reminded Bree of home.

Just four days, she reminded herself, closing her eyes, *and all of this will be behind you.*

Her thoughts treacherously turned, once more, to her husband then, to the feel of his hands on her, the slide of his hot skin against hers, and the brand of his lips. Bree's breathing quickened as she recalled the deep timbre of his voice, the way a room always shrank in size the moment he stepped into it, and the smell of him—leather, ash, and a hint of clove—that never failed to make her pulse flutter. He was the chief-enforcer, but he wasn't the callous brute she'd taken him for. Instead, he was—

Fuck. Bree's eyes snapped open. She couldn't let her mind keep traveling in this direction. She had to think about something else, anything but Cailean mac Brochan.

Growling a curse, Bree dug into her backpack. She needed something to distract herself. She hadn't finished reading Fia's diary; now seemed like a good time.

Jaw clenched, she leafed to the final entry. Despite the rain, it was dry under the sheltered oak, and there was just enough light to read by.

I received a response to my letter today—just two sleeps before I set off for Duncrag.

When Mother Gelda handed me the scroll with the wolf seal, I was giddy with excitement. The other Maids waiting for mail from their families were tight-lipped with envy. I didn't need to be a seer to read their thoughts. "How has a plain creature like Fia drawn the eye of the High King's chief-enforcer?"

Of course, we've never met.

I hurried away to my favorite spot in the gardens and opened the letter with trembling hands.

By the Gods, he is cold.

He wants a wife who holds her tongue, one who asks nothing of him. I'm forbidden from asking anything about the High King's business. He's a busy man and will have little time for me. I am to keep our quarters neat and remain industrious during his frequent absences.

I sat in the garden for a long while after reading the letter from my future husband. Suddenly, the bright day seemed dull ... all excitement drained out of me ... and as I write this, a heaviness settles deep into my bones.

I'm a foolish woman for dreaming of love. That will not be my story. Instead, I shall wed a man who will treat me like his servant.

The diary finished there. It was an abrupt conclusion, and Bree turned the page to make sure there weren't any other entries. There weren't.

Staring down at Fia's final words, Bree traced a fingertip over the cursive writing. Her belly twisted once more. Fia was dead because of her—because Mor needed a spy deep within the High King's household. No one, not even Bree herself, spared any thought for the life they sacrificed.

The woman's death had simply been a necessity.

But during her time at Duncrag, as she'd read Fia's diary, Bree had come to know her. And despite everything, it pained her that the woman had departed from Baldeen filled with dread and sadness, believing that she was to be wedded to a man incapable of caring for anyone.

"You might have liked him in the end," she whispered. "You'd certainly have caused him less trouble than me."

Putting the diary away, Bree forced down a crust of bread. The gloaming was deepening now, and soon darkness would cover the land. She thought about lighting a fire, but the wet weather would make it difficult to find dry wood. It was warm and dry under the boughs of the ancient oak. She'd be comfortable enough here overnight, and a fire might attract too much attention to herself anyway.

She was dozing against the tree trunk, close to falling asleep, when a chattering noise brought her sharply awake.

Blinking, Bree glanced about her.

Nearby, Flint had raised his head. The garron then snorted.

Slowly, she reached for one of the iron blades strapped across her front. A moment later, she caught sight of a silhouette creeping toward her through the shadows. It was shorter than an adult Marav and thickset. And as the figure drew closer, she caught sight of a pikestaff gripped in its left hand and the outline of a cap upon its head.

Bree rose into a crouch, her gaze narrowing. Shades, was that a powrie?

A chill slid down her spine then as she glanced about her. Powries were known to hunt in packs, although they usually never strayed far from ruins. Bree was in the midst of woodland and hadn't seen any buildings nearby.

Iron slay her, she should have checked properly before making camp. Tiredness and a chafing conscience had made her careless.

And as the powrie crept closer, three more shadows detached themselves from the dark wall of bramble and blackthorn on the western edge of the clearing.

They resembled stout old men, and they grinned as they approached, revealing long prominent teeth. Flint squealed in warning, but the powries ignored the pony. Their fiery-red eyes glowed in the gloaming, and lank grey hair streamed down their shoulders. The caps upon their heads were a dark red—stained from the blood of their victims—and long thin fingers tipped in claws wrapped around the hilt of their pikestaffs.

In their free hands, all four of the powries gripped rocks.

Bree's pulse quickened. She knew the tales, of how they'd stone their victims first before stabbing them with their pikes and setting upon them with their nails and teeth.

No one who fell foul of powries got a clean death. And only a fool tried to outrun them, for despite their thickset appearances, powries were said to be fast. They also liked the hunt, and a fleeing victim just excited them even more.

Bree's mouth twisted, and she drew a second blade from her knife belt.

She wasn't running.

And then, before they drew any nearer, she flung both knives. They hit two of the powries in the throat.

The creatures gave strangled squeals, reeling backward. Two bright bursts of flame illuminated the clearing, and the powries she'd hit disappeared, her knives thudding onto the wet grass.

Upon seeing their companions felled, the remaining two powries let out screeches of rage and hurled their stones at Bree.

One hit her on the shoulder, and the other grazed her right ear.

However, Bree had already drawn two more knives, and moments later, another two bursts of flame lit up the gathering dusk.

Cursing, Bree crouched there, waiting for more powries to emerge from the shadows and attack her. But none did.

Rubbing her sore shoulder, she rose to her feet and moved forward, retrieving her fallen knives. Then, she crossed the clearing and pushed her way through the brambles and blackthorn.

On the other side was the ruin of what had been a small tower with a few outbuildings. The stone was blackened with soot, indicating that the tower had been razed by fire. The four powries had likely lived here, and she'd just unwittingly stumbled into their territory.

Jaw clenched, Bree returned to the clearing and resaddled Flint. The pony was skittish now, and she didn't blame him. She'd sleep within a circle of salt tonight, with an iron blade clutched in her hands.

But it wouldn't be in this clearing. It looked as if she'd killed all the resident powries, yet she couldn't be sure.

"Come on, lad," she said, shouldering her pack and then swinging up onto the garron's broad back. She'd let thoughts of the chief-enforcer distract her, dull her instincts, but she couldn't let that happen again. "Let's find somewhere else to spend the night."

35: UNEASY

CAILEAN WALKED THROUGH the encampment, Skaal padding at his side.

Uneasiness churned within him with each stride.

What was wrong with him today? Aye, it would be a massacre at Dunmorth, but he'd done many distasteful things over the years, in the service of the High King. He'd learned to shut his mind off to it. And yet something about this campaign put him on edge. This evening, it felt as if someone had just walked over his barrow. The Reaper was close tonight and would hover at his shoulder until this deed was done.

It's her. His mouth thinned as thoughts of his wife intruded. *She's unsettled you.*

Fia had, but it was more than that. Cailean was methodical by nature, and he liked to plan his campaigns before embarking on them. This whole enterprise was rushed. The High King's hunger for vengeance had made him overeager.

Cailean's hands clenched at his sides then. He had to stop trying to rationalize this. He wasn't himself. Something had shifted within him of late, and he couldn't shake off the nagging feeling that there would be no going back to his old self.

The rain fell in a light mist, causing the pitch torches they'd put up around the perimeter to smoke. A sea of hide tents now filled the mouth of the glen where they'd stopped for the night. They'd spent most of the day riding through meadows and woodland, but from this point forth, the landscape grew wilder, as they left the Wolds behind and headed toward the Uplands.

Smoke from their cookfires stained the damp air, and the aroma of roasting hare made Cailean's belly rumble. Ignoring his hunger, he nodded to the High King's men who greeted him. He marked the wary looks they cast at the huge dog that prowled beside him. Skaal never failed to make them uneasy, but Cailean went few places without her.

He'd already decided she wouldn't approach Dunmorth Barrow though. Instead, he'd ensure that she waited on the edge of the Hallow Woods. Fae hounds were the guardians of barrows. Over the years she'd been with him, Cailean had avoided leading Skaal near one.

The warriors around Cailean were turning hare carcasses on spits over glowing embers. They clustered eagerly around the smoking fire pits, their rough voices carrying through the gloaming. There was both tension and anticipation in the air.

The High King had assured them this attack would mark a great victory against the Shee. However, like most of the Marav, they feared the Hallow Woods.

And even taken by surprise and weaponless, the Shee weren't to be underestimated.

Kennan should have been amongst his men, soothing their fears, and keeping morale high, yet he wasn't. The prince, who'd been in a taciturn mood all day, had retreated to the largest of the tents in the midst of the camp.

Although he'd rather not, Cailean sought Prince Kennan out. They needed to discuss the ambush and the best way to approach it.

He found him sitting upon a makeshift stool next to a flickering brazier, his long fingers wrapped around a cup of mead. The prince was staring into the flames, his handsome face shuttered.

He glanced up when Cailean entered. "Mac Brochan," he greeted him tersely.

"Your Highness."

The prince indicated to the stool opposite, and Cailean lowered himself onto it. Meanwhile, Skaal sat down next to him. Setting his cup down, Kennan cast a jaundiced eye over the fae hound. He then poured the chief-enforcer a cup of mead and handed it to him. "All is well?"

Cailean nodded. "It usually is while we remain in The Wolds." He paused then and took a sip of mead. "However, we'll pass Golval Barrow late tomorrow ... and that always makes the men nervous."

Kennan frowned. "As it does me ... although *Dunmorth* Barrow worries me more." His gaze returned to the flickering flames within the brazier, and Cailean watched him for a few moments.

He should have used this as an opening to discuss the ambush, yet he hesitated. There was something else that had been bothering him all day, and he wanted an answer. "Did your father choose you to lead this campaign as a reward or a punishment?"

The prince's chin jerked up, his dark eyes narrowing. Cailean had crossed an unspoken line, but he didn't care. After the events of the past few days, a recklessness burned within him. He was sick of being surrounded by half-truths, secrets, and outright lies. As such, he held the prince's gaze without flinching, awaiting his response.

Moments passed, and then Kennan reached up, pinching the skin between his brows. "Punishment. He's vexed I drag my heels at finding myself a wife." He cast him a wry look then. "It doesn't matter what *I* want … there are duties that must be fulfilled. But then you know that already."

Cailean snorted. "There always are," he replied, not bothering to hide his own bitterness. He too was heartedly sick of having so little control over his own life. His gaze met the prince's then, silence drawing out between them. "He's not just punishing you for that though," Cailean said eventually. "He blames you for the mess with the healer, doesn't he?"

Kennan's mouth pursed, and Cailean thought he might deny it. But after a few moments, he nodded. "I was foolish to tell Damhan about the armies that father has been rallying," he answered, his voice roughening.

Cailean didn't reply. After the healer's arrest, he'd learned that the healer and the prince had been lovers. A few indiscreet words after a tumble weren't a hanging offense—but in the early dawn following Kennan's admission, Damhan had slipped out of the furs and crept up onto the walls. The prince had followed him and witnessed his lover delivering a silver acorn to a huge raven, which flew off in the direction of Deeping Barrow.

It was a damning discovery—for silver acorns were normally used only by Shee royalty.

The High King had kept news of Damhan's treachery quiet, discussing it only with his druidic council. Talorc had been both humiliated and worried that a spy had been able to infiltrate his household. Damhan had lived at Duncrag for nearly two years— who knew what details he'd already given to the Shee. The High King hadn't wanted word to get out.

"My indiscretion affects us all," the prince admitted then, his gaze shadowing. "Thanks to me, the Raven Queen knows we plan to move against her … that's why father is so eager to provoke them now."

Cailean nodded, his mouth thinning. Indeed, the High King didn't want to wait for the Shee to build their own army.

Cailean left the prince's tent with a sour taste in his mouth.

His conversation with Kennan had been yet another reminder that he had no say in his future. Years earlier, he'd been focused upon his career, on working his way up through the ranks. It had never occurred to him that the High King would force his will upon him.

And now, thanks to Talorc, he had a wife.

A woman who robbed him of peace, who clouded his judgment.

A woman he'd sent away.

Cailean's gut clenched. When he returned to Duncrag, Fia would be gone. The alcove they'd shared would be empty. The scent of lavender would no longer greet him when he pushed the curtain aside. She wouldn't sit opposite him in the evenings, clumsily working upon her distaff. He recalled then, how the firelight played upon her pale skin, highlighting the scattering of freckles across the bridge of her nose and chest.

A hollow sensation settled under his breastbone.

The High King will force me to take another wife, he reminded himself then.

Fuck it. He didn't want to go through this again.

Jaw clenched, Cailean stalked toward the cluster of tents on the northern edge of the encampment. The long gloaming had ended, and night's curtain covered the world. As always, the warrior-druids kept themselves apart. His enforcers sat around fire pits, sharpening weapons, and trading insults as they waited for their supper to cook. Cailean took a seat among them with Skaal at his side. The fae hound observed the roasting hare keenly.

Reaching out, Cailean stroked her ears, and she leaned in to his touch. Usually, Skaal's company improved his mood. Not this evening though.

"Time will be tight, mac Brochan." One of his men, a druid named Tearlach, handed Cailean a skin of ale. "If we want to be in position the day before Sheathan."

He took the ale with a brusque nod. "We'll make it."

Tearlach's bushy auburn brows drew together, and he scratched his clean-shaven chin. "The High King's warriors are shitting themselves over the idea of going into the Hallow Woods."

Cailean unstoppered the skin of ale. "And you, Tearlach?"

The warrior-druid snorted. "I'm not looking forward to rubbing shoulders with The Slew."

At the mention of the 'restless dead'—malevolent spirits that dwelled within the Hallow Woods—Cailean frowned. "You're wise then."

"We'll need to ward the encampment well."

Cailean nodded. "Mac Gordain will weave a protection ballad."

"Aye." Tearlach leaned in. "But will it be enough?"

Cailean glanced across the fire, at where a blue-robed figure sat. Euan mac Gordain was drinking deeply from a horn. The chief-bard's chiseled features were set in tense lines. Euan had tried to send one of the younger bards in his stead, yet the High King had insisted the chief-bard go. And now Euan was sulking, for he'd just learned that Talorc mac Brude didn't have favorites. He'd sacrifice them all, even his own kin, to reach his goals.

The High King was right to send Euan though. Only an experienced bard, one who could infuse druid magic in every word of a song, was powerful enough to keep The Slew at bay. Nonetheless, all the members of the druidic council had done their part in readying them to ambush the Shee.

The chief-seer had spent the night in a trance before casting the bones at first light, and Gregor had held vigil with his sacrificers upon the hill outside Duncrag. Meanwhile, Annis, the chief counselor, had met with the High King well before dawn to discuss the way forward once the attack had taken place.

"Let's hope so," Cailean murmured, shifting his attention back to the warrior-druid beside him.

Tearlach pulled a face. "Try to sound more convincing, mac Brochan."

Cailean shrugged and took a gulp of ale. He wouldn't lie to his men. The spirits that inhabited the Hallow Woods wouldn't be easy to deal with. The Slew were also known as 'The

Unforgiven'—for they'd committed terrible things in life and been damned never to find peace in death. The living avoided this place for a reason.

The two men fell silent then as the aroma of roast hare drifted toward them. Supper was almost ready.

"Something feels off," Tearlach finally muttered.

Cailean cut him a wary look. He wished the warrior-druid would speak of other matters, for he didn't want to admit his own uneasiness.

Tearlach frowned. "I'm no seer … but ever since I was a lad, I sometimes get this sensation … like a stone in my gut … warning me when trouble's coming. It's rarely been wrong."

Apprehension tightened Cailean's chest at these words. "I will heed your warning," he replied after a heavy pause. "Thank you, Tearlach."

Cutting his gaze away from the druid, Cailean lifted the skin to his lips and took another gulp of ale. Meanwhile, the hare that was roasting nearby was ready and being portioned up onto wooden trenchers. The enforcers ribbed each other as they started on their supper.

But despite that Cailean's belly was empty, his appetite had deserted him.

36: ONLY ONE WISH

THE AFTERNOON SUN cast a golden veil over the world when Bree reached her destination at last.

Stopping at the edge of the woods, where Gavyn and his warriors had waited for her nearly three moons earlier, she swung down from her pony's broad back. Her gaze then slid over the hill before her, where the stone circle rose against a pale-blue sky.

Bree's pulse skittered at the sight of The Ring of Caith.

Even bathed in sunlight, this place gave her chills.

She'd arrived earlier than anticipated, for apart from rain on the first day, the rest of her journey had been under fair skies and the garron had shown great endurance. Now she'd have to wait until dawn before she could travel home.

A familiar tightness clutched at Bree's throat at the thought. She should have been looking forward to the moment she'd leave Albia, to returning to one of the Shee.

Why then, did it feel as if an iron band were tightening around her throat?

Swallowing hard, Bree turned to her garron and stroked his furry neck. "Well done, Flint," she murmured. "Let's get that saddle off you." The pony snorted, nudging her with his nose, and Bree huffed. "Just wait … you'll get your treat soon enough."

She removed Flint's saddle and bridle before digging into her pack and feeding him an apple. She'd bought a few at the last village they'd passed through. She then rubbed the pony down with a twist of grass.

"You've done your part." She watched Flint's strong jaws work as he crunched his treat. "But if you wish to keep me company until tomorrow morning, I'll not be sorry."

Swallowing the apple, the garron gave a soft whicker.

Despite the tension that rippled through her this afternoon, Bree's mouth curved. Flint had proved to be a fine companion over the past days. After being attacked by powries, she'd been more vigilant, especially when it came to choosing where to camp. Fortunately, there hadn't been any further incidents. All the same, she sprinkled a circle of salt about her and made sure to tether the pony close to where she slept each night, just in case they had to depart swiftly.

Setting the saddlery up against a nearby birch tree, Bree sat down against the trunk and pulled out an apple for herself. She ate most of it, leaving the core for Flint, who took it from her open palm.

The sun was warm on her face, yet she couldn't relax. Not this close to the stones.

Tapping her foot restlessly, she sat there for a while, leaning against the tree trunk. Her muscles were tired, her limbs heavy; five long days of travel had taken their toll. Bree's body cried out for rest, yet her mind churned.

Eventually, her gaze shifted north. The High King's army would have reached the Hallow Woods by now. The Ring of Caith lay a few furlongs east of the road that led into the northern Uplands.

Mac Brochan and the prince would be readying their warriors to ambush the Shee.

Her heart kicked painfully against her breastbone then, and she reached up, rubbing at it with her knuckles.

Iron smite her, she was tired of battling with this … guilt.

"Don't feel sorry for him," she muttered under her breath, cutting her attention away from the northern horizon. "The bastard has it coming."

Maybe he did, but her words sounded feeble, as if she was merely trying to convince herself. The truth was that with each mile she covered, the tension within Bree had coiled tighter. She couldn't stop thinking about her husband.

Her throat started to ache.

Soon, he'll be dead.

Cursing, Bree stood up. She needed to keep busy. Just one more night in Albia, and she could leave the mess she'd made behind.

She shivered then. The sun had disappeared now, for clouds had rolled in from the north. A wind had sprung up too. The Whistle, high and shrill, swept down from the Goatfell Mountains to the east.

Bree pulled up the collar of her cloak. Without the friendly face of the sun, this place had a sinister, watchful atmosphere. She'd gather some wood and light a fire. It would keep her occupied and help chase away the shadows.

Moving back into the trees, she started picking up fallen twigs and small branches. Despite the dry weather, much of the wood she found was too damp for burning; as such, she wandered farther in than intended. Presently, the trickling of water reached Bree, and she ducked under a low bough to find herself on the mossy bank of a burn in a grassy glade.

Clear water bubbled over ruddy stones, and Bree set down the wood she'd gathered and unfastened her empty water bladder from her belt. It made sense to refill it while she was here. But she'd just filled the skin, and was stoppering it, when a mournful keening sound cut through the woods.

Bree jerked upright, dropped the water skin, and drew the dagger at her hip in one smooth movement.

Still crouched, she swiveled left.

A bent figure, with its back to her, knelt at the water's edge a few yards away. It was a crone with wispy white hair, and she appeared to be washing something.

Bree stilled.

Where had the old woman come from? This clearing had been empty when she'd come across the burn.

Bree tightened her grip on the dagger. A weapon wouldn't help her though. Even without spying the woman's face, she knew who she was. The crone was neither dead nor living, but the Ben Neeya—the spirit of a woman who'd died in childbirth. It haunted the waterways of Albia, often appearing at dusk.

The Ben Neeya had never been sighted within the Shee realm, yet Bree remembered the tales. As such, a cold sweat broke out across her skin.

She was fortunate though, for the crone hadn't seen her. She was too absorbed in her washing, in singing her dirge.

Indeed, if the Ben Neeya had caught sight of Bree first, it would be *her* clothing she'd be washing—a portent of her imminent death. But if Bree caught the Washerwoman unawares and spoke to her first, she would grant her one wish.

Heart pounding, Bree cleared her throat. "Good evening."

The woman's body jerked, and she turned her head, revealing a hollowed face, rheumy eyes, and protruding yellowed teeth. As the stories told, the crone was hideous.

Bree rose to her feet and forced herself to stand her ground.

Moments passed, and then the Ben Neeya gave a bitter, wheezing laugh, her chapped hands clutching at the clothing she washed. "Ask me then," she rasped. "But choose carefully … for you get only one wish."

Bree's mind scrabbled, her heart slamming against her ribs, before she blurted, "Spare Cailean mac Brochan's life."

White-hot panic surged through her the moment the words left her lips. Of all the things she could have wished for, this was it? The Great Raven forgive her, she was a traitor to her people. She'd fallen hard for the man she'd been sent to deceive.

The Washerwoman stared back at her before a sad smile eventually twisted her lips. "I cannot grant you this wish."

Heat flushed over Bree, and she started to sweat. "Why?"

The Ben Neeya's gaze glinted. "Because I sense your conflict … your indecision. If you truly wish to change your man's fate, *you* must be the one to save him."

Bree dragged in a ragged breath. "Me?"

"Aye."

Dizziness washed over Bree then. Backing away toward the shelter of the trees, her pile of firewood forgotten, she shook her head. She wanted to deny the old woman's response, but she couldn't.

The Ben Neeya always spoke the truth.

An instant later, she lost her nerve, spun on her heel, and plunged blindly back into the trees. She crashed through the undergrowth, heedless of the low-hanging branches that smacked her in the face.

All she cared about was escaping the crone, and what she'd just told her.

By the time Bree burst from the trees, her breathing tore from her chest in ragged gasps and hysteria beat inside her like a caged crow.

Flint's head jerked up, his nostrils flaring, at her sudden appearance. But Bree paid the garron no mind. Instead, she paced before the single birch, hands clenching and unclenching at her sides.

She had to breathe—to calm down.

But she couldn't.

If you truly wish to change your man's fate, you must be the one to save him.

The Ben Neeya's rasped words echoed through her head, slicing deep each time.

Bree ground out a curse, squeezing her eyes shut. Finally, her reckoning had come.

Many years earlier, when she'd become the Raven Queen's assassin, Gil had warned Bree that her choice—her rebellion—would one day have its price. Full of arrogance and desperate to free herself from her father, she'd sneered at Gil's comment.

But she wasn't sneering now.

Was this punishment for all the lives she'd taken? Aye, she'd killed Mor's enemies without hesitation, not caring whether they deserved death or not. It was cruel, yet fitting, then that the Washerwoman had denied Bree her wish.

If she wanted to save her husband's life, she'd have to sacrifice herself. That was the truth of it. If she went to Cailean now and told him the truth, she'd be done for.

She swiveled to where The Ring of Caith loomed above her. The day was fading, the sky deepening to the color of a bruise, and the stone circle had an ominous look now: a king's broken crown.

It was her only way back home, back to her old life, but she wouldn't be taking it.

Bree gathered up the saddlery and stalked over to where Flint grazed a few yards distant. The pony lifted his head as she approached, his eyes gleaming in the half-light.

Sucking in a deep breath, she tried to calm the violent thudding of her heart. *I can't believe I'm doing this.* Reaching out, she slid her hand down Flint's muscular neck to his shoulder. She then swung the saddle onto his back and deftly cinched the girth before slipping on his bridle. "Sorry about this, lad," she muttered. "But there's one last trip I must make."

Mounting the garron, she urged him forward. Flint lurched into a jolting canter, and they circled the base of the hill. Chunks of turf flew out behind the pony's heavy hooves, and then they struck out north, toward The Hallow Woods.

37: DEEP INTO THE WOODS

THE MOON SAILED high overhead as Bree reached the southern edge of The Hallow Woods. Since leaving the standing stones, she'd ridden over bare hills and jumped the meandering burns between them. The sight of the dark tree line, looming before her, made her pulse race.

Are you sure about this? There's still time to turn around.

Bree's lips thinned.

No, she wouldn't retrace her steps. Her encounter with the Ben Neeya had shattered something inside her—something she couldn't put back together.

Instinct drove her now, fatalism settling deep into her bones.

Once she warned Cailean and told him who she really was—for she'd decided that she wouldn't hold back—he'd likely kill her.

Are you prepared to die to save him?

The question had drummed constantly in her chest as she'd ridden north from The Ring of Caith—and the answer was still 'aye'.

Recklessness had dug its claws into her now. It was both liberating and terrifying to give up her hard-won control, to rush headlong toward her doom.

It was a fitting end for her, she supposed, for Bree had never done anything in half-measures.

As soon as she entered The Hallow Woods, silence descended. The chill, high-pitched Whistle couldn't penetrate here, but as Flint slowed to a trot along the overgrown path leading through the trees, a shiver crawled over her skin. The garron snorted, and Bree leaned forward, soothing him with her hand. She wasn't afraid of this place, having roamed amongst The Slew that dwelled here many a time.

Unlike the superstitious Marav, the Shee didn't fear the Unforgiven.

However, she wasn't Shee any longer, and Bree wondered if The Slew would turn on her.

Inhaling deeply, she straightened her spine. Fortunately, the woods weren't large. It wouldn't take her long to reach the High King's army. She guessed they'd make camp a few furlongs south of Dunmorth Barrow, biding their time.

A huge grassed-over cairn that rose like a hill in the heart of the woods, the barrow's narrow doorway led into a chamber where a king of the Ancients rested. The Marav feared the cruel wights who dwelt within these places, and hated barrows, for they were Shee portals. Druid magic couldn't protect them here.

Bree's mouth pursed then. She was saving those who intended to cut down the Shee in cold blood. She was possibly condemning her own people to death—all to save one man. The cruel irony wasn't lost on her.

Once I tell him the truth, he'll order a retreat, she tried to reassure herself. *If I do this, I'll prevent bloodshed on both sides.*

Her stomach cramped then. Aye, she could tell herself that, but she had no idea how the chief-enforcer would react, or what he'd decide in the aftermath.

Just a few yards into the woods, the first of the graves loomed from the undergrowth, frosted by the moonlight: pitted grey stones, some of them as tall as her, etched with lines of odd markings. This was the burial ground of the Ancients, the people who'd inhabited Albia before the Marav—back in the mists of time, when Bree's great grandparents had been younglings.

The gravestones and markers had once sat upon a vast meadow, yet with time, trees had grown up, their roots toppling some of the stones, while others leaned drunkenly.

Bree's gaze traveled over the dark foliage surrounding the moss-covered graves, and the ivy and vines that crept over them. Nettles and ferns covered the woodland floor, creeping out over the path that wended its way through dark sycamores and twisted oaks.

And between the stones, shadows unfurled, moving like mist in the moonlight. The Slew were waking up.

Bree's pulse quickened, and Flint sidestepped, tossing his head.

"Steady," she whispered, stroking his neck once more. "They won't touch you."

Ancestors, she hoped she was right.

The chill around her deepened, and goosebumps pebbled her skin. Soon, the shadows, shapes that vaguely resembled the distorted bodies of men and women, swirled around her, their hands stretching out, fingers clawing at her.

For most of the year, The Slew lurked in graveyards—except for the night of Gateway, when they took to the skies like a swarm of corvids, shrieking their rage as they hunted for frightened Marav to feast upon.

But Gateway, which was the night when autumn slid into winter, was still a few turns of the moon away.

Bree breathed through the fear that flickered within her now. No, she couldn't let herself take that path. Her soul was still Shee, and her kind wasn't afraid of the dead.

And so, she let them touch her without flinching. And all the while, she whispered a charm, one her mother had taught her when she'd been a youngling—to soothe her pony's jitters.

Flint snorted once more, although the tension in his stocky body eased a little.

The Marav didn't know it, but The Slew fed on fear—and they'd take those who succumbed to it. Even so, Bree's skin crawled as the shadowy fingers brushed over her face and neck, plucking at the neckline of her tunic. Cruel, thin voices whispered in her ear, in a sibilant, long-dead tongue.

Keeping her gaze focused on the narrow, overgrown path ahead, illuminated by shafts of moonlight piercing the trees, Bree let The Slew slide over her, around her. She continued to breathe the charm as she rode, for Flint wouldn't make it through the woods without panicking otherwise.

A short while later, the garron halted and tossed his head. Bree swung down from his back, keeping a reassuring hand on his shoulder as she looked around her. This wasn't a pinewood, and yet the air was heavy with the resinous scent of conifers, blended with the acrid tang of ash. Druidic wards were in place just ahead of them.

"We're here," Bree murmured, gently leading Flint forward. "They've protected the path to keep The Slew out … but we can pass."

They moved forward, and the air changed once more, warming slightly. Flint let out a low huff that sounded like a sigh. Bree led him under a spreading elm and stripped off his saddlery. "We shall say goodbye now," she whispered, even as her pulse spiked. "If I were you, I'd wait until dawn before leaving the woods … The Slew are less vicious then."

The pony whickered, and not for the first time, she wished she could touch minds with him. She hoped he was canny enough to linger within the wards until morning, where it was safe.

Bree stepped away from Flint then and was about to walk on when a large shape emerged from the undergrowth.

Her breathing caught. *Skaal.*

The fae hound's eyes glowed, her long dark-green coat frosted by the silvery light filtering through the woods, as she prowled toward her. Bree noted then that the dog's hackles weren't raised. No growl rumbled in her throat.

To Bree's surprise, Skaal moved close and nudged her in the ribs with her nose.

She exhaled slowly. She should have realized Cailean's hound would be patrolling the area. Tentatively, she reached out and ruffled Skaal's thick coat. "I'm here to help him," she whispered. "But you know that, don't you?"

Skaal gave a low whine, nudging her once more. There was urgency in the hound's gesture. Aye, it was marching toward midnight now. She needed to move.

Without a backward glance, Bree slipped through the trees. Pulling up the hood of her cloak, she flitted from shadow to shadow. She compressed her lips into a grim smile as she walked. Once again, despite that she was one of the Marav now, parts of her old form still clung to her. The Shee knew how to move unseen, how to become one with the darkness.

A useful skill indeed, for she passed sentries on the way in. Two of them were enforcers, and she gave them a wide berth, choosing to pass closer to the king's men instead. She'd heard that the warrior-druids had excellent night vision, much like the Shee did, and she wouldn't risk being seen.

Even so, it took her longer than she'd have liked to make her way into the tents that had been erected amongst the ancient graves.

And as she crept forward, the faint drone of a man's voice, singing what sounded like a dirge, reached her.

Bree's skin prickled, and she halted and dropped to a crouch. They'd brought a bard with them. She couldn't see him, yet the druid was nearby, holding vigil throughout the night.

Giving herself a shake, Bree pressed forward. The bard wasn't focused on her tonight, but on keeping the encampment safe from The Slew that pressed around the wards.

She was close to the barrow now, close enough that Bree felt the vibration of the air upon her skin—a faint buzzing that was present near the portals. A primal longing arched through her then. In her Shee form, she'd be able to run into that barrow at dawn and whisper the words that would open the veil between the two realms. But as a Marav woman, the way was closed to her.

Her jaw clenched then. Shee or Marav, she wouldn't be crossing back into Sheehallion. Not after what she was about to do.

As she crept farther into the camp, smoking torches thrust up from the damp earth, casting hallowed light over the tents. Save those on patrol, there weren't many souls awake at this hour. All the same, there were fewer shadows to hide her; Bree had to be careful. As such, she crouched behind tents, waiting until the odd warrior or enforcer moved by, until daring to creep forward.

She trailed one of the enforcers heading back into the camp, hoping that he'd lead her to where his leader slept. And he did. A knot of black tents sat on the western edge of the slumbering war band, and Bree singled out the largest of them.

Her insides started to churn then at the thought of seeing her husband again. Despite that the night was cool, she was sweating heavily now.

This wouldn't be a happy reunion.

Forcing down her dread, she waited until the enforcer she'd followed ducked into one of the smaller tents. The way was clear. She had to take her chance.

Bree closed the final yards to the chief-enforcer's pavilion, ripped aside the flap, and dived inside.

The soft light from a glowing brazier greeted her.

However, a heartbeat later, the figure who'd been sleeping upon a pile of furs erupted into movement. The chief-enforcer's speed was unnatural. He rolled to his feet so fast that Bree didn't have time to react, or even the chance to push back her hood so that he could see her face.

Before she knew it, he was on her, one hand clamping around her arm while a cold iron blade pressed to her throat.

"Cailean!" she gasped, as the sting of the sharp edge nicked her skin. "It's me."

With a whispered curse, he lowered his blade, the punishing grip on her arm releasing. "Fia?"

Heart pounding, she pushed back her hood.

Her husband stood before her, gloriously naked, his tattoos glowing faintly in the dimly lit interior of the tent.

Cailean's eyes were wide, his jaw taut. "Gods, I nearly killed you," he growled.

Bree swallowed. She raised her hand to where a thin trickle of blood marked her neck. He *had*, although she couldn't blame him. He hadn't expected his wife to sneak into his tent tonight.

His gaze narrowed then, jaw hardening. "What are you doing here?"

Bree drew in a shuddery breath. If only she could give him an easy answer. Moving close, she reached out and placed her hand on his arm. His gaze darkened at her touch, and Bree's pulse leaped, for his skin was warm, and the scent of him wreathed around her, muddling her senses.

"I have much to tell you, and time is short," she whispered. "But let me start with this." Her voice caught, yet she pushed on. "You were right … everything about me is a lie."

38: GET IT OVER WITH

A GROOVE ETCHED between Cailean's dark brows, and Bree let go of his arm. "My name isn't Fia mac Callum ... it's Bree Fellshadow," she murmured, trying to ignore the nausea that crept up her throat. "I'm not a Maid of Albia. I'm not even from this realm ... I'm one of the Shee."

His face froze, and his big body went dangerously still.

Long moments passed as her husband's gaze raked over her. His lip then curled. "You're not," he replied. "I'd know if you were."

"This is no glamor," she said softly, meeting his eye. "If we pass through one of the stone circles into your realm at the dawn or dusk of an equinox or solstice, we will change from Shee to Marav. I'm one of you until I pass back through the stones." Bree drew in another, deep, breath then. "I'm supposed to go home at sunrise … but, instead, I came here to warn you."

Cailean didn't answer her, although the air between them shivered with tension.

"This is a trap, Cailean." Curse it, she had to get this out before he stabbed that iron blade he still clenched through her heart. "The Shee know you will ambush them tomorrow evening … and they will be waiting for you."

Still, he didn't move, although the fury that flared in the depths of his eyes warned her that she didn't have much time left.

"I was sent as a spy, to send back news on the High King's plans over time," Bree went on, the words tumbling from her now. "My people killed the Maid you ordered and delivered me in her place. Back in my realm, I'm the queen's assassin."

She broke off then, letting her words settle.

Sweat slid down her back, and she flexed her fingers at her sides. Part of her itched to draw one of the blades she carried, to defend herself from the wrath he'd soon unleash on her. But she hadn't come here to fight.

And then, she shocked herself by sinking onto her knees in front of him. Her pulse raced now, dizziness washing over her. Behaving so submissively went against every instinct she had. The old Bree would rather die than make herself so vulnerable.

Cailean stared down at her, his tattoos glowing now. Long moments passed before he rasped, "Why are you telling me all this?"

Bree swallowed hard, wretchedness clutching at her chest.

She wanted to tell him that she couldn't go on knowing that she'd sent him to his death, that being with him had changed her—and that no matter what happened now, she'd never regret warning him.

But the hardness in his eyes warned her from saying such things. He'd think she was trying to manipulate him.

However, she wouldn't lie either—she was done with that. "I couldn't go through with it," she whispered. "I thought my conscience died many years ago." She swallowed then as her throat thickened. "But it seems I was wrong."

Bree stopped speaking then and bowed her head. Relief weakened her limbs; how she'd hated the lie she'd been living. Her true nature was bold and direct. And now the man standing before her knew her real identity.

Moments passed, the silence swelling between them like an incoming tide.

Eventually, surprised that he hadn't said or done anything, Bree raised her chin.

Cailean was still staring down at her. His chest rose and fell sharply, although his expression was shuttered now. Only the gleam in his eyes warned her of the rage he still battled—that and the tight grip he had on his knife. His tattoos still shone, in response to his simmering temper.

"If you're going to kill me, get it over with," she said hoarsely.

A muscle flexed in his jaw, and then to her surprise, he stepped away from her and reached for his clothing. Bree watched as he pulled on his leather vest and breeches, knife belt, and heavy boots. He then sheathed his dagger and reached for his sword, strapping it to his back. After that, he donned his black cloak.

Only then did he turn to Bree once more, his face a mask of stone. "How did you get here?" he asked coldly.

"On horseback," she replied. "I left my garron on the southern edge of the wards … I don't know if it's still there."

His mouth thinned before he gestured to the tent flap. "Well then … let's find out."

Bree's pulse thudded in her ears as she followed Cailean through the encampment, through the smoke that drifted from torches and dying hearths. It was after midnight now. The chief-enforcer kept his hood down and walked south, while Bree hurried to keep up with his long stride.

She'd thought he might bind her hands and tow her along with him as his prisoner, but he didn't. He'd told her to follow him, and she did, with a meekness that surprised her. What was wrong with her these days? She didn't recognize what she'd become.

The sentries on the edge of the camp greeted the chief-enforcer, their gazes flicking to the cloaked figure that walked at his heels. Bree had pulled her hood up, drawing it forward so that her face was shadowed. Cailean offered no explanation but merely nodded to the sentries and strode on into the trees.

A short while later, they arrived at the edge of the warded area, where Flint still waited under the elm. Relief fluttered up inside Bree's chest at the sight of him. Skaal sat a few yards away from the pony, her tail thumping enthusiastically against the damp ground when she spied the chief-enforcer.

"I told you to stay out of the woods, Skaal," Cailean greeted the hound tersely. "You're supposed to be waiting on the edge of the meadows."

In response, the huge dog got up and stretched.

Despite that her guts were in knots, Bree's mouth lifted at the edges. "No one can tell a fae hound what to do," she murmured. "They go where they wish."

Her comment earned her a sharp look from Cailean before his mouth twisted.

Bree swallowed, heat rushing over her at the contempt that glinted in his eyes. "I was afraid Skaal might betray me," she admitted. "But although I'm certain she sensed who I was, she never did."

Cailean cut her a scowl. "Saddle the pony and get up on its back."

Bree hesitated. She wanted to question him, to know where they were going, yet she sensed he was holding on to his temper by a thread. Now wasn't the moment to get into an altercation.

Hot humiliation prickled her skin as she obeyed. She'd half-expected him to kill her as soon as she revealed her deception. His behavior now didn't make any sense. Perhaps he was taking her somewhere more private, away from the High King's army, so he could *interrogate* her properly before killing her. Bree's belly turned over at the thought. She'd fight him then, of course.

Maybe that was what he wanted.

As soon as Bree sat astride the garron, Cailean mounted behind her. He then reached forward, gathered the reins, and turned them south, back onto the path. Fortunately, the garron was stoutly built and able to carry them both. In the Uplands, tribespeople weighed down with weapons rode these hardy ponies into battle. Silently, Skaal padded after them.

Moments later, they passed through the wards the druids had placed, and the mild air turned cold and clammy.

Cailean's body tensed against her back.

"The Slew are attracted to fear," Bree said, careful to keep her voice low. "Show none and you will pass through untouched."

He didn't answer, although Flint gave a frightened whinny then and side-stepped. Focusing on the pony, rather than the silently fuming man seated behind her, Bree leaned forward and started whispering the charm that had calmed the garron earlier.

And like then, Flint's trembling body relaxed.

The Slew crept out from the listing, ivy-draped stones once more, their long arms reaching, their spidery fingers grasping and plucking.

Cailean's body didn't relax against hers the entire way down the path, even if the Unforgiven let him be. Nonetheless, the murmurs were harsher than when Bree had traveled through the woods on her own. The Slew were hungry for fear and frustrated not to get what they craved.

Finally, when Flint emerged from under the canopy of trees, and The Whistle shrieked in Bree's ears once more, Cailean let out a slow, relieved breath.

"Where are we going?" Bree asked then, unable to hold her tongue any longer.

"To the Ring of Caith," he replied roughly as he urged Flint into a choppy canter.

Bree's pulse jolted, and she stiffened against him. "Why?"

Cailean leaned into her, his breath feathering across her ear as he replied, "No more questions."

39: DON'T MAKE ME

THE MOON HAD set when the stone circle appeared upon the horizon, silhouetted against the deep indigo sky.

Dawn hadn't yet broken, although it wasn't far off.

Bree and Cailean hadn't spoken on the way south. During the ride, she sat in the cage of his arms as he guided the pony. The strength and heat of his body, which nudged against hers with each of Flint's choppy strides, disturbed her.

It was a reminder of how it had felt to lie with him in the furs after they'd coupled.

She'd known then that it was a stolen moment, never to be repeated. And it was, for he hated her now.

She could hardly blame him. Bree was the one who'd woven the lies, while he'd been ignorant of the truth. In his place, she would have acted far more harshly, killing him where he stood.

Even so, his insistence that they rode to The Ring of Caith mystified, and worried, her.

What was he up to?

Cailean drew up the pony at the bottom of the hill, and Bree slid from Flint's back and turned to face her husband, who also dismounted. "And now?"

He stared down at her, his face harsh in the shadows. "Isn't it obvious?"

Bree's spine stiffened at his belligerent tone. "No … enlighten me."

A nerve flickered in his cheek. "At daybreak, I'm sending you back through the stones."

Bree stopped breathing. For a few moments, she stared at him, unable to take in his response. It made no sense to her at all. "But why?" she whispered finally.

His mouth compressed into a hard line, his big body growing rigid. "The reason doesn't matter."

"But I thought you were taking me away to interrogate me … to kill me."

Something dark moved in the depths of his eyes. "You were mistaken."

She stepped closer, her chin lifting as she continued to stare him down. "Talk to me, Cailean."

"No."

Bree's pulse took off, heat igniting in the pit of her belly. The dread and shame sloughed away, anger rising to replace them. His intractability vexed her. "I didn't have to warn you."

"No, but now that you have, you can go."

"Cold bastard!" she snarled, stepping close. "Is that all you've got to say? Don't you want to know how—"

"Enough," he cut her off, the tattoos that snaked across his arms and up his neck pulsing pale silver now. "Walk back through the stones, you duplicitous Shee bitch."

Bree's lip curled, crimson dropping across her vision. Aye, here it was—the rage that had been smoldering within him ever since she told him the truth.

He was having trouble unleashing it though. She'd help him.

Whipping a knife from the belt across her chest, she lunged at him.

Cailean caught her wrist, squeezing so hard that her fingers turned numb, and the blade slid from her fingers, thudding on the dew-laden grass between them.

But she wasn't beaten.

Bree swung her free fist, punching him in the stomach before following it up with a bruising blow to his jaw.

Fury pulsed within her. The last time she'd fought this man, they'd ended up naked. But not this time. If she couldn't have his honesty, she'd have his anger. His violence. She'd make him bleed.

They tumbled to the ground, Bree's fists and knees a blur as she sought to inflict harm. And in response, Cailean's tattoos flashed in the murky predawn light. Aye, even in her Marav form, she was dangerous, and the enforcer called upon his druidic magic to fight her.

Landing a vicious blow just below his breastbone, Bree was rewarded with a grunt of pain. It wasn't enough though. Suddenly, she hated him again. He was the brute chief-enforcer she'd been sent to deceive, not the man who'd made her betray her own people. She forgot all of that, fury sweeping her up in its vortex.

Finally, he managed to quell her, his hands pinning her wrists to the ground, painfully, above her head, his heavy body crushing hers.

Bree snarled curses, squirming under his weight, until she lay there panting, her throat raw.

The red veil lifted then, and she stared up into his face.

Blood trickled down his chin from a cut to his lower lip, and a bruise was already blooming across his jaw. Yet Cailean didn't pay his injuries any mind. Instead, he gazed down at her, and the rawness of his expression made an ache flower under Bree's ribs.

The fury was gone, and the real man was unmasked before her. And the pain in those woad-blue eyes was unbearable.

Regret tore through her. "Cailean," she croaked. "I don't want to leave you … don't make me."

His gaze seared hers, even as his throat bobbed. "You must."

Something deep within her chest twisted then. "Nothing I can say will change what has been done," she whispered. "But I want you to know that I *am* sorry."

His eyes guttered, his lips parting as his breathing hitched. For an instant, Bree thought he might say something, but he didn't. And then, to her disappointment, he pushed himself up, off her. "The sun is rising," he said, his voice rough now. "It's time to go."

Indeed, the sky was starting to lighten. Dawn and sunset were always drawn out this time of year, yet the glow to the east warned her that their time was running out.

Bree rolled to her feet before she unstrapped her dagger and knife belt and handed them to him. To her consternation, her hands were unsteady. "Here … I can't take iron blades with me."

He nodded, his expression veiled. The air shivered between them now, heavy with so much unsaid.

Wretchedness twisted her insides in knots. She hadn't lied. She didn't want to go back there. Albia was cold, grey, and full of dangers, but in this realm, she'd discovered forgotten pieces of herself.

Nothing good waited for her in Sheehallion. Aye, she'd lie through her teeth when she went before Mor—she'd gotten good at that of late—but the thought made a lump of ice settle in the pit of her gut. Luckily, in her Shee form, she was stronger, more ruthless. She'd somehow survive. Her time in Albia had changed her, but maybe when she returned to her people, her heart would harden once more.

Maybe leaving Cailean wouldn't hurt so much then.

And yet, when she looked up into her husband's face, she almost crumbled.

His sharp features were strained in the glow of dawn, and his eyes gleamed. She knew then that, despite his façade, this was hurting him just as much as it was her.

"How does it work" —he asked then, his tone strained— "passing through the stones?"

She swallowed. Of course, he'd be curious. "Only the Shee can use them … and only at certain times of the year," she replied.

"And if I was to follow you through?"

Her pulse leaped. "You'd die."

Silence swelled between them, heavy with so much unsaid. And then, to her surprise, he stepped close. Lifting a hand, her husband stroked her cheek. The tenderness of his touch made her tremble.

"Goodbye … *Bree*," he said, saying her name slowly as if testing it out.

She liked how it sounded on his lips.

She managed a weak smile, even as the pain in her chest twisted cruelly. Reaching up, she traced her fingertips along the line of his jaw, committing every detail of his face to memory. "Farewell, Cailean."

Stepping away from him, she looked to where Skaal sat a few yards away, watching her with unnerving intensity. Meanwhile, Flint cropped at the grass, oblivious to her turmoil. Heart in her throat, Bree shouldered the leather pack she'd brought from Duncrag.

Casting Cailean one last, lingering look, Bree turned and walked away, climbing the hill toward the stones.

Iron choke her, she wanted to glance back over her shoulder, to meet his eye once more, but she stopped herself. There wasn't any point in making this even harder.

The Ring of Caith loomed above her, the stones' pitted, scarred surfaces illuminated by the rising sun. And as she climbed, the air grew heavy and storm-charged, as it had on The Day of the Hag.

Silence settled around her, and Bree's skin prickled.

Here we go again. She hadn't forgotten how unpleasant passing through the stones was, and dread curled in her belly.

She hadn't lied to him before—she didn't want to go back. Cailean thought he was saving her, but he wasn't. From the moment she'd ridden away from The Ring of Caith earlier, she'd told herself there'd be no returning to Sheehallion. The 'wrongness' of this act struck deep in the marrow of her bones, yet she kept walking.

She had no choice.

Clenching her jaw tight, she squared her shoulders and strode to the top of the hill, passing into the midst of the ancient stone circle.

40: TOO LATE

CROSSING FROM ONE side of the stone circle to the other was harder this time.

Bree's Marav body wasn't as resilient as her old one—only the fact that the stones recognized that she'd once been Shee allowed her to pass through at all.

She was lost in the mist, the clear morning sky of just moments earlier gone.

The air became unbearably heavy, pressing into her on all sides, and it felt as if an anvil sat on her chest.

Gasping, she stumbled forward, her hands rising to cover her ears as they started buzzing. Ancestors, it was as if hornets were stabbing her eardrums.

She staggered and nearly went down, righting herself just in time.

Her head was throbbing now, each step a monumental effort. Her body screamed, stabbing pain convulsing each muscle. The veil between the two realms was not easily breached, and it didn't welcome her.

The pain overwhelmed Bree then, and she panicked, grappling with an invisible opponent in front of her. Screaming, she launched herself forward into the breach.

The move saved her, for it closed the distance to the two largest stones on the opposite side of the circle. She lurched through them, and then she was falling, tumbling down a slope.

Bree came to a stop at the bottom, winded, on her belly. For a few moments, she lay there, gasping for breath, before her fingers splayed across the ground.

Soft, sweet-smelling grass. The air that feathered across her heated skin was warm and scented with rose.

She raised her head, her gaze lifting to where a glorious pink and gold dawn streaked the sky. Her breathing hitched, and she swallowed the sob that clawed at her chest. Not even Sheehallion's breathtaking beauty could lessen the pain.

Pushing herself up so that she sat on her haunches, Bree lifted her hands, inspecting them. They trembled, yet her fingers were longer and slenderer than earlier, her skin pale gold. She then glanced down at her body to find the tunic, which had been snug on her Marav body, was looser. The hem of her tunic now reached mid-calf instead of her ankles.

Bree lurched to her feet with a fluidity that only the Shee possessed.

It had worked. She'd returned to her true form.

She drew in a ragged breath then, waiting for the sorrow to unknot itself from deep inside her breast, for indifference and selfishness to resurface. She'd welcome them back like old friends—anything to ease this crushing agony in her chest.

But long moments passed, and a chill washed over her.

She didn't feel any different.

Cailean stared after Bree, watching as the woman, cloaked in blue, disappeared between two of the stones.

His wife had just left him, and his chest ached cruelly, as if she'd slipped a blade between his ribs before going.

It had taken everything he had to let her go, yet he had.

She didn't belong in Albia.

From this angle, at the foot of the hill beneath The Ring of Caith, he couldn't see what happened once she strayed inside. The stone circles of this realm, which had been made by the Ancients, were sacred places for druids. Discovering that their enemies could actually pass between Sheehallion and Albia through the stones was a shock indeed.

Druids carried out rites at the Rings each solstice and equinox, but they never ventured inside the stone circles at such times. To do so was forbidden. Indeed, those who had risked it occasionally over the years had never been seen again.

Until now, they'd believed that the Shee feared the standing stones, as much as the Marav abhorred the ancient barrows. But passing through the stones came at a cost to the Shee, for it turned them into one of the hated, lesser, Marav.

Cailean continued to stare up at The Ring of Caith, even as his mouth thinned. How that must have galled Bree, a proud Shee female—the Raven Queen's assassin. How she must have ground her teeth at playing a Maid of Albia.

No wonder she'd done such a poor job of acting submissive.

The sun had almost cleared the tops of the mountains to the east, the craggy spine of the Goatfells. Bree had left her passing until the last moment, but now it was done.

Shaking himself free of a wrenching sensation that felt a lot like grief—an emotion he hadn't experienced in a long while—Cailean tore his gaze away from the stones.

"Enough," he muttered. There was no point in lingering here and staring after her like a halfwit.

Bree was gone, and he had to get back to the camp or they'd think something had happened to him. And now, thanks to her warning, the Shee wouldn't take them unawares.

He had time to act, for Sheathan wouldn't take place until that evening, at dusk. When she'd told him, Cailean had considered retreating. However, he dismissed that idea now. The High King would be incensed if they didn't face their enemy.

At least it'll be a fair fight. Two enemies on an equal footing. Talorc mac Brude would get what he craved too, a battle that would start a war between their races.

Despite that impatience flickered to life inside him, Cailean's step was heavy as he crossed to the garron. Murmuring an oath, he swung up onto its back.

He was still reeling from the truth—that he'd unsuspectingly shackled himself to a Shee assassin. Had Bree originally planned to kill him, once she got the secrets her queen was so desperate for?

Cailean's hands clenched around the reins as he urged the garron forward.

The king would annul his marriage, if he explained that his wife had run back to her family. However, Talorc mac Brude would never learn of Fia's true identity.

Cailean was loyal to the High King, but he'd not betray Bree to him.

Fucking idiot. And he was. She'd betrayed him, yet he couldn't bring himself to hate her. His feelings toward her were … complicated.

He set off north, back toward The Hallow Woods. Skaal ran alongside him, keeping up easily with the garron's short stride. The impatience that had risen inside Cailean earlier bloomed bright now. He needed to return to the army, to alert them all. But first, he had to ride through The Hallow Woods again and weather the hissing, clawing Slew.

Dread curled up as he urged the pony down the path, under the branches of interlacing trees, with worn gravestones thrusting from the shadows—yet Cailean swiftly tamped it down. Bree had warned him that fear drew the restless dead. Indeed, on the way in the day before, they'd lost a handful of warriors to The Slew, their screams rending the air as the hungry spirits dragged them off their horses and into the undergrowth before devouring them.

None of the enforcers had been taken though, for they knew how to master terror. And Cailean did now.

Even so, he breathed easier when he reached the warded area. Swinging down off the pony's back, he turned to where Skaal had halted beside him. "*Stay* here," he ordered, the rumble of his voice cutting through the dawn chorus that chattered around him. The fae hound gave a low whine, and Cailean bent at the waist, lowering his face to Skaal's. "This won't be a battle between Marav," he said, catching the dog's chin. "Protecting the Shee is in your blood; I'll not put you between us."

He stared into the hound's golden eyes. Of course, Skaal couldn't understand him, yet sometimes the intelligence he glimpsed in her gaze made him believe she could. Skaal's company had filled a void over the years; the sound of the hound's snoring at night had made him feel less alone. She was all he had now, and he would not risk her in a fight between Marav and Shee. Whenever he'd hunted Shee over the past few years, he'd left Skaal back at camp—and, usually, she heeded him.

"*Stay*," he repeated before straightening up and stepping away from the fae hound. Then, he turned and made his way through the trees toward the tents.

The absence of sentries immediately alerted him that something was wrong.

Shortly after that, the birdsong stopped, and an eerie silence settled over The Hallow Woods. Skirting around a cluster of leaning headstones that sprouted from the roots of a gnarled sycamore, Cailean slowed his step.

A moment later, he drew the sword that was sheathed across his back. The rasp of iron against leather sounded obscenely loud.

Cailean walked on, and when the first of the tents hove into sight, with no guards to be seen, his heart lurched violently against his ribs. When he'd left, he'd heard Euan chanting. But now there was nothing but pregnant silence.

Many of the tents had collapsed, and those that remained upright listed drunkenly. The smoke from dying torches blended with a wreathing mist. Cailean's breathing grew shallow, and he summoned his magic. A moment later, his senses sharpened, and his limbs tingled, his fingers flexing against the hilt of his sword.

Cailin's nostrils flared as he inhaled the scent of crushed grass and cloying rose. He knew that smell well, had hunted it often enough over the years.

Shee.

He crept forward, his tattoos searing his skin as they pulsed to life. His muscles tightened, readying him for battle.

But there was no battle to be had. He'd arrived too late. The fighting had ended. The bodies of Marav men littered the damp ground, and if any Shee warriors had fallen, they'd been carried away.

Pulse thudding in his ears, Cailean walked through the ruin of the High King's war band. Many men lay dead in their tents, while others, half-dressed, weapons in their hands, sprawled by the cold fire pits. And among the dead, he found his enforcers, including Tearlach. The warrior-druid lay upon his back, his throat torn open. Marking the grievous wounds of those scattered around him, Cailean realized they'd been vastly outnumbered. Even iron and druid magic hadn't been enough.

Euan mac Gordain was among them. Staring sightlessly up at the trees, his mouth agape, the chief-bard had an ax buried in his chest.

Blood roaring in his ears now, Cailean kept moving, heading toward the heart of the camp, where the bodies were piled thick, to the pavilion where the prince had slept.

Unsurprisingly, Kennan was dead too.

Naked to the waist and barefoot, two knives still clutched in his hands, the prince sprawled face down at the entrance to his tent. His long dark hair fell in a curtain around him, soaking into a puddle of blood. Kneeling next to him, Cailean felt the prince's neck, just to be sure. There was no pulse, although his skin was still warm.

He'd missed the ambush by only a short while.

Sitting back on his heels, Cailean surveyed the devastation.

Fire pulsed in his gut. Bree had warned him of a counter-ambush, but she had failed to tell him that it would come so early. Had she known? If she had, why hadn't she told him?

To save you, a voice whispered to him.

Bile surged up, scalding the back of his throat.

Gods, the bitch could twist him around her little finger. And the worst of it was that he let her.

Instead of sending his deceitful Shee wife home—instead of lingering to watch her pass through the stones—he should have taken her prisoner and readied his men to face the Shee. After that, he'd have dragged her back to the High King and handed her over to him. A prize indeed.

But he hadn't.

Instead, he'd let her play him for a fool … again.

To be continued …

AUTHOR'S NOTE

I've been writing books set in Ancient and Medieval Scotland for years now … and have always wanted to create a fantasy world based on this fabulous country, steeped in history and myth. So, I finally did!

Scottish folklore has a dark and foreboding quality to it—full of dangerous creatures that will foretell your death or lure you to your doom. It's just crying out to be used in Fantasy. Not only that, but Scotland's cold, rainy, misty climate lends a certain brooding atmosphere.

I moved to Edinburgh in January 2024, and since then have immersed myself even deeper into the setting of my books. This country has it all: forgotten graveyards, lonely ruins, ancient stone circles, mist-wreathed mountains, dark woodlands, and desolate moors. There's so much to be inspired by.

When I created Albia, I wanted a Fantasy world reminiscent of Ancient Scotland and the Pictish kingdoms that once thrived here—a world where I could bring mythology to life.

Of course, because it's fantasy, I've played with folklore a little and made several flourishes of my own!

Many of the names within this duology come from Scottish Gaelic. It's a beautiful language yet written quite differently from how it's pronounced. As such, I have changed some of the spelling in the novel, to make it more phonetic, and therefore more accessible to readers.

Below is a glossary of people and places from the novel and a bit of background on meaning and the original spelling:

- **Albia:** a variation of 'Alba', the Scottish Gaelic name for Scotland.

- **Ben Neeya**: the Bean Nighe (see note below about 'the Washerwoman').

- **Caisteal Gealaich**: the Shee queen's stronghold. It means Moon Castle. I left the original spelling for this one (it's pronounced *castel galeech*).

- **Sheehallion**: Original spelling is 'Schiehallion'. Located in Perthshire, it's one of Scotland's most prominent mountains and rich in legend. Its name derives from the Gaelic Sith Chaillean meaning 'The Fairy Hill of the Caledonians.'

- **Feannag**: Cailean's black stallion (The name means 'crow'). I left the original spelling for this one too. (it's pronounced *feearnarg*).

- **Skaal**: Cailean's fae hound ('sgàil' means 'shadow').

- **The Marav:** the name for the mortal race that inhabits Albia. Comes from 'Marbh' or 'mairbh' which means a dead person/people.

- **The Shee**: the name for the fae race that inhabits Sheehallion. This name is based on the Daoine sìth (pronounced: *doonyuh-shee)*, the Scottish name for the fairy race.

- **Tivesheh**: is the name of Bree's white stag (the name means ghost and the original spelling is 'taibhse').

In this novel, I use 'mac' with Marav names. Of course, this is from Scottish Gaelic, which meant 'son of'. In Pictish times, 'mac' was used as a separate word in a name with the father's name following. This was the origin of many Scottish surnames we see today.

Drualus is the old Scottish Gaelic name for mistletoe.

The dice game 'Liar', is based on an ancient game:
https://www.lore-and-saga.co.uk/html/dice.html

My inspiration for The Hallow Woods comes from Warriston Cemetery in Edinburgh. Partially overgrown, you walk through dappled shade, climbing ivy, and banks of nettles, past where headstones and crosses covered in moss peek out of the undergrowth. Built in 1845, this huge Victorian cemetery spans 11 hectares and consists of a large terrace, serpentine paths, catacombs, and a neo-classical bridge. And although there's some restoration work underway, it's literally a place time has forgotten.

The societal structure of Albia is based on the ancient kingdoms of Ireland and the Pictish kingdoms of Scotland, where a High King ruled several lesser kingdoms governed by 'overkings'.

The creatures that are mentioned or feature in BOUND BY DECEPTION, and their Scottish mythological origin:

Fae hounds are a variation of the Cù-Sìth (pronounced *ku-shee*), a ghostly hound from Scottish folklore that roamed the Highlands. The name means 'Fairy Dog', and the Cù-Sìth were said to be the size of a small bull with dark-green shaggy fur and a coiled or braided tail

People believed the Cù-Sìth was a harbinger of death—much like the Grim Reaper. Although mostly a silent hunter, this giant dog would sometimes let out three blood-curdling howls. If you didn't get away before the third howl, you'd be overcome with fear and die from sheer terror.

Ben Neeya: The Bean Nighe (pronounced *ben-nee'-yeh*) also known as 'the Washerwoman', is an old woman seen wandering near streams and pools, where she washes the bloodstained clothes of those who are about to die. The Bean Nighe is sometimes said to sing a mournful dirge. She is often so absorbed in her washing and singing that she can at times be caught unawares. If a person sees her before she spies them, she will reveal who is about to die and will also grant three wishes. In my tale, I've altered things slightly, so that she grants you one wish.

Powrie: also known as a Red Cap, or a Dunter, is a type of malevolent, murderous goblin found in Border folklore. He is said to inhabit ruined castles along the Anglo-Scottish border, especially those that were the scenes of tyranny or wicked deeds, and is known for soaking his cap in the blood of his victims.

Find out more:

https://folklorescotland.com/the-fearsome-redcaps-of-the-scottish-borders/

Aughisky: The each-uisge (Scottish Gaelic, meaning "water horse") is a water spirit found in the Scottish Highlands (anglicized as aughisky or ech-ushkya). It usually takes the form of a horse—similar to the kelpie but far more vicious. Unlike the Kelpie (which inhabits streams and rivers), the each-uisge lives in the sea, sea lochs, and freshwater lochs. The each-uisge is a shape-shifter, disguising itself as a fine horse, pony, or handsome man. If you mount this creature while it's disguised as a horse, you are only safe out of sight or smell of water. Otherwise, your skin will stick to the creature's, and it will pull you down to the deepest part of the loch and tear you apart.

Find out more:

https://about-mythical-creatures.weebly.com/each-uisge.html

Corpse candles: also known as will-o'-the-wisps or fairy lights. In Scottish folklore, will-o'-the-wisps are variously depicted either as mischievous spirits (typically fairies), or even the ghosts of the dead, eager to lead travelers off their path and to their death. The lights typically appear close to a bog, marsh, or swamp, places where straying off the beaten path can become dangerous – or even deadly.

Find out more:

The Slew: The Sluagh Sidhe, or 'Fairy Host': spirits of the unforgiven or restless dead who take to the skies at night searching for humans to pick off.

Find out more:

The Botach: The Gaelic word bodach (pronounced bot-ach) can mean 'old man' and also 'specter, ghost'. In ancient Scotland, it was the name of a mythological 'bogeyman', who comes down chimneys to steal children. He was also seen as an omen of death. The bodach was said to slip down the chimney and steal or terrorize little children. He would prod, poke, pinch, pull, and in general disturb the child until he had them reeling with nightmares. According to the stories of most parents, the bodach would only bother bad or naughty children. A good defense would be to put salt in the hearth before bedtime. The bodach will not cross salt.

Find out more:

Wulvers: a Scottish mythological creature that is part human, part wolf. The wulver kept to itself and was not aggressive if left in peace. They would often guide lost travelers to nearby towns and villages. There are also tales of Wulvers leaving fish on the windowsills of poor families. Unlike their werewolf counterparts, the Wulver is not a shape-shifter.

Find out more:

Gods and Goddesses of Albia

The FIVE

The Mother: Goddess of enlightenment and feminine energy—the bringer of change

The Warrior: God of battle, life, and growth, of summer

The Maiden: Young goddess of nature and fertility

The Hag: Goddess of the dark—sleep, dreams, death, winter, and the earth

The Reaper: God of death

Gods and Goddesses of Sheehallion

The Ancestors

The Great Raven

Festivities of Albia

Earth Fire: Salute to new life and the first signs of spring

Day of the Hag: Spring Equinox

Bealtunn: Passage from spring to summer

Mid-Summer Fire: Summer Solstice

Harvest Fire: Festival to salute the harvest

Gateway: Passage from summer to winter

Mid-Winter Fire: Winter Solstice

Five 'paths' of druids

Enforcers: wear black and are the warrior-druids who serve the king.

Sacrificers: wear red and carry out ritualistic sacrifices to keep the Gods happy

Counselors: wear white and are the sages; you go to them for wise advice

Seers: wear green and are masters at divination

Bards: wear blue and sing and entertain; they tell lore and wield power through song and music

The arch-druid: wears gold and is the one deemed to be the most wise

Initiates: wear brown and spend their first months studying druidic lore and readying themselves to develop their 'gift'

The four winds of Albia

The Whistle: high and shrill

The Sharp Billed Wind: pierces the land like a sharp-beaked bird

The Sweeper: whirling gusts that strip branches from trees

The Gales of Complaint: scatters food and crops

Source:

https://weewhitehoose.co.uk/study/the-cailleach/

DIVE INTO MY BACKLIST!

Check out my printable reading order list on my website:

https://www.jaynecastel.com/printable-reading-list

ABOUT THE AUTHOR

Multi-award-winning author Jayne Castel writes epic Historical and Fantasy Romance. Her vibrant characters, richly researched historical settings, and action-packed adventure romance transport readers to forgotten times and imaginary worlds.

Jayne is the author of a number of best-selling series. A hopeless romantic in love with all things Scottish, she writes romances set in both Dark Ages and Medieval Scotland, and Romantasy with a Celtic vibe.

When she's not writing, Jayne is reading (and re-reading) her favorite authors, cooking Italian feasts, and going on long walks with her husband. She's from New Zealand but now lives in Edinburgh, Scotland.

Connect with Jayne online:

www.jaynecastel.com

www.facebook.com/JayneCastelRomance

https://www.instagram.com/jaynecastelauthor/

Email: **contact@jaynecastel.com**